Diana Comet

AND OTHER IMPROBABLE STORIES

Diana Comet

AND OTHER IMPROBABLE STORIES

Sandra McDonald

Lethe Press

LETHE PRESS
MAPLE SHADE NJ

Published by Lethe Press
118 Heritage Avenue
Maple Shade, NJ 08052

www.lethepressbooks.com | lethepress@aol.com

This is a work of fiction. Names, characters, places, and incidents either are the product of the author's imagination or are used fictitiously. Any resemblance to actual events, locales, organizations, or persons, living or dead, is entirely coincidental and beyond the intent of either the author or the publisher.

Cover Image by Niki Smith

ISBN 1-59021-094-8 | 978-1-59021-094-9

"Graybeard and the Sea" appeared in part as "Bluebeard and the Sea," © 2004 by the author. Originally published in *Talebones*, Summer 2004 | "Diana Comet and the Disappearing Lover" © 2009 by the author. Originally published in *Strange Horizons* as "Diana Comet," March 2009 | "The Fireman's Fairy," © 2007 by the author. Originally published in *Realms of Fantasy*, December 2007. | "The Instrument," © 2004 by the author. Originally published in *Chizine*, January 2005. | "Women of the Lace," © 2006 by the author. Originally published in *The Town Drunk*, Fall 2006. | All other works are previously unpublished and original to this collection.

Library of Congress Cataloging-in-Publication Data

McDonald, Sandra, 1966-
    Diana Comet and other improbable stories / Sandra McDonald.
        p. cm.
    ISBN 1-59021-094-8 (pbk. : alk. paper)
    1. Short stories, American. I. Title.
    PS3613.C3874.D53 2010
    813'.6--dc22

                                        2010013962

Dedication

In October of 1998, a gay college student named
Matthew Shepard was beaten, tortured and left to die
on a fence in rural Wyoming.

The men charged with his murder used the
"gay panic defense."

These stories are dedicated to those people
whose gender or sexuality should be held
as sacred as anyone else's.

Table of Contents

Prologue 11

Graybeard and the Sea 15

Diana Comet and the Disappearing Lover . . 23

Pieter and the Sea Witch 53

In the Land of Massasoit 81

Fay and the Goddesses 91

Diana Comet and the Lovesick Cowboy . . . 113

What You Wish For 143

The Goddess and Lieutenant Teague 149

The Fireman's Fairy 177

Nets of Silver and Gold 209

The Instrument 215

Kingdom Coming 221

Diana Comet & the Collapsible Orchestra . . 243

Women of the Lace 273

Diana Comet

AND OTHER IMPROBABLE STORIES

Prologue

"Every day they're throwing away more books," the man said, standing at the bow of the fine sailing ship. A brilliant dome of stars cast white light onto the limitless sea before him. "Hundreds of them. Thousands! Throwing them away like dirty rags or scraps of rotten meat, just because no one wants to learn Dynish anymore. Who knows how many stories have already been lost? Tales of lovesick cowboys and river goddesses and tiny little orchestras that fit into the palm of your hand. About countries where women march off to war and corpses won't stop talking, and how fairies save the hearts of men. If I don't go back, more books will be destroyed and lost to us forever."

His companion said nothing. A salty breeze stirred the sails, and somewhere an unsecured line slapped against a mast. The man drank from a bottle of apple wine and grimaced at the sweet taste.

"I've fallen in love with two firemen, both of whom were ashamed to admit their feelings," he continued. "But somewhere out there is a man who isn't afraid, or who can live with his fear. I won't find him if I stay here."

The captain of the ship, a nun in a black habit and white tennis shoes, listened to this conversation from nearby.

She felt no remorse about eavesdropping. Her unnaturally long lifespan, coupled with a life of secrets and hardships, had burned most shame right out of her. She leaned over the railing of the good ship, keeping a sharp eye out for whales.

"I'd take you with me, but you're too big to fit into my apartment. I don't think I could even get you up the stairs," the man said.

The breeze picked up, flapping the wings on the Captain Nun's ornate cornette. She had heard stories of nuns with such headgear who could fly away on the wind. It seemed improbable, but it was her hope that one day she would indeed find herself aloft above the world.

The man sighed. "I hope you find happiness one day."

The Captain Nun retreated into a dark alcove as the man passed. She went to the bow herself and spoke to the man's friend. She confided, "He has great work ahead of him. I saw it in a dream. From every corner of the world he will collect books of forgotten lore and wonderful secrets. Books that could be dangerous if they fall into the wrong hands, and even more dangerous if they go unread. Surely a creature as old as yourself understands how important that is."

Only the breeze answered; the breeze and that unsecured line, and the slap of water as the hull sliced through it, and the flap of a silver fish which broke free from the depths and then fell back down again.

"Well, sulk if you want to," the Captain Nun said. "I need a drink."

And so she went to her cabin, poured herself a generous libation, and opened up a dangerous book.

Author's notes

1. In 1989, Aaron Lansky won a MacArthur genius grant for his amazing work in saving thousands of Yiddish books from the trash heaps to which they were increasingly being delegated. Since then, millions of such books have been rescued and collected. Support this effort at yiddishbookcenter.org.
2. Have you read any dangerous books lately? What makes a book dangerous? Would you go to jail over pages and glue, words and ink?

Graybeard
AND THE SEA

*G*raybeard longs for the sea. The great glittering blueness of it fills his vision but remains out of reach beyond the boulevard, the seawall and stretches of pale brown sand. He cannot turn his gaze from the ocean. He cannot reach it with his hand. He imagines that the sea tastes like salt, seaweed, melted sunshine, a soldier's chapped lips, a virgin's blushed cheek. If only he could stretch out his tongue and dip it in the waves, he would be a man more at peace with his imprisonment.

"You're not a man," a seagull tells him, circling lazily.

"Are you Omar?"

"Never heard of him."

Graybeard isn't sure he's heard of Omar, either. He wishes he could scratch his head in thought. "If I'm not a man imprisoned, what am I?"

The gulls lands atop the roof of the brick bathhouse nearby. The brisk autumn breeze ruffles her feathers. On the horizon, the sun is just rising from the sea in streaks of red and gold. The red looks like fire. Fire frightens Graybeard. The great ocean is mostly dark, but the whoosh of the waves breaking on time-worn pebbles is like the pulse of his own blood through his own veins, if he had any.

"Graybeard's Castle! Ten cents admission, step right up, full of crazy mirrors, moving stairways and secret passages. You're one of the oldest attractions here."

"Attractions?"

The gull flaps her wings. "Dance all night at the Nautical Gardens! Tour the wonders of the Exotic Bazaar! Be amazed by Howard the Lobster Boy! Mermaid shows, diving horses, a roller coaster—it's all here."

Graybeard thinks that over. Dimly he remembers lights and music, summertime heat, the smell of beer and fried dough. Fireworks over the waves. "Am I popular with the crowds?"

"I suppose."

All he can see of himself is the splintered tip of his nose and the casual repose of his right arm. His chin rests neatly on his fingers, which are long and beige and weathered by the elements. He has no knuckles. Two gaudy purple bracelets encircle his wrist. "Who made me?"

"Who made any of us?"

"What does the sea taste like?"

"Like dead fish. Like rotting whale carcasses and diesel oil and human sewage." The gull launches into flight and sweeps in to land on Graybeard's arm. "I prefer frozen custard, candy kisses, clams dipped and fried in butter."

"Will you help me?" Graybeard asks. "If I don't taste the sea, I will die."

"Do you have a plan, a scheme, a strategy? Have you learned a magic spell, did an old gypsy tell you how to break a curse?"

"No."

"Silly piece of wood. Don't ask me to help you if you don't have a plan."

The gull flaps away to find breakfast.
Graybeard makes a plan.

Winter moves in with heavy air, snow on the sand, howling winds that batter his face. The only people he sees are souls swaddled in coats, hats and gloves as they take their morning constitutionals. Automobiles glide by but rarely stop. Graybeard spends the long nights sniffing for the fearsome odor of smoke and listening to the creaking rafters and roof behind him. Wooden groans fill the air so loudly that he imagines himself at the bow of a great clipper ship steering its way across uncharted depths.

One gloomy morning he hears footsteps under his chin and calls out. "Hello?"

A pause, a flurry of receding steps, and then a scrawny knock-kneed boy appears on the sidewalk below. He's eleven years old, maybe twelve. Soft eyes, weak chin. The kind of boy who gets picked on by bullies, Graybeard thinks, though he's not quite sure what a bully is. Boys with slicked-back hair and wide smirks, perhaps. Strutting for laughing girls who pin up their hair and wear poodle skirts.

"Don't be afraid," Graybeard says.

The boy peers up at him. "Who are you?"

"Graybeard. Who are you?"

"Cubby," the boy says. He has a gap in his bottom teeth and his face is dirty. "You can talk!"

"So can you. Will you bring me a cup of seawater?"

"What for?"

"I want to taste it."

"Tastes awful," Cubby says. "Swallow it and you die. Someone tried to drown me once, so I know. How come you can talk?"

"I don't know," Graybeard says. "Will you help? You're my plan."

"I'm your what?"

"Find someone to help me. That's my plan."

The kid spits on the sidewalk. "Does the magic genie talk? How about the dragon at the roller coaster?"

"I don't know. Go ask them, if you must."

The boy springs away. Graybeard wishes he hadn't made the suggestion. But the next morning Cubby returns, shivering in his thin coat and ragged shoes.

"You got anything I can eat?" he asks.

Graybeard says, "I don't eat."

"Humph."

"Did you eat breakfast at home?"

"Don't got a home," Cubby says. "I ran away."

Graybeard thinks he would like to run away. First to the sea, and then to whatever's on the other side of it: cities, empires, golden deserts, jungles full of monkeys, mountains that scrape the sky.

"Would you like to stay here with me?" Graybeard asks. He doesn't mean to be mercenary about it, but surely friendship will lead to a cup of seawater carried across the boulevard and poured on his lips.

"Maybe. Just for a little while."

Cubby takes up residence in the tower that Graybeard can't quite see, somewhere off to his left. The boy spends most of his time foraging for food or searching for treasure.

He returns home bearing candle stubs, broken toys, pornographic magazines, women's underwear, an army blanket, and stolen pies left on windowsills to cool. When he lights a candle stub for illumination, Graybeard feels a thin sweep of terror.

"Don't burn me," he warns.

"I won't. I'm careful."

Cubby sometimes cries himself to sleep at night. Graybeard pretends not to hear, but some inexplicable protectiveness makes him wish he could fold in upon himself and keep the boy safe. One day Cubby disappears until dusk, and just when Graybeard begins to worry, he returns carrying a bottle of blood-red wine.

"Found it stashed behind the carousel," Cubby says, with a burp.

"Can I try some?" Graybeard asks.

Unsteadily Cubby crawls out along Graybeard's forearm. The wind is bitterly cold, the light rapidly fading. The sky is beginning to reveal its stars.

"Don't slip, Cubby."

"I won't." The boy reaches Graybeard's chin and pauses to peer down at the sidewalk. He leans over and pours a cap full of liquid into Graybeard's mouth.

"Not like paint, but like the stuff that peels paint away," Graybeard says. "I'd rather taste the sea. Could you bring me a cup of that?"

Cubby swallows a gulp and sits down. "This makes you warm. The sea just makes you cold."

"Are you sure you wouldn't rather be at home? Your mother and father must miss you."

Silence for a moment, and then, "Dad died in the war. Shot down over the Big Nip Sea. Mom married this guy from the mill, but he's no good."

"No good how?"

Cubby just shrugs. Drinks some more.

"There's a place," he says. "I heard about it. In Massasoit. That's a big city, the biggest one in the world. You have to stow away on a sailing ship to get there, or jump onto a freight train. This place takes in kids like me. You know. If you don't have a home, or you don't like the one you got."

Graybeard is dismayed. "Will you go there?"

"Maybe." Cubby drains the bottle and then dangles it over Graybeard's fingers toward the pavement below. He doesn't drop it. "Are you the real Graybeard? The one who married and killed seven wives?"

"I don't remember any," Graybeard says. "But I do recall having a murderous cousin named Blue."

"I'm not ever going to get married," Cubby says, and drops the bottle. It breaks with a distant and lonely sound, like the sea.

A moment later the boy weaves his way back inside the tower and goes to sleep wrapped in his thin blanket. Graybeard can't see him, but ever since Cubby's arrival, Graybeard has grown more aware of interior sounds and smells, of the air that fills his rooms, of his own shuttered dormers and windows. He thinks he is becoming smarter, perhaps. He is mulling over that idea the next morning when a black car parks at the curb and a fat man emerges, chewing on a big brown cigar.

Graybeard remembers this cigar-chomping man. He usually comes in the springtime, accompanied by laborers in white caps, and as he walks along he barks out orders for brooms, mops, a screw to fix a railing, fresh paint on the ticket kiosk, new flags for the tower. He is the enemy of mice, bats, runaways, vagrants, and Graybeard himself.

"Wake up, Cubby," Graybeard whispers. "You have to go!"

"Huh?" the boy asks.

"Run!"

Cubby escapes by squeezing out a side door, but the cigar-chomping man finds his treasures and throws away everything but the dirty magazines. New padlocks and chains are installed on the doors. Graybeard doesn't see Cubby again until a few nights later.

"I just came to say goodbye," Cubby says. "I'm going away."

"Will I ever see you again?"

"Don't know. But I brought you this first, because you're my friend."

The boy crawls out on Graybeard's arm with a green bottle in hand. Graybeard itches all over with anticipation. He feels the first cool splash inside his mouth and sees, on the dark horizon, a dozen white porpoises arc into the air. The seawater is saltier and better than soot-tasting rain, but before he can register all the flavors it is gone, absorbed into his wood.

"More!" he begs. "More!"

"Can't." Cubby climbs down to the sidewalk. "Got to go. See you around, Gray."

Graybeard stares out at the ocean. One thing is for certain: he needs a new plan.

A short time later, a runaway boy named Cubbert Salaman hops a freight train and lights out for the famous city of Massasoit, where our tale must follow.

Author's notes

1. During its heyday, Revere Beach in Massachusetts was famous for its wooden roller coaster, amusement rides, dance halls, movie palaces, and the narrow gauge railroad that brought visitors in from the surrounding cities. Much of it was destroyed in the Great Hurricane of 1938.

2. Cubby's father, Captain Erman Salaman, survived being shot down over the Big Nip Sea, but was caught and imprisoned in a hellish POW camp. While prisoner, he wrote a series of poignant letters to his only son. He died of dysentery and is buried in an unmarked grave. The letters are in the bottom of a dusty box in a forgotten museum, waiting to be rediscovered.

3. Richard III is a person cruelly maligned by history books, but the crimes of Gray's cousin Bluebeard are all true.

Diana Comet

AND THE DISAPPEARING LOVER

Two ship's porters came knocking on Diana Comet's cabin door. She adjusted her blouse, gave one last tuck to her dirty parts, and opened the door with a sunny smile.

"Good morning, ma'am!" Henry, a small man about fifty years old, doffed his cap. His young assistant quickly did the same. "We've come to collect your luggage for Customs."

"Of course, Henry. They're all ready for you."

She let both men inside the luxurious first-class cabin to tend to her extensive collection of trunks, cases, and hat boxes. It was possible that Diana had overpacked, but three weeks of dining and promenading had required an arsenal of corsets, dresses, shoes, hats, and jackets, all in summer colors and fabrics. In the city of Massasoit she anticipated needing clothes for dining, for the theater, and for inevitable business engagements. She had no idea what they held fashionable in this corner of the Empire but she was determined to be stylish and proper.

And she couldn't very well confront James while dressed like a pauper, after all.

"Henry," she said, as the younger porter hauled her possessions toward the door. "You grew up here in the city. What's the fastest way for me to get from our arrival pier to Old Slit?"

He paused from consideration of the checklist in his hand. "Why, ma'am, that's easy enough. You'll want to hire a private coach. Look for one bearing the emblem of Foster & Sons. They are reliable, dependable, and with enough financial inventive, quite discreet."

From the ship's wheelhouse came the long blast of the *Arctica*'s horn. Diana had spent the ocean transit reading books, travelogues and diaries by travelers who'd made the brave journey before her. She was ready to take on the city's dangers and thrills—its con artists with their charming smiles, its disease-infested boarding houses, its murdering thieves who would happily slit her throat to steal her diamond necklace. Excitement swirled through her belly at the prospect of combat.

"Foster & Sons. I'll do just that, Henry. And if I arrive at Old Slit wishing to interview the hard-working men and women employed in its finest mansions?"

Henry shook his head in polite but paternal admonishment. "Ah, Miss Comet. You don't want to get too close to those Corish. They can't be trusted."

Another horn blast came as the *Arctica*'s engines, rudder, and paddle wheels turned them into the harbor. Beyond the curtained portholes, Diana could see clipper ships and fishing trawlers. The coast was a green blur in the morning sunlight.

"I need their input for my pamphlets," Diana said, which was entirely plausible. As a champion of the underclass, she was always in pursuit of the truth.

Henry looked unconvinced. Diana reached for her lace purse and withdrew a shiny half-dollar.

"The taverns on Water Row," he reported as he tucked the coin into his pocket. "But it won't be safe for a woman of your beauty, Miss Comet."

Diana resisted the urge to tap the five-inch blade strapped to her left thigh.

"Trust me, Henry," she said. "I can take care of myself."

Once her luggage was removed, Diana went out on deck. The salty air and bright sun weren't good for her complexion, but it wasn't every day she got to see such a wondrous skyline of brick and stone reaching toward the clouds. The sprawling city stretched north and south along the harbor. Bells rang out, clear and heavy, from towers specially constructed to hold their mammoth weight. Enormous ships bearing passengers, cargo and immigrants arrived and departed in clouds of smoke and steam. She didn't see the same beautiful minarets and towers as back home, but there was a different, industrial kind of beauty in the labyrinth of factories and mills, industry and production and housing.

"Half a million people live there," said ancient Miss Harvegstraem from under her ostrich hat. Like Diana, she was traveling alone. They had spent many teatime hours in conversation about art, books, and politics. "It is a city best appreciated from afar and not its foul gutters."

"Yet you return time and time again," Diana reminded her.

"She is an addiction in my blood, even if the damned Corish are ruining everything built by my Dynish grandfathers. Once you've spent a day in her streets, you'll never return to your own exotic lands." The ostrich feathers wavered in the breeze as the dowager slid Diana a sly glance. "Then again, I'm not sure return is your goal."

Diana opened her mouth in a small "o" of surprise. "I don't know what you mean."

A grim smile flashed her way. "You claim to be on assignment from New Dalli's largest newspaper, but anyone who's been to the country knows its notoriously cheapskate editors would never fund a trip this far. As a journalist, you seem unaccountably wealthy and accustomed to the habits of the stuffy upper class. You've already told me you have no intentions of traveling beyond Massasoit. I ask myself, what could bring a wealthy, beautiful, independent woman halfway across the world except true love either thwarted or pursued?"

The city drew nearer in its splendor and squalor. Diana could smell offal and sewage now, and behind the ringing bells was a distant, constant noise like rolling thunder.

"Pursued," she admitted, finally.

Miss Harvegstraem tilted her head. "Let me guess. A handsome visitor, both well-spoken and highly educated. Scion of some wealthy family. He came to you under the cover of darkness, promising sweetness and fidelity, stealing your hard-protected virtue."

Diana almost laughed. Her virtue had disappeared, by her own choice, in a small hot apartment overlooking the grandest square in New Dalli on a day of high prayers. She'd been fourteen years old, hairy and skinny and awkward. Nowhere near the woman she was today.

Miss Harvegstraem continued, "Right before the engagement was announced he was summoned home to steward his family's fortunes through some unexpected crisis. He swore with his hand on his heart that you would soon be reunited. He sent long, romantic letters on fine stationery. But then the letters stopped. Now your missives go unanswered."

Diana was silent. She watched some young boys paddling a rowboat through lanes of sea traffic, showing either great courage or careless disregard. Their small wooden boat bobbed on the blue-green waves precipitously.

"They're not worth it, my dear," Miss Harvegstraem said.

Diana gripped the railing tightly. "This one is."

Because it was inconceivable that James had lied, or been otherwise deceptive, or had somehow forgotten her. Of that she was sure. And so here she was, halfway around the world indeed, about to step off into a strange new adventure to win back her man: James Tremaine Hartvern, elder son of the wealthiest family in all the city of Massasoit.

Miss Harvegstraem said, with terrible gentleness, "He'll only break your heart again."

Diana shifted her leg and felt the weight of her knife. "He can try."

The *Arctica* docked at Pier 12, an enormous stretch of planking that led to the Customs and Immigration Hall. Inside, officials waited at high desks to pass judgment on the thousands of Corish passengers petitioning for entrance. The immigrants, most clad in peasant clothes and carrying cardboard suitcases, waited in snaking lines to be inspected for disease, infirmity, or mental impairment. Their noise—tears and laughter, argument and relief—rose to the cathedral-like ceilings and enormous dusty windows. Diana queued in the much shorter line for first-class passengers and had her papers inspected by an officious man wearing a silver monocle. It only took a few moments to be granted a visa for six months, and the ink on her application was still wet when she stepped past thick turnstiles into the riotous lobby.

The noise of the crowd there set her pulse racing, and the stench of so many unwashed bodies reminded her of the bazaars back home. Immigrants freshly admitted were accosted by friendly strangers promising the best accommodations, the most lucrative jobs, all avenues of support. These were traps, Diana knew. Hapless newcomers were more likely than not to end up in fetid tenements, working for slave wages in factories or slaughterhouses or brothels. Every successive generation of immigrants, no matter what city or what century, found themselves exploited in similar ways. Such was the way of the world.

That didn't mean Diana had to stand by and participate through inaction, however. As a porter loaded her luggage into a Foster & Sons coach, she saw two young Corish girls, sisters by the look of them, falling prey to a pretty lad with a fast tongue. She paused in her step up to the coach to eavesdrop.

"True enough, the landlady's like my own dear sweet mother," he was saying in the Corish language of Faelic. "Cleaner beds you'll never find. Fresh breakfasts and a lunch pail filled with her own cooking. Girls like you, you need a safe place! In a good neighborhood, too."

The girls, no older than fourteen and sixteen, looked undecided. Diana wondered if they'd traveled alone across the ocean or come with an adult who'd died in transit. More than a few of the *Arctica*'s steerage passengers had done just that, their bodies wrapped in shrouds and jettisoned late at night.

"We do need a safe place," the younger girl said, her hands twisting in worry.

The older girl touched the wooden rosary around her neck. "We don't know you at all. How can we be sure you're telling the truth?"

"Girls like you remind me of my sisters back in County Corey," the boy said, all dimples and earnestness. "I only wish someone like me was there to take care of them. Won't you come now, before she rents the beds to someone else?"

The younger girl tugged on her sister's sleeve. "We should go with him."

"You should not," Diana said, stepping forward and speaking in Faelic. "If it's safe accommodations you seek, set your sight on the largest church spire in the city and ask charity of the parish ladies. This is a city that thrives on the ignorance of country rubes."

The older sister said, "We don't take charity."

"And we're not rubes!" the younger one said.

"You most certainly are," Diana said tartly. "And this boy here will no doubt have you spreading your legs for a dozen men by midnight, each one reeking of ale and sweat, their fingers and other dirty things spearing you wide."

The youngest girl turned red in the face. The lad, recognizing there would be easier marks in the crowd, stepped sideways and was lost in the throngs. Diana turned back to her coach, satisfied at one small crisis averted, but the older girl stepped forward and tugged on Diana's long sleeve.

"A fine lady like you needs maids, ma'am," she said, her gaze earnest. "Liddy and I work hard and we're honest and we can be useful."

Diana sighed. "You mistake me for an employer."

The younger girl, Liddy, said, "Mary, don't. We don't need her."

Mary ignored her. "We'll work cheap, ma'am. Anything you need."

"Of course you'll work cheaply." Diana considered the two of them. Young, not quite pretty, much too skinny, but there was potential in their braided hair and high cheekbones. Two farm girls fleeing the Famine. Not so different than Diana's own arrival in New Dalli, so many years ago.

"I'll regret it," Diana said, "but go ahead. Climb aboard."

The first stop they made was in Old Slit, that prestigious enclave of brownstone mansions. Diana was mostly unimpressed, but she enjoyed watching the awe on Mary's and Liddy's faces as they took in the grand architecture and flourishing gardens. Diana had the coachman present her calling card to the butler at the Hartvern mansion. The card was accepted without comment. Next they journeyed to a lower-class shopping district and a small store where both Liddy and Mary were outfitted with cotton dresses suitable for servants. Young Liddy asked for lace on her cuffs, which was totally unacceptable, but Diana admired her spunk. Mary studied her own sallow reflection in a warped mirror and said, "Who'd have thought this, on our first day in the city?"

The girls were close-mouthed on the subject of their parents back in County Corey, but admitted they'd had no schooling. Neither could write, or read, or do anything beyond basic sums. Diana brooded on that at the cordwainer's shop, where the girls were outfitted with proper shoes. Then they were off in the coach to Gravesner Square and the elegant New Dalli embassy, where Diana presented her credentials.

"Ah, Miss Comet!" said the tiny dark-skinned Secretary in his long white robe. He bowed to her three times while ignoring the girls. "Most welcome are you! We received your letter and have prepared a room. His Majesty the Duke is most regrettably traveling on business, but Prince Harami most sincerely invites you to dinner at four o'clock prompt."

She responded with a curtsey. "I'm honored by His Highness's hospitality. These two girls are in my employ. Please arrange to board them with the embassy servants, and if you could, recruit a tutor."

"A tutor!" The secretary gave her a scandalized look. "For two Corish farm girls?"

Sternly she said, "Yes. That's exactly what I said."

The girls were sent off to the kitchens. Diana supervised the moving of her luggage to the embassy's residence wing. Her room had high alabaster ceilings, brilliant curtains of red and gold, and fine furniture carved from New Dalli's great teakwood forests. The windows looked down on Gravesner Square and she could hear bells again—Massasoit was a city of bells, apparently, jangling all hours of the day.

Her doors locked, the curtains drawn, Diana loosened her clothing. The padding and support under her blouse had chafed a little during the day, leaving a red mark. She soothed cream into the heated skin. She had to unwind her dirty parts in order to use the chamber pot, but as usual she averted her gaze and covered them again as quickly as possible. With a jade hand mirror she inspected her face for any stray hairs that might have sprung up since the ship's arrival, and once satisfied, rested her ugly square feet on a cushion to ease the lingering ache from too-tight shoes.

The last of James's letters was in her traveling purse. Diana unfolded the cream-colored paper and reread it for the hundredth time. *Your deepest secrets are safe in my heart*, he'd written. He didn't care what covert jobs she performed for the New Dalli monarchy, or what ugliness she concealed under the finest of fashions and fabrics. She lounged back in her divan, listening to the clip-clop of traffic, the great grinding city of industry. Eventually she reaccoutered herself appropriately and met Prince Harami in his gold-and-turquoise dining room.

"Miss Comet," he said, rising from his damask chair. "As beautiful a seductress as ever."

"Your Highness," she said, and allowed him to take her hand. "You handsome bastard."

Harami grinned widely. He was of true New Dalli ancestry, an honored line that went back a hundred generations. Strongly built, handsome, and kind. A man she might have lusted after if he didn't already have three wives, each more beautiful than the last.

They sat at the table around bowls of fresh fruit and nuts. Against the turquoise wall, a golden parrot eyed them from its cage and stately perch. Harami said, "First, news of your love. Have you any?"

"I was hoping you'd have an answer to that."

He frowned. "It is most regrettable. And it saddens me to tell you what I've heard. They say it was an elopement. With a minor actress from the theater."

She lifted her chin and met his gaze squarely. "I don't believe it."

Harami spread his hands a bit, half apology, half acquiescence. The parrot behind him lifted one claw and examined it with interest.

"I have made many discreet inquiries, and the answer is always the same. They ran off to the south. You of all people know a man's heart cannot be predicted." Harami took her hand. "Except mine. You don't need him when you could have me, my dearest."

Diana shook her head. "I won't believe it until he tells me himself. Can I count on your support?"

"Of course! The assets of this embassy are at your disposal. You need only ask." He paused and squeezed her fingers. "In return, I must ask of you a small favor."

She withdrew her hand. "The last time you asked me for a small favor, I had to rescue your nephew from an Empire prison. What's wrong now?"

"Nothing! All I ask is that you obtain for me a small golden object. One of several hundred floating around this city. Not of much worth on their own, but invaluable for the prestige and favor they carry. I have tried all diplomatic channels, to no avail. I have petitioned the great mayor himself, only to have him regretfully decline. Now I turn to you."

Diana was intrigued. "What kind of object are we talking about?"

"A badge." Harami leaned forward. "Diana Comet, I want you to obtain for me an official badge from the Massasoit Fire Department."

The situation was thus: whenever the fire bells rang, volunteer firemen ran to the city firehouses, grabbed their gear, and dragged, by horse or by hand, pumping engines to whatever conflagration awaited them. Something was always burning down. The city was full of ash-holes, ash-houses, blocked fire chimneys, improperly tended stoves and shoddily made steam boilers. Crowded tenements and factories often fell to the careless flames of candles, oil lanterns, or poorly doused tobacco pipes. Breezes carried embers across tinder-dry roofs and into stables. Over the last few years the city had grown enormously with the influx of industry and immigrants. Everyone agreed that the time had come to have a proper organization of ladder, hose, and chemical companies, with employed and trained firemen subject to new rules of bureaucracy and professionalism.

The trouble, as Harami explained, was with the fire gangs. These were the men and boys who turned out regularly to alarms and caused no end of trouble with their misguided efforts or general hooliganism. Some of them were genuine volunteers who followed the firemen to offer assistance. Others were intoxicated louts, secret arsonists, or thieves and pickpockets seeking to take advantage of chaos. The fire companies themselves were fiercely competitive, with captains and engineers determined to be the best or fastest in the city. Sometimes rivalry turned to violence. Just the previous month, members of Engine Company 13 had taken hooks and shovels to the men of Engine Company 17 when both showed up at a saloon blaze on Orr Street. Three men had been killed.

"I don't understand what this has to do with badges," Diana said.

"The mayor and Common Council have decided that policemen must now respond to all fires," Harami explained. "The police are charged with guarding the fire zone. Only those firemen, alderman, wardens, and officials carrying numbered badges from the Fire Department will be allowed past the barriers."

Diana gazed at him in bewilderment. "And you want one?"

"I want one!" Harami said. "Such bravery! Such danger! If the goddess allows me a second life, I should like for my spirit to be reborn in this city so I can grow up to be a fireman. Until such grace, I will be happy with a badge of distinction."

Diana wasted little time on wondering what, exactly, he would do with it. Her impression of Massasoit, in just the few hours she'd been within its precincts, was that it was as stringently and ridiculously segregated as any city of the Empire. Harami was no safer walking alone amid such fire hooligans than those two Corish girls Diana had rescued. She was sure that he merely wanted to hold and possess something denied to him. In that regard, they weren't really that different.

"I won't leave this city until such a badge is in your hands," Diana promised.

That night, while the rest of the residence slept, she shed her supports and bandages and wig. She tidied up the brown wisps of her original hair with the tip of an ivory comb, then donned a jaunty cap. It was all a necessary evil. The body in the mirror, plainly garbed in trousers and a workman's shirt, was nothing but a tool. One she could put aside or utilize as needed in her career, no matter how much it disgusted her.

She went out the rear window of her suite and down a garden trellis. It was a half-mile or so of darting down streets and across parks until she reached Old Slit. Further east she found Water Row, where rowdy drinkers had clustered at tables to drink and painted wenches brought kisses and ale. The bawdy, profane language was heavily tilted toward Faelic.

"Such a pretty lad you are!" one rough man exclaimed as Diana cornered her way to the bar. "What'll it be, boy?"

"A pint of bitter," Diana said, in the low voice she'd trained herself out of years ago.

While the landlord poured the ale, Diana carefully withdrew a package of sulfur matches and began laying them in a row. She lined up fifteen of them and peered at them intently. The man beside her, a burly man with stringy hair, said, "What's that, then?"

"A bet my Pa taught me," Diana said. "For the beer. You take away one, two or three matches. I do the same. Keep going. Whoever leaves just one match on the table is the winner."

The man squinted at her past the film of alcohol. "Easy!" he proclaimed, and took away two matches.

Diana took away two more, leaving eleven on the wooden bar. "My auntie, she works for the House of Hartvern. Sally Hawes. Do you know her?"

He burped and withdrew one match. "Hartvern bastards. I work for Cosstlen."

She removed one match more, leaving nine. "Cosstlen's finer, I hear."

"Hartvern's a bucket of scum," he said, pawing away two matches. She took two, leaving five behind.

Her burly companion squinted and tilted his head. If he removed one, she would take away three and be the winner with one left on the table. If he removed two or three, she could easily counter and again he would lose. She could see him puzzling through it, reaching the inevitable conclusion. His callused hand came down clumsily and scattered them all.

"Try again," he growled.

She bested him in the next round and was challenged by another man who'd been watching. He was a groom who'd worked for Hartvern before being hired away by the House of Nemmsen. Diana beat him easily. It was a shame, really, that none of them had ever had training in modular arithmetic. Soon she had more ale than she could drink, and an earful of gossip. But it wasn't until the end of the night that she met a tall, handsome man named Eremiah who was a footman for Vencent Hartvern, James's older brother.

"Never heard of a Sally Hawes," he said, peering at the seven matches remaining between them. Carefully he took away one. "Been there three years, I have. No Sally at all."

"I must be mistaken," Diana allowed, and slid another match away. "I could have sworn it, though. She fancied herself in love with one of the rich sons. James, was it? The one who's ill?"

Eremiah said, "Haven't seen him in months. Went to the country, they said. With a girl he knocked up."

She let him win, graciously bought him a beer, and tried to leave.

"Don't go!" he said, catching her arm. "Play again!"

She twisted free with ease.

Eremiah slapped her on the side of the head and grabbed an ear. His grin was lopsided and dangerous. "Come on, boy! Stay a while."

Diana hated to resort to violence. And if possible, she didn't want to expose herself as dangerous. Carefully she grasped his wrist and used the two-finger poke that Master Wong had taught her in New Dalli's Central Orphanage. Eremiah gasped and let her go.

"Keep your hands to yourself," Diana said, and slipped off.

Back in the embassy she slept for a few hours but was up again at dawn, glad to put her bosom back on. Again she hired a coach from Foster & Sons, and again she had her calling card presented to the butler at Hartvern House. After that she headed off to the Department of Fire Suppression. Charm and a small bribe got her to Chief Abbot, a genial man with a long salt-and-pepper beard.

"My dear lady," he said, once she had presented her fabricated story of woe. "Your elderly and sickly father sounds like a hard-working man with a genuine interest in our mission, but he does not qualify for a department badge. Only firefighters, wardens, watchmen and official volunteers can carry the seal of Massasoit."

Diana put on a pout. Her leg shifted slightly, revealing a sliver of lace stocking. "It would be a great comfort to him in these last days. All of his life he's been a keen supporter of the volunteers who keep this city safe. I assure you I would return the badge when he expires."

Chief Abbot's gaze stayed resolutely upward. "Madam, it's impossible. Every day I have politicians, cronies, newspaper reporters, insurance men, and fire aficionados petitioning my office. Please accept my regrets."

She hated men of integrity. Diana returned to the embassy mulling over her options. She found Mary cleaning her room, which was an unwelcome surprise.

"Who told you to tidy up?" Diana snapped.

Mary dropped the pillow she'd been fluffing. "Sorry, ma'am. You don't want fresh bedding?"

Diana's trunks were always locked. A quick inspection showed they hadn't been tampered with. Carefully she reined in her temper. "I'll let you know what I want. Aren't you busy enough in the kitchens?"

"Yes, ma'am." Mary's hands fluttered over the disarrayed sheets, but she didn't straighten them. "They're very kind. We've learned lots about the city, and it's only been a day!"

"What about the tutor I asked for? Have you met him or her?"

"No, ma'am. Not yet."

Diana hung her hat on a hook. She would have to speak to the embassy secretary. It would be all too easy for him to "forget" her goal of having the girls educated. "Have you explored the neighborhood?"

"Just a little. Minnie, she's the cook's help. She took us to market for eggs and cheese this morning."

"And did you pass the firehouse on Mercery Street?"

"Yes, ma'am! It's a big brick building with giant arches. The firemen let children climb on the engine."

Diana sat in an armchair and gave the girl a long look. "Did you talk to any of the firemen, Mary? Any handsome young lads with a roving eye?"

"Oh, no, ma'am," Mary flushed a little. "We were very busy to market and back."

"Tomorrow morning I want you to go to market again," Diana said thoughtfully. "And I want you to talk to them. I want you to make friends with the lads. Be close-mouthed about yourself, but find out everything you can. And if that entails a kiss or two, a lad's hand on your arm or neck, then you're really no stranger to that, are you?"

Mary's gaze dropped a little. "No, ma'am. Not a stranger."

"I am not advocating you let yourself be taken advantage of. The trick to a woman's power is knowing what little things can be given away without worry and those that you must hold closer, as tightly as possible. Do you understand?"

The girl looked relieved. "Yes, ma'am. May I ask why you want me to make friends with the firemen?"

"No." Diana leaned back and closed her eyes. "But you may finish straightening that bed."

For the next three nights Diana returned to Water Row. A succession of magic tricks involving matches and a boiled egg earned her more gossip. Everyone agreed that James Hartvern had run off with a pregnant actress, though no one could agree where. A groom had heard something about Lyremouth, a pastoral hamlet several miles upriver best known for its insane asylum. A porter had heard gossip of Westershire, where the Hartvern family kept a stone house on a remote island in the lake. One of the bakers told Diana that he'd heard a frightful argument from Vencent Hartvern's library the day before the elopement.

"What were they arguing about?" Diana asked.

The baker shrugged. "Thick walls, that house has. But I think it was another woman. Never heard her name. So how *do* you make the egg jump out of the glass without touching either one?"

Every morning Diana presented her card at Hartvern House. Silence was her only response. Afterward, she would begin her daily rounds in a Foster & Sons coach. In the streets of Massasoit she saw more poverty and filth than she'd ever seen back in New Dalli. Poor women scrounged in the streets with gaunt babies on their backs. Former slaves labored long hours in the sun to erect buildings for the rich. Diana didn't need to read the newspaper to know that people were dying of cholera, of syphilis, of any number of diseases, not the least of which was the tragedy of broken hearts and spirits. Yet there was something energizing about this growing city, an indefinable energy that was as inspiring as it was cruel.

Her mission for Harami vexed her. Diana met with aldermen and watch wardens, offering discreet incentives and encouragements to no avail. The closest she came to success was when the embassy's district counselor, an officious man named Kandekist, opened his leather wallet and showed her his badge.

"Impressive, isn't it?" he asked.

Diana had held jewels and diamond crowns; she wasn't impressed by an oval of copper and scrap inscribed with a seal and three-digit number. Things men held dear never ceased to amaze her.

Dutifully she said, "It's quite lovely."

"Miss Comet, let me be frank." Kandekist heaved himself out of his chair, rounded his oak desk, and loomed over her in a domineering way. "As much as we respect your Prince Harami, and I'm sure your folks back home like him a lot, the Fire Commissioner's not going to give any badge to a man of his color. There aren't any blackies in the department and there's never going to be. Is that clear?"

She resisted the urge to grab the badge, kick him in the groin, and make good an escape. "Perfectly, Mr. Kandekist."

His leg brushed against hers. "Doesn't mean you and I can't talk about it more, though. My wife's away visiting her sister. What do you think?"

"I think you should stay home alone and play with your shiny piece of metal," she said.

By the time she returned to her rooms at the embassy, she was hot and tired and in desperate need of a chamber pot. She was in the middle of unwrapping her dirty parts when young Liddy knocked and let herself in without waiting for acknowledgement.

"Oh!" Liddy exclaimed.

"Out!" Diana thundered.

The girl fled with a slam of the door. Exposed, humiliated, Diana quickly pulled on her dressing robe. How much had the wretched girl seen? It was impossible to say. She tiptoed to the door and listened. Heavy breathing on the other side of the wooden panel convinced her Liddy hadn't gone anywhere. Crossly Diana opened the door.

"Have you no manners?" Diana demanded.

"I'm sorry, ma'am!" Liddy's eyes were red. "They told me I had to bring this to you urgently!"

She offered a pale blue envelope. Diana took it but said, "I should send both you and your sister away."

"Please don't!" Liddy said, panicking. "We've nowhere else to go!"

That wasn't true. There were many places two poor, uneducated Corish girls could find refuge and companionship in the city. She said, "Whether I send you away depends entirely on you. Are you the type of girl to gossip and wag tongues over her employer's tragic scars and injuries? Have you no sympathy for childhood catastrophes and stolen innocence?"

Liddy curtseyed. Tears swelled. "Ma'am! I won't. I mean, I do. I won't tell!"

Diana looked down her nose at her for several long seconds.

"Go back to the kitchens and be useful," Diana said.

She closed the door in the girl's face, retreated to the divan with the envelope, and glanced at the return address: Hartvern House. It was a long time before her hands stopped trembling enough to slit the envelope open.

❧

The footman who opened the library door was none other than handsome Eremiah, though he didn't recognize her. Diana gave him the barest glance.

"My dear lady," Vencent Hartvern said, rising from his desk. "Thank you so very much for coming."

Diana allowed him to kiss her gloved hand. "It's lovely to finally meet you."

They sat by the cold hearth with the windows open to the fragrance of the rose garden. Diana's gaze touched upon the framed prints and playbills that hung on the walls. Vencent Hartvern was a known supporter of the Broadvern theaters. Vencent said, "I must apologize again. My mother's not accepting visitors these days, and I've only recently arrived from our summer house. As for my brother...well, the situation is very unfortunate."

Vencent bore a strong resemblance to his brother. Diana found it disconcertingly to see the same chin cleft, slight jutting of the nose, and habit of leaning forward in a chair. She asked, "How unfortunate?"

He fidgeted with his pocket watch. "James is one of the smartest men I've ever known. Book smart, that is. In affairs of the heart—will you forgive me if I'm blunt?"

She graciously tilted her head.

"In affairs of the heart he often finds himself drowning and casting for lifelines. I believe that he very much enjoyed your company in New Dalli. And that he had every intention of honoring his promise to you. It was only after the journey home that he sobered to the reality of his responsibilities. He can no sooner marry you than I can follow my love of theater onto the stage. We each have the burden of our family name."

"I heard it was love of the theater that derailed him," Diana said. "An actress, to be precise. An actress in a delicate and embarrassing situation."

"Lord, no!" Vencent's cheeks bloomed red. "Who says that? How dare they! It was nothing of the sort. Business, that's all. Family business."

Somewhere in the house, a door closed with a heavy thud. A hay cart passed in the street with a distinctive rattle and the whinny of horses. Diana said, "I understand completely, Mr. Hartvern, the misery and grief that such rumors cause. And you understand, of course, that I count on James as a man of integrity to deliver news of our broken engagement himself. When shall I see him in person?"

Vencent rose and went to his desk. "I'm sorry to say he's no longer in the city. He won't be back for several months. He did, however, leave you this letter." He held up an envelope. "In it, he bids farewell."

❧

My dearest, James had written at the beginning. At the end he concluded with, *I'm sorry.*

Diana read the letter a dozen times as the sky darkened and gas lamps flared in Gravesner Square. She imagined that he had been secreted against his will by his brother and was trying to convey his location between the lines, but found no evidence. She decided he had suffered some horrible blow to the head and lost his memories, but the letter contained just enough personal recollection to indicate otherwise. Silver letter opener in hand, she considered stabbing it through the envelope's heart, just as she'd been stabbed.

The next day passed in a blur of despair. The following days were no better. As much as she considered putting on her best dress and hat and going out to explore the city, the heaviness of futility weighed her down. Harami sent her invitations to dinner, all of which she declined. The embassy secretary came by with a basket of fruit, but she turned him away at the door. She forgot entirely to ask him about the Corish girls and their tutor. She refused to read the newspapers delivered to her door beyond scanning ship timetables, looking for a suitable liner back to New Dalli. Finally her misery was disturbed by a knock and the arrival of Mary, her face flushed.

"I did as you asked, ma'am," she said. "I made the acquaintance of the firemen in Company 17. Walked by three times a day with my best smile until they noticed me. One of them's named Tommy Doyle, from County Corey. He says he wants to marry me!"

Diana was too weary and heartsick to point out what a terrible idea it was for the girl to marry someone she barely knew. Her expression must have betrayed her, though, because Mary said, "It's not a trick! He's a good boy, they all say so. Sweet and kind and he doesn't kiss too hard at all. He took me to meet his mother. Sweet as a rose! He even gave me a token to prove his love."

She pulled a shiny gold badge from her pocket and held it aloft.

Diana said nothing.

"I mustn't lose it." Mary turned the badge so that it caught the lamp light. "He'll get in awful trouble. But he said I could hold it until he gets me a ring tomorrow."

Young love. True love. Nothing was more fragile or hopeful. Diana raised her hand gingerly and touched the warm metal. There was no mistaking the city seal or the distinctive lettering.

The distinctive lettering...

She turned back to James's letter. Pulled out all the others he'd sent her. The handwriting was strong and powerful—but there! She should have seen it earlier. The slant was similar, as were the shape and size of the letters, but the forger had put just a little too much space between the words themselves.

Diana shrieked a little.

"Ma'am!" Mary said. "Are you all right?"

"I am more than all right." Her blood picked up speed in her veins. "I'm determined, Mary. And undaunted. Do you know what a formidable combination that is? Don't answer. I have arrangements to make. You have a love token to return come morning. Somewhere out there is a man who needs rescuing, and time is running short."

"Is that why you asked me to befriend the firemen?"

"Not at all," Diana said. "But I do believe your newfound friends can be put to good use."

Just past the hour of one a.m., after the taverns had let out and most honest citizens retired to sleep, a hay wagon burst into flame in the square in front of Hartvern House. The tightly packed material's flammability was heightened by cartons of lantern oil, some bits of lumber and a bale or two of cotton. The driver and horse were nowhere in sight when the footmen of Hartvern dashed out of the house armed with buckets of water. The conflagration was far enough from the surrounding stone buildings to be of little danger, but the flames and noise were enough to bring out

Fire Company 17, the local warden, a drunken alderman and the District Counselor, Mr. Kandekist, whose tryst with a farrier's wife had been so rudely interrupted by the fire alarms. The local police kept all unauthorized personnel at bay—or all unauthorized save two.

The first of these was a small man, slim and shadowy, hired just a few hours earlier on the secret recommendation of the New Dalli embassy. This deft man, who gained access to the scene using a fire badge borrowed from a young Corish girl, was able to slip his hand into Counselor Kandekist's pocket and steal his wallet. Kandekist wouldn't realize the theft until the next neighborhood inferno, and then had to petition the Fire Department for new credentials.

The second unauthorized person, dressed like a man, was viewing the blaze with satisfaction from the rooftop of Hartvern House. She shimmied down a gutter, pried open the window to Vencent Hartvern's study, and climbed inside in order to rifle through the contents of his desk. Her search yielded nothing.

She sat back, annoyed. All this effort without result was making her cranky. Diana eyed the great bookcases full of leather volumes, any of which might be hollowed out. She studied the tacked-down rug, under which might be a floor safe. Books could be sorted through and wall safes could be cracked, but she didn't have much time. In the end she rose and glided to the wall, where the framed theater playbills had been artfully arranged. Centered in the group was a framed sketch of the famed tragedienne Lucy Avonner, and her autograph in big black script.

Outside, the firemen were pondering the mystery of the abandoned cart and congratulating themselves on a job well done.

Diana pulled down the wooden frame and turned it over.

Taped to the back was a doctor's letter from the Lyremouth Asylum for Men.

James Hartvern struggled to wake against a haze of sedatives. He had been dreaming of New Dalli, that dusty old city of markets and temples, with its daily calls to prayer and the secret smiles of the woman he loved. Since his involuntary commitment he'd had many dreams, all of them crushed by the cold light of morning. He pulled now against the restraints holding him to the bed and squinted at the moonlit room. An attendant had come in while he was sleeping and was peering at him from the foot of the bed.

"Who are you?" James yanked at the straps holding down his arms. "What do you want?"

The stranger came closer. He was a slim man, young, wearing common clothes and a jaunty cap.

"Did my brother send you? Come to kill me at last?"

"Never," the stranger replied softly.

He came closer to the bed. James couldn't see the color of his eyes but he had the fleeting impression they might be blue. Blue speckled with gold. He shook his head at such errant fancy and lifted his head defiantly.

"Do I know you?" he demanded.

"Oh, yes," the stranger said, and fell upon James to deliver a bruising kiss to his lips.

James's first instinct was to bite the man's violating mouth. Memory stopped him. He knew the taste of those lips and tongue.

"Diana," he breathed.

She pulled back an inch or two. "I came for you."

"I knew you would!"

"But I had to come like this," she said with a downcast gaze. "Ugly and plain. There are no women here at all."

James arched upward to kiss her cheek. "Wrong. You're here. The most beautiful woman I've ever met no matter what you look like on the outside. And I would say that even if I didn't need you to untie me from this bed."

By midnight they were on the roof, embracing by moonlight. Come dawn they were in a private carriage racing back to Massasoit. Diana shimmied up to her rooms and refused to see James again until she had re-donned her wig, breasts and best gown. James hired a lawyer and had Vencent roused from the family home and business on various charges, including kidnapping, forgery, and forced imprisonment. Three months later, James and Diana married. Though Diana delighted in her satin gown and lace bustle, she fretted that she wouldn't be able to give her husband the heirs he deserved.

"We will have a hundred heirs," James told her. "There is need and we have a fortune to spend."

Which is how they came to found the Hartvern Academy, which to this day still stands in Gravesner Square though all the other mansions and brownstones have long since been torn down and replaced. Here all children are welcomed, loved, and educated. Recursive math is taught to all, as is the importance of tolerance, world travel, and knowing how to perform tricks with matches and eggs. Girls dress like boys and boys dress like girls; that is the lasting legacy of that finest of women, Diana Comet.

Author's notes

4. In some versions of this story, Diana confronts that titan of theater, Miss Lucy Avonner, and is impressed by the other woman's intelligence and fierce independence. During her theater years, Miss Avonner appeared in more than two dozen productions and received numerous awards and accolades. Her dressing room at the Gyre Theater is said to have contained a secret passage to the fairy-world, to which she would occasionally flee in a bid to escape the rigors of the stage. That secret passage is now bricked over, and a fast food restaurant covers the site.

5. Violent clashes between volunteer fire squads are well documented in Massasoit's history books. The city is still full of ash-holes.

6. The Corish people are a fine and proud race whose contributions to the growth and success of Massasoit cannot be underestimated.

7. Many, many children in New Dalli owe their virtue and continued survival to Master Wong's two-finger poke. That esteemed gentleman, now more than two hundred years old, can be found in the back room of a cell phone store in Central Square, but he is visible only to children.

Pieter
AND THE SEA WITCH

"**D**earest Valeria—arrived safely!—fort is wonderful—"

Pieter wrote as quickly as he could, because the ferryman who'd brought him to the island pier seemed determined to set off again immediately. The thin, sour-faced man had tossed Pieter's bag onto the planks, unloaded a large crate of supplies for the other soldiers at Fort Defiance, and was trying to climb back into his boat over the objections of the sergeant who'd met their arrival. Pieter couldn't hear much over the keening wind, but the sergeant was waving his arms in agitation.

"Twenty coppers—" the sergeant yelled. "—whiskey!"

"—no more!" the ferryman insisted.

Pieter balanced his pencil and pre-stamped postcard on one knee, wondering what else he could write to his twenty-year-old wife so far away in Massasoit. Here he was, a man of the army, and she was stuck at home with two babes in arms and another on the way. He wouldn't tell Valeria about his three-day train journey to Cardyr with coughing, sick companions, or the flea-infested barracks he'd bunked in for a week after that, or the nauseating trip out here on a heaving, churning winter sea. Better that she think he'd had a fine time of it and was even now settling down to a good hot meal with his new comrades.

The sergeant yelled, "Thirty! No more!"

"I said no!" The ferryman hopped back into his long, wide boat and took up the oars.

Pieter waved his postcard. "Wait!"

The ferryman ignored him and rowed away from the pier. The black ocean, choppy with waves and roiling with fog, carried him off in seconds.

The sergeant cursed loudly. Like most sergeants Pieter had met during his brief enlistment, this one was thick around the middle and had an unruly gray beard. He didn't look physically fit enough to defend his country from much more than an old woman and her darning needles, and in no way did he stand as a model of patriotism, cleanliness or good order.

From the look on the sergeant's face, he didn't find much to admire in Pieter, either. How ridiculous. Pieter had trimmed his beard that very morning, had polished up the seven buttons on his coat, and had even made sure he tied his boot laces with the proper number of knots.

"Come on," the sergeant said, spitting to the side.

He turned on the scuffed heels of his boots and stalked along the pier toward the great granite pentagram of the fort. Pieter, a mere corporal, slung his bag over his shoulder and followed with the heavy crate in his arms.

The hike to the West Gate took only a few minutes on a dirt path flanked by seagull dung and dead wildflowers. No trees adorned the shoreline. The last elms had been felled decades earlier to heat the fort during the Second Siege of Cardyr. The island itself, a half-hour's walk from end to end, held little strategic importance these days and was manned only out of a quirk of the army payroll and master planning documents. Three men only, each serving at least six months' rotation.

The whole place was said to be haunted. Pieter liked that. Given the bleak, harsh landscape, he could almost even believe it.

The heavy crate shifted in his arms. The strain pulled his shoulders and sides. He hadn't done hard physical work since his years as a child laborer in the blacking factory. Nevertheless he struggled on, sweating under the wool of his coat. Once he and the sergeant stepped inside the fort's high gray walls, the wind was diminished though not eradicated. Pieter glanced around at the acres of faded stone and ragtag grass.

"You're Majorowicz?" the sergeant asked, stopping to gave Pieter a head-to-toe scrutiny. "I thought you'd be older."

"No, sergeant. I'm Pieter Kowalik."

The sergeant looked irritated. "Idiots! They're supposed to send Majorowicz."

"He fell ill. Dengue fever, they say. I might be new to the army, sergeant, but I promise I can—"

"Idiots," the sergeant said again. "And you're an idiot, too. Who told you to carry that crate?"

"I thought—"

"Put it down. That's Runney's job."

Pieter gladly unburdened himself. The sergeant stalked off again, crossing the parade grounds with short, annoyed strides. On his way he passed a scrawny, unhappy looking goat grazing on the grass. The creature ignored Pieter completely.

"That's Nellie," the sergeant said. "She bites."

Past the parade grounds sat a squat brick guard-house of more recent and ugly architecture than the surrounding fort. Pieter followed the sergeant past the heavy door. Inside he found an office, a lavatory, a storage room and the main room, where a set of bunk-beds and a single bed had been wedged against the wall opposite a large pot-bellied stove. The air smelled like burning coal and old tobacco. A large cupboard provided food storage, and beside it stood a square dining table with three sturdy chairs. The place was clean enough, if austere. Given the chance, Valeria would have probably hung yellow curtains on the window and put a rug on the worn floorboards. Maybe placed dried flowers in a vase on the table.

Pieter missed her so terribly that he had to blink several times to clear his vision.

"Oh!" A buck private cleaning the stove rose in surprise. "He's early! Georgie, you said not until suppertime!"

The sergeant scowled. "That's Sergeant Tayborn to you, Runney."

Private Runney's expression turned blank for a moment. Though he was younger than Pieter, his hair was thin and he didn't have many teeth. The dirty rag in his hand shook for a moment, and then his face lit up with awareness. "Sergeant Tayborn, yes, sir! I always address my superiors by their rank and family name, sir!"

"Not a 'sir,'" Tayborn said petulantly. "I work for a living. That's your bunk, Kowalik. The bottom one. Runney, go get the crate in the yard."

Pieter carefully unpacked his knife, books, pens, clothing and sewing kit. He was aware of Tayborn eyeing his belongings from his chair by the hearth. He hoped the sergeant wasn't a thief.

"What are the books for?" Tayborn asked.

Pieter touched the stack reverently. "Well, the Eveland Bible, of course. I read four scriptures a day. This is a book of essays and poetry by an anonymous gentleman of Massasoit. Quite good, but woefully unappreciated. And this my diary, for notes and observations during my stay."

Tayborn scraped a clump of dirt from his boot. It landed on the floor with a thump. "Regular man of letters, are you?"

"I've had some education."

"Then what are you doing in this godforsaken army?"

Pieter would have told him about the wages young authors earned and the debts they incurred upon publication, but just then Runney returned with the crate and they all explored the bounty. The Cardyr quartermaster had sent dried and salted meat, a tin of sweet drops, two pairs of socks, a box of ammunition, kerosene, cheese, crackers, hardtack, biscuits, coffee, tea and a jar of peaches. Some of the items were wrapped in newspaper. Tayborn and Runney started to throw the paper sheets into the stove, but Pieter rescued them.

"I like to read any news of Massasoit," he explained. "My family's there."

Tayborn paused in his examinations. "Parents?"

"My wife and children."

The jar of peaches slipped from Runney's hand and smashed to the floor.

Tayborn ignored the soiled fruit and said, in a strangled voice, "Wife?"

"Valeria. We married three years ago this month—"

"Did you tell them?" Tayborn took a menacing step forward. "Did you tell the army that you had a wife? The battalion commander knows?"

Pieter backed up under the glare. The corner of a bunk bed dug into his hip. "Yes, I told them. I don't know about the commander. He's new, they say."

Tayborn's fists clenched. "Married men can't serve here. It's the rule. It's the curse."

Runney nodded wildly. "She'll come for you!"

Pieter forced himself to laugh. "Curse! You know, they warned me you'd try to play a joke or two—"

"Don't be an idiot," Tayborn said. "If you want to live—if you want your wife to live—you'll shut your mouth and listen to what we say."

The fire in the stove did little to warm Pieter as he listened to the story. Runney had thrown away the broken glass but carefully washed and saved the peaches, which sat plump and swollen in a bowl on the table. Rain splattered against the glass windows and the skies roiled with thunderheads.

"It was exactly one hundred years ago," Tayborn said, sucking on his pipe. "The battalion here was a thousand strong with soldiers, ironsmiths, carpenters and masons. The First Siege was at its height. Every hour of the day they manned the battlements, and every day of the week they fired the cannons at the Kilvemi ships trying to enter the harbor. Later, of course, the whole place became a prisoner of war camp for the Kilvemi bastards. On a bad day, you can still smell their piss. The captain of the fort was named Daren Santolv. It's all his fault."

Runney leaned forward in his chair. "He was married!"

"Shut up," Tayborn said. "I'm telling it."

Runney flinched and sat back.

Tayborn continued. "Yes, he was married. To a fine lady of Cardyr. Every month she sent him food and liquor, and new clothing come winter, and sweet cakes for the men. She comforted the men's wives in times of trouble, and supported the war effort with letters and rallies. They said she was beautiful and kind, but stern when needed. Any man would be glad to have her. But Captain Santolv was only a man, after all. A lonely man. He had weaknesses."

The windows rattled in their panes. The coals in the stove glowed somberly.

Tayborn drew deeply on his pipe. "One day, maybe a year or so after they'd been parted, Mrs. Santolv put on men's clothing and smuggled herself here to see her husband. She wasn't the first, of course. There'd been women here before—girls dressed as boys to support the war, or nurses brought out to help the garrison doctor, or others brought out to comfort the men in other ways. But Mrs. Santolv, she didn't tell her husband that she was coming. She wanted to surprise him and celebrate Deadwinter. A surprise it became, indeed. She made her way to his quarters and saw him fast asleep. But he wasn't alone."

Runney's cheeks were pink. "He was a sodomite!"

Tayborn glared at him. "Shut up! That's not how the story goes."

Pieter leaned forward. "Did she kill them? Her husband and his...lover?"

"No. She fled his obscene betrayal and ran in the rain to the North Wall," Tayborn said. "They tried to stop her, but she stripped off her clothes and leapt to her death. Broke her back and drowned on the rocks. They fished her out the next day. Blue as that blanket over there, with seaweed in her mouth and her eyes already plucked out by crabs. A terrible shame. Then, the next night, the guards found a set of wet footprints leading from the walls across the courtyard to Captain Santolv's quarters."

"And she killed him then?" Pieter asked.

"Who's telling the story?" Tayborn demanded.

Runney blurted out, "He killed himself."

"Damn you both!" Tayborn exclaimed.

"Sorry," Runney said, sniffling loudly.

"Sorry, sergeant," Pieter echoed.

Tayborn glowered. "Too late for sorry now. Just like it was too late for Captain Santolv. They found him with his hand clutching his own knife, which he'd used to cut his very own throat. The door was locked from the inside."

Silence but for the crackling fire.

"Surely it's nothing more than a tall tale," Pieter said.

"Surely not!" Tayborn exclaimed. "The Sea Witch that was once Mrs. Santolv rises out of the waves every Deadwinter Eve. That's tomorrow night. She climbs out of the sea naked as the day she was born, and walks through walls and doors like they were nothing at all. The list of her victims is as long as both your arms and both your legs put together. She'll come for you, Pieter Kowalik, no doubt about it."

"You have to leave." Runney's eyes were round and bulging. "There's no time left."

"How?" Pieter asked. "The ferryman won't be back for a week."

Tayborn nodded grimly. "There's an old dory. For emergencies. You'll have to row yourself back to the mainland and beg the garrison commander to reassign you."

"He won't be pleased," Pieter said slowly.

Runney said, "But you'll be alive!"

The wind against the windows went suddenly still. Pieter took his time answering.

"Gentleman," he said. "You tell a convincing story. A lesser man than myself, someone of no letters, might be swayed. But I know the stories of the Sea Witch. Late at night, hers is a popular tale in the barracks. Mrs. Santolv found her husband, yes, but not in the embrace of another man. Instead, it was a garrison nurse. Or perhaps a low woman, one brought out to sell herself for pennies here and pennies there. She murdered her husband and his companion right there, then leapt to her doom. Or maybe Captain Santolv killed her himself, threw her to the rocks, and then killed himself. Everyone knows, of course, that her vengeful spirit rises on Deadwinter Eve. Or Summerpole. Sometimes the last Wolf Moon. She kills married men, or maybe only men who've been with a low woman. Or maybe both. It all depends on the needs of the storyteller and the man he's trying to scare."

Runney gaped at him.

Tayborn's ears had gone bright red at the tips.

"What does that mean? What storyteller?" Runney asked.

Pieter settled back smugly. "It means your ruse is up! I know that the legend of the Sea Witch is used as a prank whenever any new soldier gets posted to this island. The men already here persuade him to row back to the mainland, or parade the island with his clothes inside out, or perform some other outlandish stunt. I was forewarned, gentlemen."

Tayborn got to his feet so forcefully his chair skittered backwards. "I find your comments insulting, Private Kowalik. When the Sea Witch comes for you with her terrible gaze and cold hands, don't expect me to raise a helping hand!"

He stomped out of the guard house without even taking his coat.

Runney covered his face with both hands.

Pieter asked, sympathetically, "You didn't know?"

Runney's head shook. "Sergeant Tayborn and Sergeant Coomey, they told me. When I got here two months ago. They said I was doomed, but there was a way to save myself."

"You're married?" Pieter tried to picture Mrs. Runney, no doubt short and stout and not much smarter than her husband.

Runney reached for his dirty handkerchief and blew his nose "Right before I came here, because the baby was coming. The sergeants told me that I could ward off the Sea Witch if every morning I went naked up to the North Wall and sang her a love song. So I do. To protect me. But now you're here and she'll come anyway."

Pieter said, "No. You're missing the point. There's no Sea Witch at all."

"How can you be sure?" Runney asked.

"Because I'm a man of learning. We don't believe in common superstitions, fascinating though they may be. We dissect them with logic and good sense. Though, I tell you, this is all very inspiring. I've decided just now that I'm going to gather up as many of these legends as I can and present them to the world. It will make for fascinating reading."

Runney gazed glumly at the stove, humiliation plain on his face.

Pieter, full of his grandiose new plan, let the silence linger. His first book had failed, yes, but this new one would capture the public's imagination and recoup his losses. He would embellish it with tales from the trenches of war, of heroic men on impossible quests, and of beautiful women who stood by their men through the most savage of circumstances.

Finally Pieter pushed out of his chair. "Tell me, do we conduct rounds here? Is there a schedule?"

"Sometimes," Runney said unhappily. "If you'd like."

"I'll do them," Pieter said magnanimously. "The fresh air will do me good."

The rain was still pouring down on the parade grounds, but Peter's oiled coat and hood protected him well enough. He wound his way through the old ammunition rooms until he was far enough away that the others couldn't hear him laugh. And laugh he did. At poor Runney's gullibility, and the expressions on Tayborn's face when Pieter unmasked the charade, and the way the miserable weather had cooperated with setting the mood for the tale. He imagined any number of young soldiers as the butt of the Sea Witch prank. It wasn't the only military legend he'd heard in the Cardyr barracks—there were also tales of haunted battlegrounds, phantom trains, and cursed weapons of war—but this was one of the best, and Tayborn told it masterfully.

He continued on his self-appointed rounds, happy for exercise and historic surroundings.

The rooms smelled dank but were mostly dry. Some still showed outlines of furniture on the floor. Old plumbing jutted from walls, the toilets and sinks long gone. Others had boarded-up windows or rusted old bolts on the floor. All were empty. One of the largest chambers had an arched ceiling, brick columns and sealed-up slots where the cannons had once aimed at the horizon. He thought it was the most melancholy of all the ones he'd seen so far, so poignantly removed from war and usefulness of its time.

His explorations didn't end there, but they did end with something that added to the legend of the Sea Witch.

"That was a nice touch," Pieter said, at supper. "The wet footprints. You must have made them when you went out for the crate, is that it, Runney? Your feet are small enough."

Tayborn and Runney both blinked at him. The mood had been sullen since they'd sat down for their evening meal of salted pork, potatoes, fresh bread, and peaches. Pieter suspected Tayborn would hold a grudge for days, if not weeks, for spoiling the joke.

"What footprints?" Runney asked.

Pieter sighed. "In the garrison office. Thirteen small steps, like a woman's."

"Show me," Tayborn growled.

They donned their coats and traipsed through the evening gloom with lanterns in hand. The old office had no furniture and decorations, only a wooden sign over the door to mark its former importance. The wet prints began beneath a heavily shuttered window and trailed toward the door before they disappeared.

"Oh!" Runney said. "She's already here!"

"Enough," Pieter said, mixing his exasperation with amusement. "They're the same size as your feet, Runney."

"The marks aren't his," Tayborn said.

Runney lifted his left foot, pulled off his boot and unrolled his gray filthy sock. "Not me! See?"

Pieter stared at the stumps of toes.

"Two winters ago." Runney rubbed the little knobs of flesh. "It got awfully cold at Fort Pierce. Do you want to see my other foot?"

Pieter slipped a glance toward Tayborn's large boots. No match there, either. He remained firm. "You made them some other way. A plaster mold on a stick! A sponge shaped like a woman's bare foot."

Tayborn crossed to the chamber's window. He unlatched it and peered down. "Nobody human could scale this wall. It's twenty feet, smooth as a baby's head, to the rocks and water."

"I don't know why you persist," Pieter said.

Runney said, "She's really here, isn't she?"

Tayborn shook his head and headed back to the guard shack.

Their entertainment options for the evening were limited to card games, Tayborn's fiddle, Runney's wood carving and Pieter's books and diary. To show what a good sport he was about the whole thing, Pieter played three games of dead man's bluff and gracefully lost half a copper on each. Afterward he retired to the bottom bunk and carefully penned an account of the day, keeping in mind that he might not be able to trust his companions to respect his privacy.

That night he didn't sleep well. The sounds of the shaking windows and the rain on the roof conspired against him, as did Tayborn's snores and Runney's restless tossing back and forth in the bunk above Pieter's. The stove put out some warmth, but his nose ached with the cold and he'd left his sleeping cap back in the East Cardyr barracks. When Pieter did doze off, he dreamt of Valeria sewing in her chair by the window, squinting against the fading light of day as she mended his uniform shirt.

"Dearest," she said. "Remember your promise."

When he woke he couldn't decide which promise she'd meant; their marriage vows, his oath of enlistment, or some other contract spoken or unspoken. He rolled out of bed and saw Tayborn and Runney had both gone outside. Pieter washed up with cold water and peered at the gray drizzly sky. It occurred to him that today was going to be as miserable as yesterday, and that whole weeks of this weather awaited them on this barren rock cut off from the comforts and diversions of civilization.

He had known what to expect, but found the reality of it disconcerting. Six months of bleak boredom lay ahead. No wonder Tayborn and Runney seemed so worn and short-tempered. Over in Cardyr, the Deadwinter Carnival and festivities would mark the turning of the year. Here, they would mark another notch on a dreary calendar, a grim reminder of all the weeks and months they still faced.

Tayborn stomped in just as Pieter pulled his pants over his long johns.

"God-awful weather," Tayborn said, and added a few more curses.

"Sergeant," Pieter said. "Such language insults the Book of Eveland."

Tayborn replied, "If you don't like the colorful language of a common soldier, Private Kowalik, feel free to rip the pages out of your precious bible and stick them in your ears."

Runney burst in before Pieter could think up a suitable retort. "Nellie's gone," he announced breathlessly. "Vanished!"

"Don't be stupid. A goat doesn't just vanish," Tayborn said, sitting by the stove.

Runney sneezed and wiped his nose with his fingers. "I searched everywhere."

"Kowalik, you go look. Runney, show him. Don't either of you come back until you find her."

Pieter pulled on his boots and the rest of his clothes and accompanied Runney outside. The chill wind snuck past his collar and raised goose bumps on his back. Six months of this, he thought grimly. With a lout like Tayborn and an idiot like Runney, or whatever uncouth men replaced them. It seemed like a terribly unjust sentence for a crime he hadn't even committed.

"See?" Runney asked, shivering. "No Nellie!"

There weren't many places for a goat to hide on the island. The lower warrens of the keep were all locked, the rocky outcrops offered no purchase, and the animal certainly hadn't climbed into the dory and rowed herself away.

"Where do you keep that boat, anyway?" Pieter asked.

Runney took him to the east shore, where a small pier and boathouse jutted into the waves. It wasn't much of a building—gray, ramshackle, caving it on itself. The doors were long gone and the place smelled like rotting fish. More importantly and ominously, the boathouse was empty.

"What'll we do?" Runney asked, his face starkly pale. "What if we need help?"

Pieter glanced across the high waves toward the mainland. "We could light a bonfire."

"There's no wood. Only a few pieces of furniture."

"Isn't there a flagpole of some kind?" Pieter asked. "A distress flag?"

Runney shook his head hard. "The pole fell over three summers ago."

"Of course it did," Pieter said.

Back in the guard house, Tayborn didn't take their news well. "What do you mean, the boat's missing?"

"Boat and goat both," Runney said. He smiled unexpectedly. "Boat and goat. They rhyme!"

Tayborn slapped the side of Runney's head. "Shut up." He swung on Pieter. "That's your doing, is it? Thought you'd pull a prank in return by setting a poor helpless goat adrift on our only means of escape?"

Pieter resisted the urge to back up under the hostile glare. He would not let himself be intimidated. "I would do no such thing. Besides which, I was here all night. You would have heard if I'd left. Both of you were outside when I woke! To where, I wonder?"

"I always walk in the morning," Tayborn said. "Rain or shine. Keeps my legs from aching. Where were you, Runney?"

"Up on the North Wall, singing to her," Runney said.

Pieter and Tayborn stared at him.

"I know you said she's not real," Runney told Pieter. He chewed on his bottom lip with his rotten teeth. "But you, Sergeant. You wouldn't lie to me all these months, right? So I thought it best to keep doing it. Especially since tonight's Deadwinter Eve."

Tayborn grimaced. He sat in largest chair by the stove and opened his tobacco pouch. "Every man has to decide for himself what to believe and what not to believe, Runney. But you might as well realize you're not even married."

"He's not?" Pieter asked.

"I am!" Runney insisted.

"Don't be foolish," Tayborn snapped. "You told me and Coomey all about it. There was an angry father and a pistol, but no priest. It ain't official without a priest. Even if she's a slip of a girl getting big with child. You fell for the prank anyway. Every morning, Coomey and I laughed our asses raw watching you sing buck-naked on the North Wall."

Runney's expression twisted. "I don't understand. How can there be no Witch? What about Nellie, and the boat, and the footprints?"

Pieter hung up his coat.

Tayborn stuffed tobacco into his pipe.

"I don't believe either of you anymore," Runney said, face crumpling into tears, and went back out into the rain.

Peter went to his bunk. He pulled out his Eveland Bible and resolutely began reading his four scriptures for the day. He still hadn't had breakfast, but he didn't feel settled enough to swallow tea or toast.

"You're just going to sit there?" Tayborn demanded.

He took his time answering. "You're the sergeant, sergeant."

"You're the one who's gone and stirred up all this trouble," Tayborn snapped. "You think I don't know you made those footprints on your own? Your feet are small enough to be a woman's."

"All you needed was a plaster cast and a wooden pole," Pieter said. "I'm sure that there's many a prop left over from all the soldiers who've served here during the years."

Tayborn's face grew mottled. "I've told you exactly the story of the Sea Witch as it was taught to me. Maybe it is just a myth. A ghost story that's become a convenient way to scare the new men. But not only is tonight Deadwinter Eve, it's also the one hundredth anniversary of her death. Come midnight, you're the one who's going to pay the price of disbelief."

"Or maybe not," Pieter said. "Maybe she's coming for you, and anyone else here who's lain with a low woman. Which, I assure you, is something I've never done."

Tayborn grimaced. "You're wrong. It's the married ones she goes for."

"I guess we'll find out tonight," Pieter said, and turned back to his bible.

The weather grew worse as the hours lengthened. Pieter read and composed entries in his diary and read, for perhaps the hundred time, the book he'd penned as an anonymous gentleman of Massasoit. That it had failed to find any audience whatsoever still made his heart ache. The two critics who'd given it any notice at all had been uniformly dismissive. "A failed transparent attempt," said one. "Forgettable prose and ideas," said the other. Valeria had made him promise not to go challenge each man to a duel.

"Your pride," she'd whispered one night. "Such a fearsome thing."

Yes, he had a lot of pride. But no money. Instead, children hungry for dinner and a wife who couldn't be expected to support their family sewing piece work. So here Pieter was, pulling an army salary, listening to the wind worsen as Deadwinter Eve drew inexorably nearer.

Tayborn played cards by himself. Runney stayed out in the fort somewhere and didn't even come in for mid-day dinner, which Tayborn and Pieter prepared and ate while ignoring each other. Come the gray light of late afternoon, during a break in the weather, Pieter put aside his misgivings and went outside. He searched the old ammunition rooms, the enlisted quarters, and the officer's chambers. In the garrison captain's private quarters he imagined where Captain Santolv must have been lying with a prostitute when his wife opened the door. He could almost hear Mrs. Santolv's shriek of surprise. Or maybe that was the wind, the damned ceaseless wind, tormenting Pieter as it must have tormented soldiers here for centuries.

He hurried back to the guard house under a sky thickening with fog.

"I can't find him," Pieter said, the first words he'd spoken in hours.

Tayborn grimaced. "Fool. Probably went underground, hiding like a little child."

"Are we going to let him?" Pieter asked.

"You want to coddle him, is that it?"

"He could be in trouble somewhere. Fallen and hurt himself."

Tayborn clearly didn't like it, but in the end he rose to the responsibilities of his position. They took lanterns and keys to the rusty old doors. The restricted warrens were worse than Pieter imagined. Dark as a coal pit, or how he imagined a coal pit would be. No windows at all here. Just dungeons of stone and moss where Kilvemi prisoners had once languished and rotted in their chains, waiting for the end of war. The storm outside created eerie whispers inside. Pieter fought a rising sense of dread. He told himself it was impossible to hear the dead or feel their fingers reaching for his arm.

"Stop playing games, Runney!" Tayborn shouted. "That's an order!"

No answer from Runney. No answer from the ghosts.

It took hours to finish their fruitless search. The sky had gone pitch-black while they were inside, and the storm drove rain like needles into Pieter's face. At the guard house they stripped out of their wet clothes and built up the coals in the stove, to no avail. Pieter could not get warm.

"Supper will make things better," Tayborn announced. "I've been thinking about tinned sardines all day."

Pieter opened the food cupboard.

His gasp made Tayborn push him aside to take a first-hand look.

The four shelves had been cleaned out of sardines, biscuits, jams, beans and tea. All their food, in fact, had utterly vanished. There was only seaweed and handfuls of wet sand, and the cracked-open body of a crab, and the picked-clean skeleton of a large fish.

"What did you do?" Tayborn demanded.

"How could I do anything! I was with you!" Pieter returned, fury rising. Again he'd been fooled by their plan. "This is your doing! In collusion! You and Runney can't give up this damned prank!"

Tayborn swung a punch at him. Pieter saw it coming but couldn't duck in time to save himself. He'd never been any good at fighting as a child, and against a man as large as Tayborn he had no hope at all. The first punch slammed into his jaw, spinning him into the wall. The second landed hard against his side, driving pain like a sledgehammer through his ribs.

"Stop!" Pieter cried out. "I beg you!"

Tayborn stopped, but not before landing a few more punches that left Pieter bloody and hurting on the floor. Tayborn stomped away. The sergeant breathed hard through his nose and mouth, like a bull. Pieter clung to one of the cupboard's open doors but didn't have the strength or inclination to get back on his feet. He feared another punch, or maybe a kick, if he angered Tayborn more.

"Admit it," Tayborn said, his fists opening and closing.

Pieter said, "Yes. I did it. I made the footprints with my own feet. Trying to be…" The words came hard. "I was trying to be clever."

Tayborn nodded.

"But I didn't do anything to the boat!" Pieter added.

Another nod. Without remorse Tayborn said, "I did. It was an accident. I keep a flask of whiskey in its stern. Two sips, every morning. Medicinal. But this morning the line broke under my weight and it was all I could do to leap back to the pier before the waves took the boat away."

Pieter slowly sat up straighter. His side flared with pain, and he could taste blood in his mouth like a sickening liquor. "The goat?"

"Stupid animal probably fell into the sea. Thing was half-blind to begin with."

"And the food?"

Tayborn's gaze shifted past Pieter to the shelves.

"Runney's idea of a joke," Tayborn said. "Wherever he is. Here I thought he was the fool, but he's been fooling me for months with that pretense of idiocy. Man's brilliant. Utterly brilliant."

With that, Tayborn straightened a chair that had been knocked aside. Pieter got himself to his feet and limped to his bunk. He pulled out his diary but his hand shook too badly to journal the day's events. He desperately wanted tea, or maybe some of Tayborn's whiskey stash, but all they had was hot water from the kettle on the stove. His stomach ached with hunger and two teeth felt loose on the right side of his jaw.

"I'm going to sleep," Tayborn announced. "So I can dream all night of strangling Runney tomorrow."

It was the smartest thing Tayborn had said since Pieter's arrival. After washing his bruised face carefully, Pieter settled into his own bunk and huddled under the blankets. The only light came from the red coals in the oven. Outside, the Deadwinter storm raged and howled. Pieter thought of Valeria at home in their lumpy bed, the boys nestled in beside her, all the cats and rats and other vermin settled down for the night. Valeria would be wearing her green nightgown and wool socks, and each of the boys would be snug in caps and swaddling. Their rented house in one of Massasoit's poorer neighborhoods was only a temporary setback; with the army pay he was sending back to them, Valeria would soon be able to pay off their debts and afford better lodgings.

The door opened and slammed against the wall like a pistol-shot.

"She's here!" Runney shouted from the doorway. He was soaking wet and wild-eyed and elated, though not sane. "Don't you see? She's real after all!"

The woman behind Runney stepped forward with seaweed around her ankles. She was no slip of a girl forced into marriage by an angry father. Her blue-green skin shone with a hard inner illumination, and sea snakes moved through her long black hair. Her eyes glittered like silver fish scales. On her face was the terrible smile of a shark.

"She came," Runney said, oblivious to Pieter and Tayborn's horror. "She heard my singing and she came. Isn't that wonderful?"

The battalion commander looked out his window at the flat gray water of the harbor. Fort Defiance was a bare smudge on the horizon. Behind the commander, the ferryman shuffled his weight from one foot to the other but kept his hands clasped behind his back.

"And he insisted on this crazy story?" the commander asked.

"Sir. Yes, sir. That the Sea Witch came on Deadwinter Eve and killed Sergeant Tayborn for the crime of lying with low women. But she loved Private Runney because of the songs he'd been singing to her, so she took him into the sea and made him her husband."

"You saw Tayborn's body."

The ferryman's voice shook. "It was a terrible sight, sir. But there was no sign of Runney."

The commander stroked his bearded chin. "You left Private Kowalik out there."

"I didn't think it safe to row back with a madman!"

"Excellent decision." The commander turned briskly. "Who else have you told?"

"No one, sir. I came straight here. This is his written account of what happened, which he begged me to deliver. Here's a letter and postcard he asked me to post to his wife." The ferryman handed over the documents, twined with string and still damp from the journey. "I haven't read either."

The commander sat in his chair but left the ferryman standing. "Your discretion is appreciated. This is a terrible tragedy. A tragedy for us all. At the same time, an opportunity! You have proven yourself a man of courage and quick thinking. We need men like you working at the consulate in Kilvemi. Such an embassy we have there. You've heard of it?"

"Yes, sir." The ferryman's expression brightened. "Food like a feast at every meal. Tropical beaches and dancing girls—" He caught himself. "I mean, excellent entertainment."

"And excellent opportunities for financial gain," the commander reminded him. "I am at this very moment penning your transfer letter."

The commander scratched his pen against paper for several moments. He sealed the letter and handed it over.

"Present that to the quartermaster and he'll advance your pay. You will leave today. Outstanding work, son."

The ferryman took the parchment. Hesitated. "What of Pieter Kowalik, sir?"

The commander sighed. "The time has come for Fort Defiance to be decommissioned. Its illustrious history can no longer be an excuse for the sad state of disrepair and the cost of keeping men posted there. This tragedy, should it become known, would only stain its legacy in the minds of the public and press. I shall have the manning document changed and the supply roster amended immediately. The island shall be placed off limits to military and civilians alike. Private Kowalik shall be recalled and quietly discharged after he admits that Sergeant Tayborn and Private Runney killed each other in some petty quarrel that got out of hand, and that he disposed of Runney's body for pity's sake. Can I count on your continuing discretion?"

"Yes, sir! I shall tell no one."

"Good. You're dismissed. Give my regards to Kilvemi."

When the ferryman was gone the commander returned to his window. He was new to this posting, eager to make a good name for himself. The scandal of murder and insanity would hardly encourage his goals. Meanwhile, a few unremarkable soldiers gone astray could easily be overlooked among the thousands of others who came and went from Cardyr each year. Fort Defiance itself was easily overlooked as well—one sad little island and neglected bastion with no source of fresh food, and the rest of the winter season remaining to bring storms and hardship.

He put Kowalik's letters and postcard into a metal trash can and watched the paper burn to gray ash.

Afterward he donned his coat and cap and set off for home, where his wife and five children were waiting for him. After supper, by the light and warmth of the hearth, he would smoke his pipe and tell them stories; stories of brave soldiers and old wars, perhaps. Of heroes and battlefields. Perhaps he would tell them a ghost story or two, given the Deadwinter season. But he would not tell them, nor would he ever tell anyone else, the story of Pieter Kowalik and the Sea Witch.

Author's notes

1. A young writer named Edgar Allan Poe, in debt after paying for the publication of his first (unsuccessful) book, enlisted in the United States Army in 1827 and was stationed at the old fortress Fort Independence in Boston Harbor. This is not his story.

2. Several of the names in this story are pulled from the tangled vines of the author's family tree. If you are related to the

Majorowiczs or Kowaliks of Boston, why not drop her a line?

3. Valeria Kowalik was devastated by the mysterious disappearance of her husband Pieter, but with three small children to care for, she had little time or energy to fight army bureaucracy. She later married a fireman and bore five more children, all of them boys. She died at age forty during an influenza epidemic.

4. Very few first editions of *Poems by a Gentleman of Massasoit* are known to survive, and they often bear mysterious watermarks.

5. Nellie the goat survived this story unharmed, through means unknown.

In the Land
OF MASSASOIT

After a night of noisy, rattling travel on a freight car, the boy Cubby woke to a cold spring sunrise. He hunkered down by an open doorway, coat wrapped tightly and hands jammed in his pockets, and watched as the landscape of sea marshes evolved into mile after mile of wooden shacks, poorly made houses, scrap heaps, junk yards, small factories, belching smokestacks. His stomach ached with hunger but the miasma of a passing slaughterhouse nearly made him gag. When the train went around curves he saw the jagged and imposing skyline of Massasoit waiting for him mercilessly. The excitement he'd felt upon leaving Cardyr—free at last!—was tempered now by the sickening realization there was no one in the city to care for him at all—not his sad mother, not his ill-tempered stepfather, not even the talking head of Graybeard on the ocean boardwalk.

The train gradually slowed as it approached the freight yards. Cubby saw hobos leap from other cars and guessed that there would be security guards in the yards, men with billy clubs and mean eyes. He jumped as well, rolling on the gravel railbed, and survived with only a few scrapes on his palms. After passing under a chain-link fence, he wandered through neighborhoods of squat houses and dirty sidewalks. His journey took him past old men curled up on wooden benches and scrawny, sick-looking dogs sitting in alleys. He was cold and felt weak all over. He was sure he'd be dead within a few days, but it seemed like a good idea to keep moving anyway.

Organ music, sporadic but cheerful, drew him to the open doors of a enormous brick church at the corner of Duchess Street. From the outside, the building looked so new that the mortar was probably still wet. Inside, dozens of empty pews led to a mahogany altar heavy with fresh flowers. Above the altar hung pale wooden statues of three men nailed to wooden crosses. The statues' eyes were blazing white. White with wrath, Cubby thought. Like they could see clear through him to all the dirty secrets in his soul.

He was only twelve years old, but he had one or two secrets worth burning over. Cubby turned around. A man's voice boomed down at him from the organ loft, stopping him in place.

"Hello, little traveler!" the man said. "Sit down and take that load off your feet."

Cubby squinted at the railing. He couldn't see anyone up there. "Who says I'm a traveler?"

"We get many young men passing through from the train tracks," the man said. His words were followed by three dramatic chords of music—dark, majestic, full of mystery. "We minister to all who walk through the door."

Cubby gazed at the open doors. "Doesn't seem like many are walking in, Reverend, sir."

A wooden bench scraped on the loft floor. Footsteps tapped on an unseen set of stairs. A red curtain parted, and the reverend emerged—tall, handsome, wearing a dark suit. Not much older than Cubby's stepfather, who had once tried to drown him.

"The immigrants in this neighborhood need persuasion from their heathen religions," the reverend announced somberly. "Even now, they're picking out their fancy hats and pretty shoes to wear to the services of blasphemous goddesses. Into this sin and desolation I was sent by my superiors to establish on oasis of spiritual salvation. My name is Sawberry Chicken."

Cubby tried to stifle a giggle, but was not entirely successful.

"The surname Chicken has been in my family for many generations," the reverend said, with a twinkle in his eye. "What's your name?"

"Graybeard," Cubby said.

"Another unusual name," Reverend Chicken said. "Would you like to join me for breakfast, young Graybeard? I have tea and bread, strawberry jam, some lovely fresh eggs, and the morning paper to peruse."

Cubby was tempted, oh so tempted, by the prospect of hot food and strawberry jam. It wouldn't be a kindness, he supposed, to keep the holy man company on this lonely Sunday morning. But surely the reverend's resemblance to his stepfather was an omen that should not be ignored.

"I promise I won't try to proselytize you," the reverend said.

"That's a big word," Cubby said warily.

"It means I won't talk about religion."

"Well, that's okay, I suppose."

Breakfast was everything Reverend Chicken promised, and a bit more, too: bread toasted in a skillet, freshly churned butter, sugar for the tea. The rectory kitchen was a warm and sunny refuge. As promised, there was no talk of god or goddesses or anything religious. The minister browsed through the newspaper and murmured comments to himself about the state of the world these days. When Cubby had eaten as much as he could, he excused himself to use the bathroom and then kept on walking, right out the side door, through a garden beginning to bloom and out to the main street.

For most of the day he wandered through Massasoit, walking south from the immigrant neighborhoods into more elegant streets of brownstones, crossing from streets full of food stalls and aggressive merchants to quieter residential havens. He stopped to admire the elevated electric trains, which thundered over avenues on great metal supports. He hurried past tenements where kids his age played jackstraws, watched by housewives smoking cigarettes on stoops. Madmen ranting at invisible enemies, he avoided. Late in the day he spent some money on a hot pretzel at the corner of a park so big it looked like a wilderness. He supposed he was going to have to sleep in that park for the night, and the prospect filled him with dread. Better that he should have stayed with Reverend Chicken, but the good minister was several neighborhoods away, and Cubby didn't think he could find his way back without a map.

He entered the park under a large arch of iron, circled a stone reservoir of water, and found shelter in a thicket of trees near the bronze statue of a soldier on a horse. The soldier, with his droopy mustache and wide-rimmed hat, stayed silent as darkness descended. But under the light of the silver blue moon, the horse spoke in a low and sad voice.

"Little boy, these woods are no safe haven for children," the horse said.

Cubby was too tired to be surprised by yet another talking statute. He blew breath on his hands, trying to warm his fingers. "There's no place else for me to be."

The horse added, "And you shouldn't talk to strangers. My name is Kanthaka."

"That's a strange name for a horse."

"It's an honorable name of great historic significance," the horse sniffed. "Will you bring me some of that grass? I have longed to eat it for many years."

Cubby wasn't in the mood to fetch grass, but perhaps the grateful horse would tell him secrets of survival. He ripped out fresh shoots by the roots, climbed the base of the statue, and pushed them up into the horse's open mouth.

"Tastes like spring," the horse murmured. "Tastes like new life."

"I'm looking for a place," Cubby said. "A safe house for kids."

"Will you bring me more?"

Cubby climbed down. Twice more he brought Kanthaka grass, and then a most amazing thing happened. The metal in the horse's legs began to stretch and buckle and shriek. The front legs, already high in the air, rose up even more. The statue of the rider toppled backward and landed with a solid thunk. The horse twisted free of the pedestal, leapt through the air, and landed as a creature of muscle and flesh, with a sleek coat of black hair. Steam poured from its nostrils as it pawed at the dirt. Its tail swished furiously.

"Many years," Kanthaka said. "Many years I have waited for release. My gratitude, young child."

With that, the beast galloped across the park's expanse and disappeared into the far woods.

Cubby felt swamped with disappointment, but maybe the animal meant to come back to him. He huddled against a nearby tree and drew his knees to his chest. He waited. Come morning he was stiff with cold, and wearier than he'd ever been in his life. With shaking fingers he counted how many coins he had left. He was unfolding his cramped legs when a gray squirrel bounded over to him.

"Kanthaka says you should head ten blocks south, three blocks east, around the fountain, down Kensington Mews, two blocks past the firehouse, across Gravesner Square, and to the mansion across from Bellingham Park. That's Hartvern House. Ask for Miss Diana Comet and she will shelter you from harm."

Cubby blinked at him. "What?"

But the squirrel had already bounded away.

Cubby set off on foot, fortified by a hot toddy from a man pushing a cart with a great white eagle painted on its side. South took him down narrow canyons between shops, hotels, museums, dance halls, theaters, saloons, and residences. During the next sixteen hours he asked directions of seven strangers, three of whom who only spoke foreign languages, two of whom were drunks, one of whom was mentally ill, and the last of whom was marginally helpful. He was almost run over by a bus. Two schoolgirls giggled scornfully at his shabby clothing. Three schoolboys tried to bully him. A burly man with sinister intentions followed him for three blocks until Cubby vaulted a fence into a private garden. The gardener, a lonely old woman with poor eyesight, mistook him for her grandson and gave him crumpets. She told him stories about a war he'd never heard of, and then gave him erroneous directions to Hartvern House. He ended up at the tough waterfront, where he narrowly escaped being shanghaied by pirates. It was, all in all, an eventful day.

As the city succumbed to night and prospects for safe haven looked to be at their lowest, he passed a three-story house where bright red flames had begun to shoot out the windows. He shouted for help, dashed inside, and was responsible for the safe evacuation of ten innocent adults and children. The fire captain from Engine 13 gave him a hat and a badge as rewards, and upon learning of his homeless circumstances, drove him to Hartvern House. The firemen let him ride in the back of their gleaming engine, the lights blazing and sirens blasting despite the late hour

"This young lad's a hero," said the fire captain, depositing him into the care of the lady who answered the door. She was tall and dark-skinned and looked like she was quite accustomed to answering the door in the middle of the night.

"We'll take good care of him," she said.

She brought Cubby inside, tucked him and his soot-covered blanket on a sofa in the library, and brought him some hot apple cider. Cubby looked at the fine furniture and tall cases of finely bound books. He wondered if this really was a place he could call home.

"I'm supposed to ask for Miss Comet," he said, his throat hoarse from smoke.

"Miss Comet's not here," the woman replied, sitting in an armchair across from him. She was wearing a long green housecoat and plain slippers, and her voice had a strange drawl to it, but there was something commanding about her nevertheless. "Some say she's dead of old age, while others believe she's found a magical fountain of youth and is sailing the globe on a pirate ship. My own well-informed belief is irrelevant. Meanwhile, the mission of Hartvern House continues. I'm Mrs. Fayella Maytree Avery, her heir apparent. You may call me Miss Fay."

Cubby gulped at the hot cider. "Her hair parent?"

"Her successor," Miss Fay explained. "Tell me. Are you truly an orphan, or are you a runaway? Think carefully before you answer."

He wanted to lie, but his courage curled up and died in the face of her direct gaze. "My mom's alive," he mumbled.

"Do circumstances prevent you from feeling safe at home?"

He looked down at his shoes, which were ashy from the fire. "If you want to say it fancy like that."

"Are you familiar with *Poems by a Gentleman of Massasoit* or the collected works of Mr. Whitney Waltman?"

He supposed she meant books. In a low voice he admitted, "No, ma'am."

"Do you think you can be happy in a place where children are encouraged to think freely, behave as individuals, engage in free will, eschew tradition, and confound harmful gender and racial stereotypes?"

Cubby's head hurt. "Ma'am?"

Miss Fay took pity on him. "I'll ask again tomorrow, when you're not so obviously exhausted and coated with grime. Come now. You shall bathe and go to sleep, and we'll have this discussion again in the morning."

She rang a bell to wake the housekeeper, and sent him off to hot water and a clean bed.

Then, long after the grandfather clock in the hall chimed midnight, Fay sat in the dark room, sipping tea, thinking about her first fateful encounter with Miss Diana Comet.

Author's notes

1. Over the course of the next fifty years, Reverend Chicken's church became a pillar of the neighborhood. Over the course of fifty more, it fell into disrepair and disrepute. It eventually changed denominations and was partially renovated. Then aliens invaded Earth from outer space.
2. Reverend Chicken himself has been the subject of three biographies, two films, a Broadway musical, and two videos on YouTube.
3. The horse Kanthaka is a nod to Buddhist mythology and to the horse Athansor in Mark Helprin's magnificent novel *Winter's Tale*.
4. One of the children Cubby saved from the house fire went on to become a famous science fiction writer. You have not read her books.

Fay
AND THE GODDESSES

The choirmaster scowled at Fay and arched his gray, neatly groomed eyebrows. "How old are you, girl?"

She resisted the urge to tug on the sleeves of her new green dress. Pa had bought her the dress especially for this audition, though he'd had to borrow the money from Uncle Coll. Her new leather shoes, or at least new-to-her, squeaked on the hardwood floor of the church hall as she took a tiny step forward. Dust motes floating in shafts of autumn sunlight made her want to sneeze.

"I'm seven years old, sir," she said.

"We don't take applicants until they're eight."

The pianist, tall and white-haired and nearly as old as the choirmaster, lifted her chin from her music. "She's Deacon Maytree's niece."

"*Junior* Deacon Maytree," the choirmaster said with a sniff. He ran his thin fingers down the chain of his watch and into his pocket. "What songs do you know, child?"

Fay's hands were sweating. She started to wipe them on her dress, remembered that she wasn't supposed to, and instead clasped them behind her back. "I can sing 'Sweet Mamma Goddess Mine.'"

He rapped on his podium with his baton. "A heathen song! Don't you know anything proper?"

She almost protested that Grammy wasn't a heathen, no sir, and she and Fay sang that song every summer out in the fields. But from the way the choirmaster was glaring at her, she didn't think he'd listen. The pianist popped a peppermint in her mouth and glanced around the hall as if hoping someone more interesting might have silently snuck in.

Meekly Fay said, "I can sing 'Oh I Am Your Lamb.'"

The choirmaster continued to scowl. "Fine. Sing that. Miss Cawthorne?"

Miss Cawthorne lowered her fingers to the piano keys, waited a beat, and began to play.

Fay sucked in a deep breath and waited for her entrance. When the measure came, she sang just like Grammy had taught her to—loud enough to be heard over shovels and picks and chains, long enough that heaven would be pleased.

"Stop that!" The choirmaster shouted, and smacked his baton down again.

She stopped. Miss Cawthorne raised her fingers.

"This is the sacred ground of the Stern Loving Mother," the choirmaster said. "Not some hoe-down honky-tonk backyard hootch shack!"

Miss Cawthorne said, "Mr. Abbot. Such language."

The choirmaster's nostrils flared. Very precisely, he said, "Sing with grace, child. Sing as softly as a true lamb would."

"But lambs don't sing," Fay said, bewildered.

Miss Cawthorne started to play again.

The choirmaster raised his baton.

She tried singing like a lamb, which she supposed meant quiet and meek-like, not down on all fours with her nose in the feed. Fay didn't think the choirmaster much liked her singing, and Miss Cawthorne looked more interested in her peppermints, but when the music stopped both of them nodded, just a little bit.

The choirmaster said, "You can join the Children's Choir. But only if you promise to never again sing any of those blasphemous country hymns."

"Yes, sir," she said. "Thank you!"

On the walk home with Pap, she reasoned that the choirmaster only meant she couldn't sing country hymns when she was in the Stern Loving Mother's church. Surely he hadn't meant she couldn't sing them when she spent the summer months with Grammy. Summers were for the fields and Grammy's ratty little shack, which always smelled like tobacco and corn. The rest of the year was spent here in the city, with Pap and Fay and Uncle Coll snug in Uncle Coll's little brick house. The house had indoor plumbing, and a shed out back where Pap kept his liquor juice. Uncle Coll disapproved of liquor juice.

"How come they hate the Water Mamma here?" Fay asked Pap, just as they were crossing the street.

Pap made a harrumphing noise. "They just have different ways here in the city. You know that."

"The Stern Loving Mother is very beautiful," Fay admitted. She thought of the great ebony statue that hung over the church altar. "But ain't she harsh? The Water Mamma, she loves everyone."

"Don't you let your uncle go hearing talk like that," Pap warned.

"No, sir," Fay agreed. Uncle Coll did not take kindly to discussions about religion.

He squeezed her shoulder. "But you did good today. Your ma would be proud."

That Sunday, Fay began singing with the Children's Choir. They practiced for an hour before every service, singing scales and memorizing lyrics. They all wore black robes over their best clothes, and on special occasions wore fresh flower pins, too. Up in the choir loft they had to enter very quietly, no fidgeting allowed, and then file out again when their turn was done.

"Rank and file, very precise," Uncle Coll told her. "Like a little army of singing angels."

"Weren't many angels in the army I served in," Pap grumbled.

Fay liked being a soprano because she got to sing melody, whereas the altos usually got stuck with harmony. Reverend Dexter's beautiful daughter, Noranne, complained about harmony all the time. Choirmaster Abbot would hear none of that.

"Melody's easy," he said. "Harmony takes work and a complex understanding of music."

Noranne preened.

"Sounds like your choirmaster's an uppity little man," Grammy said come June, after Fay moved back for the summer and regaled her with stories. Grammy poured herself more sweet tea. "That church is a bunch of stiff know-it-alls with fancy hats and ain't-I-better-than-you lipstick. Still, they'd be downright fools not to recognize the Water Mamma in your voice. You've got a voice for the heavens, girl."

Fay was pleased. Despite her other winter accomplishments—she'd grown two inches, and received all A's in school—she was most pleased to hear that Grammy liked her voice.

"How come there aren't any kids singing in our church here?" Fay asked.

Grammy lifted her skinny, bent body from her chair. "Let's go find out."

The white clapboard church at the crossroads didn't have a fine organ like Uncle Coll's church did. Just hand-clapping and foot-stomping and a dozen women sweating heavily under royal red robes. Fay had always envied their big hair and big voices. Miss Lina, in charge of the choir, listened to Fay sing Grammy's favorite, "The Devil Don't Treat Me Nice."

"Well," Miss Lina said, afterward. "That was fine. But a little stiff."

"Stiff?" Fay asked.

"You don't just sing with your voice, little girl. You've got to sing with everything you've got. Put your hips into it. Wave your hands. You think the Water Mamma wants you to stand there like an upright corpse? Be a tree! Bow in the wind!"

Fay tried singing like a tree. She swung her hips around and waved her arms.

Miss Lina nearly fell over in amusement. "Well, then. Maybe you could just be a little sapling for now."

By age twelve, Fay understood the theological differences between winter and summer. Ma's ma and her folk believed the Water Mamma lived in rivers and lakes and the sea, which Fay had seen only in picture books. The Water Mamma had green flowing hair and eyes like silver fish scales. Pap's people believed instead in the Stern Loving Mother. She lived above the clouds with angels and cherubs at her side. Both the Water Mamma and the Stern Loving Mother were locked in eternal battle with the Lady Devil, who spouted smoke from her fiery horns and told nothing but lies, lies, lies.

"Your voice is a sacred gift from the Stern Loving Mother," Uncle Coll said one night, just after she'd turned thirteen. "Like all sacred gifts, it has to be given back. It'll help the Stern Loving Mother beat down the Lady Devil and keep us all safe."

Fay paused over her addition and subtraction. "If she needs it so bad, how come she gave it to me in the first place?"

"Don't get smart, young lady," Uncle Coll said.

Standing by the gas stove, warming his hands by the blue gas flames, Pap said, "Coll. That's enough."

"Girl has to have respect." Coll pulled at his tie. He put one on every morning for work at the bank and didn't take it off until bedtime. "Giving back is a joy."

Pap turned his broad back to them. "Not her time yet. Not until next year."

She'd heard of Giveback but it was always something vague and far away, like marriage and paying taxes and letting a boy kiss you for reasons other than a dare. Her Sunday School teacher would only say that it was an honor and an act of devotion. Fay's classmates had nothing to share but gossip. "It's when they cut off all your hair," Sue-May Clark told her. "Or maybe it's when you marry the Stern Loving Mother's oldest son."

"What if you're a boy?" Fay asked.

"If you're a boy, you get to marry Her yourself." Sue-May paused. "Or maybe you have to cut an extra hole in your pee-stick."

She heard that Joey Elks, who was all the way up in high school, had given back his ability to run faster than all the other boys. Afterward he could still play football, but he wasn't very good at it. Sweetpea Johnson, once the prettiest girl in town, had given back her beauty. Now the boys thought she was just so-so. Noranne Dexter, even more beautiful now that she was growing curves and breasts, was going to give back her artistic ability. Every Sunday her finely detailed drawings decorated the church newsletter. One of her drawings had won a city-wide competition.

Fay caught up to her after school one rainy day. "Aren't you scared?"

"Scared of what?" Noranne asked, peeking out from under her red umbrella. She had the prettiest brown eyes Fay had ever seen, and if she liked you she smiled in a way that was warmer than the sun.

"Giving back to the Stern Loving Mother. Is it going to hurt? Can't you say no?"

Noranne flicked her gaze away. "Silly country girl. You don't know anything."

The next Sunday, Fay lingered after mass and hid behind the heavy velvet curtains of the choir loft. She watched as Noranne approached the altar in a white dress and lace veil. Her father lifted up a golden chalice. The sleeves of his fine purple robe wrinkled just a little.

Reverend Dexter asked, "Do you, child of the Stern Loving Mother, give your gift back freely and without reservation, for all the days and nights of your life to come?"

Down in the pews, Noranne's mother and aunts pressed handkerchiefs to their faces. The air was heavy with the smell of lilacs and vanilla candles. Fay leaned closer to the railing and bit her upper lip with worry.

"I do," Noranne said.

Fay couldn't watch any more of it. She left the loft, hurried out of the church's side door, and knocked right into an elderly white woman wearing a smart blue traveling suit. The woman went sprawling into a patch of grass, her hat askew and her purse spilling over.

"Hooligan!" the woman accused. "Scoundrel!"

"Oh, ma'am!" Fay said, genuinely contrite. She fussed over the old woman and helped collect the contents of her handbook—lipstick and compact, a comb with a pearl handle, a notebook filled with fine black handwriting. "I'm sorry! So sorry!"

"You should be a football linebacker," the woman groused, once she was back on her feet. Upright, she wasn't quite as old as Fay imagined, though her hair had a lot of gray in it and there were wrinkles around her eyes. The woman adjusted her hat and peered down at Fay. "Here I am, trying to make the best of an unexpected sojourn, and I'm attacked in broad daylight."

"I didn't mean to!" Fay protested.

"You shall have to make restitution for my unsettled state. You'll have to buy me a cup of tea," the woman announced. "And cookies."

Fay's mouth dropped open. "But I don't have any money."

"Then I shall have to buy the tea and cookies, and you can pay me back someday. Come this way."

Within minutes they were sitting in a corner booth in the dark, fancy restaurant of the Hotel Claremont. Fay was glad she had on her Sunday best, though it seemed inadequate compared to the stiff black vests and white shirts the waiters wore. The waiters were very nice to the woman in the blue suit, who introduced herself as Miss Diana Comet of Massasoit.

"That's mighty far away," Fay said, as she eyed the fine china of her teacup.

"Yes, extremely. My husband and I are on our fourth honeymoon, but he's currently over at the garage observing the repair of our automobile. The spirometer or capacitor or something similarly unfathomable burst into flames just as we were leaving town this morning. Give me a horse and carriage any day."

"If you're married, ma'am, why's your name Miss Comet?"

"You are an inquisitive child, indeed." Miss Comet stirred sugar in her tea with precise movements. "I keep my maiden name as a sign of feminine independence. Now, what's your name, and what puts you in the business of waylaying innocent strangers?"

Fay didn't think a rich city woman would understand. It probably wasn't even worth trying to explain. Nevertheless she described Noranne's ceremony, and did the best she could with the subject and dilemma that faced her in less than a year's time.

Miss Comet listened with grave attention. "We don't have these goddesses in the north. Dare I say I'm extremely suspect that they even exist. Nevertheless, I've heard of stranger customs than this Giveback, and children's souls are always being tested in unusual ways. What will happen if you reject this church of your father and your Uncle Coll? Will they beat you, imprison you, force you to capitulate?"

The lemon cookie that Fay was nibbling on suddenly tasted like talcum powder. "No, ma'am! I don't think so. But Uncle Coll, he might be so mad he'll make us leave. You can't be a deacon and have a blasphemer in the house."

"What of your grandmother? Will she condition her love on your commitment to this Water Mother?"

"Water Mamma," Fay corrected.

"Mother," Miss Comet insisted.

Fay said, quietly, "It's what my own mother would have wanted."

"I don't envy you your position," said Miss Comet, just as a sleek black roadster pulled up to the curb outside.

Fay knew such automobiles were most often driven by tycoons, movie stars, or even the Lady Devil herself. She watched through the big glass window as the driver got out. He was a tall, handsome man who walked with a limp. He came into the restaurant and soon was standing by their table.

"James," Miss Comet said, "May I introduce Miss Fay?"

James bowed at the waist. "My pleasure, young lady."

Fay giggled.

"Darling, you know I would never rush you," James said, taking Miss Comet's hand and kissing it. "However, we must leave town now if we're going to make it to the mountains before dark."

"Of course," Miss Comet said. "But first you must tell us, my love. What do you do when you're stuck between a rock and a hard place?"

"Paddle for shore," James advised.

"You have always been my boat," Miss Comet said, and Fay just shook her head. Sometimes adults said very strange things.

Three months later, after the turning of the year, Pap came to Fay's bedroom and gave her a dime. "For one of those milkshakes you like so much," and she thought he was feeling guilty because he'd been drinking too much liquor juice lately.

Fay looked up from her schoolbooks. "Pap, do I have to? Give back my singing voice when the summer's over? Because Nellie Hutchins and Bella Grindel both had their birthdays, and they're in the choir, and they didn't have to give up their voices."

He scratched the side of his head. "Nellie and Bella don't sing fine like you. That's the difference. It ain't a sacrifice if you don't have much to give."

"Will I be able to sing at all?" Fay fretted.

He dropped a rough kiss on her forehead. "Worry about it later, little girl of mine."

Fay didn't spend Pap's dime on a milkshake. She put it in the small cigar box that also held her baby teeth and the only photograph she had of Ma before the sickness took her. Later she added the quarter Mrs. Dannon gave her for singing in the Equinox Concert, and the silver half-dollar she was paid for singing at the Mayor's birthday breakfast. She liked counting the money. She liked the weight of it in her palm, and the prospects it represented.

"Girl like you could be a famous singer some day," the Mayor had told her. A singer like Ella Herald, whose scratched vinyl records Pap liked to play when Uncle Coll was away at church meetings. Like Millie Mae Brown, who posed for magazine covers wearing pearls around her long graceful neck. But Ella and Millie Mae were sinners. They smoked and drank and ran around with married men, or so Uncle Coll said. They cavorted with the Lady Devil.

Sometimes Fay pretended Ella Herald was her mother, who'd run off from home to be famous and was going to send for her any day now so they could live together in a fancy house full of music and cats. Any day now.

School let out in early June. Fay dragged her feet all the way home. That night she said, "Pap, I don't want to go to the country tomorrow. Sue-May Clark is having her birthday party next week, and she said there's going to be four different kinds of cupcakes. And I'll miss the Armistice Picnic. The mayor said he'd give me a whole dollar if I sang the national anthem."

Uncle Coll stirred sugar into his after-dinner coffee. "Seems to me the girl's got a point."

Pap was sitting in his big armchair, the evening newspaper in his lap. He shook his head. "Promised her grandmother."

"But they're all dumb in the country," Fay said. "Dumb and poor."

Pap stood up so quickly the newspaper slid to the floor. "Shut your mouth. Your Ma was country folk, and damn proud of it."

"Frank," Uncle Coll said mildly. "No blasphemy."

They locked gazes, Pap and Uncle Coll, and then Pap left the house to take refuge with his liquor juice.

Fay moped all night long. She kept silent the next day when Pap walked her downtown, refusing to meet his eye in any way. He put her on a bus that smelled like gasoline and handed her a paper bag containing a ham sandwich and big red apple.

"You're growing up fast," he said roughly, standing hunched over in the aisle.

She turned her face to the window.

"Your Ma, she sang like you. First time I heard her, I was on the army bus and we stopped for soda at a little country store. She was out back, singing hymns as she washed out the milk bottles. Worst thing I ever did was take her away to the cold hard city."

Fay broke her sulky silence. "Do you think she listens, Pap? That she can hear me up in heaven?"

"I'm sure she hears you all the time."

"But especially when I sing?"

Pap tugged on her ear. "Don't get too boastful."

The bus jolted and rattled through the muddy countryside for five hours. At the end of the ride Fay walked up the path to Grammy's shack and was met with warm arms and a toothless smile. Grammy made her special corn cake for dinner and listened to all of Fay's winter stories. The sun went down in the fields, turning the night black and noisy with insects.

"Do I really have to giveback my voice when I go back to Pap and Uncle Coll?" Fay asked as she lay on her straw bed.

Grammy sucked on her pipe. The little red embers glowed from across the room. "That's a decision only you can make. The Water Mamma would never ask you for such a sacrifice, child. What does your daddy think about it?"

"Daddy does whatever Uncle Coll wants."

"I know. Don't I know." And after that Grammy was silent, and the rocking of her chair lulled Fay to sleep.

In the morning Fay went to work with her aunts and uncles and cousins, filling burlap sacks with cotton. The late rains had left some bolls only half-open. Her hands and fingers got all scratched up as she pried them out. The days were ten hard hours long, sometimes twelve. She sang heathen songs with the others and worried plenty about her Giveback. Grammy said nothing more on the subject.

"It doesn't make sense to me," Fay told Miss Lina at the crossroads church one afternoon, after her work for the day was done. "Why's it bad to be good at something?"

Miss Lina said, "Them city folk, they don't want people to be good at things. Makes the mediocre majority feel poorly about themselves. But the Water Mamma, she loves everyone at their best and brightest. She won't ever ask you to give up anything but the sin of luxury."

"Luxury?" Fay didn't know anyone in the country or the city who drove fine cars or wore expensive furs. Only Mille Mae Brown and Ella Herald, featured in the magazines. She kicked her heels against the hard pew beneath her, then stilled her ankles. "Is drinking milkshakes a luxury?"

Miss Lina said, "Anything that's not simple and direct."

Fay had never considered that Grammy's wretched little shack was a deliberate choice. That sleeping on the floor battling heat and bugs was an act of devotion.

Miss Lina tugged on one of Fay's braids. "You want to escape the clutches of that Mean Loving Witch, you get yourself baptized in the Water Mamma's name. This Sunday, Reverend Hatt will be doing the dunking in Big Weed Creek. Dawn time. After that, your Pa's people won't touch you at all. You won't have to give back anything."

In the days that followed, as she worked and sweated hard to fill her sacks, Fay tried to imagine herself toiling in the fields for the rest of her life. She'd be able to sing, sure, but what good was that? Her cousins and uncles and aunts sang about loneliness and heartbreak because that was all they knew. When they got sick there was only one doctor to send for, and he was half-drunk all the time. They had to walk three miles each way to get to the country store. They didn't have schools, and could hardly read or write, and never even looked at the newspapers.

Miss Lina hadn't said Fay would have to live in the country, but Pap and Uncle Coll would be mighty mad if she returned to the city with a water swirl on her forehead. Even if Uncle Coll let her stay, all the people at church would turn their backs. Reverend Dexter and Choirmaster Abbot wouldn't let her sing anymore. The mayor himself might not even look her in the eye. Water-folk weren't good for anything but cleaning toilets and taking out the trash for proper folk.

Saturday night, as they ate fried catfish and sweet potatoes for dinner, Grammy said, "I know you talked to Miss Lina. You going to the creek in the morning, little girl?"

"Should I?" Fay asked.

"It's a hard thing, surrendering the gift of luxury. It's nothing I wish lightly on you. But what's your other choice? Go back to the city and give your voice to that witch?"

"She's not a witch," Fay said. The Stern Loving Mother was kind and gracious. It wasn't her fault she was locked in eternal battle with the Lady Devil. "And maybe I can keep a little of it. Just a little."

Grammy spat in the dust. "Never once have I told you which goddess to pick. Never once did I say this one or the other. It's all up to you."

Fay slept poorly that night. She dreamed of Uncle Coll in the city church, holding a golden chalice in his hand. The parishioners sat properly in their pews with manicured hands on their bibles. The stained glass windows glowed beautifully. In the dream Fay felt safe and loved. Then Grammy's snores or crawling bugs or a barking dog in the field would wake her, and it took hours and hours to get back to sleep. Again she stood in Uncle Coll's church, and everyone was smiling at her. Fay opened her mouth to thank them for their kindness but no sounds came out. Instead the Stern Loving Mother was singing with it, was singing with Fay's stolen voice, and Fay climbed up the statue to wrestle it back—

Grammy shook her arm.

"Time for the dunking," Grammy said.

Groggy with weariness, Fay pulled herself to her feet. Blue was beginning to chase black up the horizon but the full moon cast a wide silver path. She and Grammy followed fifteen or so other women down the long road to Big Weed Creek. The water was about five feet across, running fast and deep. Thick reedy stalks flanked it on both sides. They looked sharp enough to pierce Fay's skin if she stumbled too close. Though it wasn't cold out, she shivered.

"Sisters and brothers," Reverend Hatt said from knee-deep in the water. He was a tall man with milky-white eyes. Blind since birth, they said. "We come in Her name. We came to Her Waters."

The sun rose majestically, burning the edge of the world gold. The cotton fields stretched far and wide on top of the dark earth.

"Who comes to Her Hands? Who asks for Her Blessing?"

A line of women in cotton shifts edged forward. Hatt took them one by one. First he pulled a supplicant into the water. Then he put his right hand on her scarf-covered head. In the old language he shouted out words Fay didn't know. When he was done shouting he would push the supplicant down into the water and hold her there for a few seconds, or maybe a moment longer, depending on how the Spirit of the Water Mamma moved him. One woman thrashed and grabbed at his hands before he let her come up, sputtering and choking. A water swirl glowed on her forehead.

While the dunking continued the witnesses sang and shouted, and waved their hands in the air, and stomped their feet in the dirt.

"Go on, girl," one of them said to Fay, and pushed her hard on the shoulder.

In that moment she knew the truth.

"I can't," she said to Grammy. "I'm sorry."

Grammy's face turned fierce. "Get on, then. Get!"

She sprinted back up the road to Grammy's shack, shoved her things into a sack, and started walking three miles toward the general store. Her breathing was fast and her legs trembled. Sweat drenched her thighs and her eyes burned under the bright rising sun. She told herself she was going to a better place now. Not to luxury, but to kindness and security in the Stern Loving Mother's arms.

"Then why you weeping, girl?" asked a woman from nearby.

Fay turned. Parked by the side of the road was an old black car, rusty and dusty, and leaning against the hood was a middle-aged woman in a plain blue dress.

"I'm not crying," Fay said.

"Sure you are." The woman stood upright, one hip arched to the side. Confidence poured through her voice. "Seen it a million times, I have. Girls like you weep when their hearts are broken. When the end of the world's in sight. Or when a boy knocks a baby into you."

Fay wiped her face with her hand. "No. It's not that."

The woman swiveled on one foot, her thighs and legs and back all fluid and languid. The driver's door creaked open under her hand. She slid in behind the steering wheel and leaned out the open window.

"My name's Lucinda Hatt," she said. "I come down here once in a while, see if I can't persuade my daddy to stop dunking people in the creek. Lost cause, I say. But hope, she springs. Springs all over."

Fay's tears had stopped. She felt calmer, but also a little emptier.

"Come on," Lucinda said. "I'll give you a lift. It's not safe for a girl like you, all alone out here in the heat and loneliness."

Bag in hand, Fay glanced down the long straight road toward town. Heat made the air shimmer and blurred her vision.

"I much appreciate it, ma'am," she said as climbed in.

The woman turned the ignition key. "My pleasure."

The worn vinyl of the front seat was hard, but it sure beat walking. The road unwound beneath the car wheels and the loud hum of the engine was a lullaby. Fay dreamed she was back in Big Weed Creek, stepping forward to Reverend Hatt's embrace. He pushed her down in the water. The cold river filled her ears and closed over her head. In the currents she heard the sweet voice of the Water Mamma, calling her home. But the voice was drowned out by music, loud and jarring, that yanked Fay out of her doze. She jerked sideways and nearly hit her head on the window frame.

Lucinda's fingers reached for the car radio and turned down the volume knob.

"That's rock'n'roll," she said. "Ever hear it before?"

Fay listened hard. The words didn't much make sense—"Do la la" and "Sha ra ra"—but the beat itself caught her heart and made it pound just a little faster.

"Who sings it, ma'am?"

"Why, singers just like you. Singers with fire in their bellies. The man I work for is the president of the Poor Dumplin recording label. You ever hear of it? No? They've got the biggest stars, the biggest fame. Headquartered in a fine luxury suite. You walk in, they serve you ice cold water in crystal glasses. The rugs come from New Dalli and the bathroom faucets are pure gold. You sure you've never heard of them?"

"No, ma'am."

"I guess they don't listen much to rock'n'roll out here in the sticks. But your pappy, I bet he listens to it. Big man like him, made little by the city. I guess he'd know, yes indeed."

Fay blinked hard. The car around her was slowly changing. The worn dashboard became darker and prettier, fresh off the assembly line. Cracks in the leather seats repaired themselves. The dirty windshield began to gleam. Lucinda Hatt's plain cotton dress turned to frilly silk, low on her chest and high on her thigh. Red lipstick on her lips now, wet enough to fall into.

"What do you know about me or my pappy?" Fay asked.

"I know enough." Lucinda's red fingernails tapped the steering wheel. "I know a thousand girls like you. Dirt-poor in the country or soul-poor in the city. You want a husband, girl? Some fancy upright man who'll beat you when the doors are closed in your tidy little home, or some country boy who'll have you wiping baby snot and doing his laundry all day long?"

Fay scrubbed her eyes. The long nose of the car was now gleaming black. The loud engine was a soft purr.

"You're not the minister's daughter," she said, and her voice trembled.

Lucinda grinned wide and eased the car to a stop. Nothing but fields surrounded them, wide and open. "Maybe once I was. Now, I'm a woman of independent means."

The sky was a blank stretch of blue untainted by clouds. Heat crawled out of the dirt and through the open windows, baking Fay's skin. When she put her hand on the doorknob, it was icy cold beneath her fingers. Cold like the Water Mamma's creek, cold like the Stern Loving Mother's gaze. She thought of Pap sitting in his chair reading newspapers, and Grammy in her chair smoking her pipe.

"This world is cruel to girls of color," the Lady Devil said. "It stomps them down and grinds them into the dust. You make your choice and live with it for the rest of your life, girl. Come with me and I'll show you the world."

Fay was silent for a moment, imagining the possibilities. Then, very carefully, she opened the door and stepped out onto the dusty road. Her knees were trembling, but her resolve was strong.

"Thank you for the offer, ma'am," she said, politely. "I appreciate your interest."

A frown, a wrinkle. The Lady Devil hated losing. "Where you going, girl?"

Fay started walking. She figured the trip would be long and hard, but the road was clear enough. "Paddling for shore."

Author's notes

1. Does this story inaccurately portray, represent, depict, or otherwise characterize characters of color? Discuss.
2. Uncle Coll, it should be recognized, had his own problems to deal with. As Junior Deacon he was invariably responsible for all the jobs the Senior Deacons did not want, which included self-flagellation and suffering from instruments of mortification in the name of the Stern Loving Mother. On his deathbed, Uncle Coll wished for oblivion and not any kind of afterlife. Such wishes often go unfulfilled.
3. Lady Devil perfume is available in fine stores everywhere.

Diana Comet

AND THE LOVESICK COWBOY

*I*n about five minutes the lovesick cowboy was going to lurch off his lumpy bed, grab his pistol, stumble out to the balcony of this fleabag hotel and shoot every last bullet down into the saloon across the street. Justifiable homicide, some slick lawyer might say. No man should have to listen to *Campside Traces* a dozen times in a row on a broiling hot summer day. Murdering the piano player would be doing the entire town of Goldstone a favor, and maybe afterward the mayor would pin a hero's medal on Sam Landan's chest.

Landan didn't want medals. He'd had medals, once upon a time. They were scattered now, like silver and gold birds, lost to pawn shops or barroom bets on the journey west. All he really wanted was his Isaac, who was out there in the hills hopefully just as miserable and lonely as he was. But unless that stubborn fool saw reason, Landan would have to make do with alcohol.

That wretched song began again. Maybe it would be more expeditious to shoot himself instead of the pianist. He wouldn't have to walk so far, and there was less chance of hurting someone innocent. Then again, the walls were so flimsy any bullet through his temple might just arc through the plaster and hit his neighbors—the ladies of ill repute over in room 206, or the recluse with the awful cough over in room 202. To be a true gentleman he'd have to shoot up through his chin. Luckily the ceiling already had so many holes in it that one more wasn't likely to make a difference.

Instead of shooting himself he grabbed the whiskey bottle and drained the last precious gulp. His last swallow coincided with a brisk knock on the door. Surely a mistake. The room was paid up through the week, and nobody in town had business with him. But there was that knock again, brisk and demanding, so Landan staggered over to turn the doorknob.

The woman in the hallway was beautiful and proper in a way that made him think he was hallucinating. Despite the heat, she was impeccably dressed in a royal blue jacket, ankle-length skirt, and fancy leather shoes. Her dark hair was swept up and pinned under a satin hat decorated with lace. She was in her mid thirties or so, not so much older than Landan, but obviously from the world he'd long put aside—the world of cities and boulevards, fancy tea parties and ballrooms filled with fine folk.

"Captain Samuel Landan?" she asked optimistically.

"Not anymore." Legs unsteady, he leaned against the doorframe. "Who are you?"

Undaunted, she said, "My name is Diana Comet. I've come from Massasoit. I want to hire Captain Landan to take me out to the Circle W ranch in Kelly's Pass."

Landan liked the word *hire*. More money meant more whiskey. The Circle W, that was no problem. Long haul to get there, but he'd heard good words about the place from the men who worked the pass. Yet despite the positive omens, this fine-looking city woman in her very fine attire seemed like a series of headaches waiting to happen; she'd harangue him about drinking, maybe try to get him to go to church, and heaven help him if she ever found out he was a sinner and a sodomite.

"He's not for hire," he said.

"I hear differently," Miss Comet said. "And I pay very well."

"Sorry." Landan closed the door in her face.

After dark, with the noise of miners and cowboys filling the town and a powerful thirst urging him on, he slapped tepid water on his face and went down to see what money he could win at poker. To his surprise, Miss Comet was waiting for him in a chair across from the front desk. She held a book in her lap. She seemed serenely unconcerned with the drunken men careening about in the company of perfumed and painted women.

"I'll buy you dinner," she said.

He considered. "Buy me whiskey."

"Dinner and one whiskey. Shall we?"

She led him down the street to the town's only reputable hotel, where the dining room had red velvet paper on the walls and a waiter in relatively clean clothes served them chicken with potatoes. He couldn't remember the last time he'd eaten with polished silverware. Miss Comet let him have his one whiskey, and then despite every urge in his body he ordered coffee.

"What do you want with the Circle W?" he asked.

Her expression was somber. "I've come to check on the welfare of an orphan boy sent there a year ago to find a new home."

"The Circle W's closer to Flagpole than here. You could have taken the stagecoach straight through."

"The coach broke an axle on the way from Elizabeth City," she said. "And the next one's not due for two days. I need a local guide to get me to the Circle W."

Landan sipped his bitter coffee. "Are you a missionary?"

"A philanthropist."

"That's a fancy word, ma'am."

"Not too big for Captain Landan. He attended East Point. Graduated near the top of his class. A most promising officer, they said."

Landan hadn't thought about the academy in a long time. He remember the grand granite buildings, the sweeping parade grounds, the view across the North River to the sprawling metropolis of Massasoit. The city was a dream of spires and chimneys soaring upward, and steel bridges flinging outward, and a lingering haze of smoke and steam and the noise of multitudes. The river itself, strong but complacent in summer, churned and teemed with thunderous ice during the winter. The memory of so much water seemed to him surreal and slightly obscene after all the dry land of mining country. Isaac had never been anywhere east of Texana; Landan had tried to describe the North River to him once, as they both lay naked and sated by the edges of a creek, but he'd flatly refused to believe in such a sight.

He reached for more coffee. "You can't believe everything people chatter on about, Miss Comet."

"If it's a matter of money, I assure you that you'll be promptly and accurately paid. If it's pride, rest assured that I've seen men fall into worse conditions after honorable military service during war. If it's an addiction to liquor that keeps you here, then simply say so and I won't bother you any further."

Her gaze was forthright, her voice clear, and for the first time in a long time Landan realized he was in the presence of a woman of candor and ambition. She was also the most beautiful woman he'd seen since the war. Yet there was something in her chin, or maybe the symmetry of her eyes, that nagged at the edges of his frayed nerves. Maybe he'd seen her portrait somewhere, or known a cousin of hers. His brain itched. It was the same kind of itch he got when he needed a drink, or when he missed Isaac's touch on his body, and the way they'd entwined in too-narrow beds.

Miss Comet lifted her chin. "Would you like me to ask again tomorrow, after you've thought it over?"

Landan pushed aside memories of Isaac. He cleared his dry throat. "Who said I was this Landan fellow anyway? Maybe I'm an impostor."

"The editor of the *Goldstone Times* described you perfectly, and said he'll vouch for you entirely."

Damn all writers, he thought without rancor. Damn the people who found out your secrets and then told them to the world. Maybe even damn the liquor that loosened his mouth, made him admit stories of the war he should have kept quiet.

Grudgingly he said, "I don't come cheap. And I'll need an advance to pay for my room and incidentals."

"Money's not a problem," she said. "But there won't be any drinking on this journey, Captain. I need you sober and committed to the job."

She put a small silk bag on the table between them. Inside it, Landan found a fistful of shiny silver dollars. It was more than he'd seen in a long while. He wondered how rich she really was.

"No drinking on the job," he agreed, and took the bag. But the night was still young, and the job several hours away.

Morning came like an artillery blast to the brain. Landan's skull and body both ached as he glared at the generous breakfast in front of him. Eggs, toast, bacon and hotcakes. He wanted to vomit. He didn't trust himself to speak and so kept his mouth shut while Miss Comet prattled on to an elderly couple at the next table. She had descended the hotel staircase dressed in a riding skirt, tailored green jacket, high leather boots and a hat wide enough to cast a shadow on an entire herd of cattle. Landan thought it was ludicrous. Riding was hot, sweaty work, and she sure was a city slicker if she thought she'd be comfortable in that get-up.

Still, he wasn't one to talk much about clothing. His only pair of trousers had worn thin at the knees, his shirt stank to his own nose, and there was a hole in the toe of his left boot. He'd shaved and doused water over his hair, and was as presentable as he intended to be, but he was well aware that he was one shabby, sorry-looking companion.

To hell with it, he thought to himself. She hadn't hired him for his handsome looks.

After breakfast, they went directly to the stable where she'd already made arrangements. For him, she had hired a gray gelding with a streak of white between his eyes. For

Miss Comet herself, a lad brought out a sleek brown pony in high spirits. Trailing both was a sad-looking brown mule already loaded up with food, water, oats, bedrolls, two tweed suitcases, a bright yellow carpetbag and three sturdy hatboxes.

"What's all this?" Landan asked, perplexed.

Miss Comet said, "One must always be prepared."

Landan scratched the mule's ears, commiserating silently, and then double-checked the saddle and straps on his gelding. Miss Comet mounted her pony with the boy's assistance and sat serenely until he was done. She showed no trouble in her saddle as they rode down the street and past the town cemetery. The sun was relentlessly bright even at such an early hour, the rolling landscape dry and dusty.

"I love travel," she said once they were past the town limits. "It tests the soul, scours the body. Makes a person new again. Don't you think so, Captain?"

He'd done a fair bit of traveling in his time, and nothing had made him new. He was impure, through and through, had known it since he was a boy. Couldn't be cured.

"I'm not a captain any longer," he said. "Just call me Sam."

"'Captain' sounds so much more interesting," she said. "My husband served in the war as a captain, too."

Landan's gaze dropped to her gloved hands. He hadn't seen a ring on her during dinner.

"When you wear expensive jewelry, people try to steal it," Miss Comet observed. "Like those gentlemen following us even now."

He had noticed the signs, but was surprised she had, too. Two men on horseback about a quarter-mile back.

Thieves who'd marked her back in town as an easy target. "I figured they'll wait until we stop for a rest, circle around, cut us off."

Miss Comet sighed. "Violence is such a blunt instrument."

Instead of waiting to be ambushed they took to a small ridge, waited for their followers, and scared off the scruffy would-be-thieves with some well-aimed shots. Landan was impressed with Miss Comet's grace and composure in the face of armed robbery. Later they ate lunch by an arroyo. He wanted to scoff at the delicate cheese sandwiches she'd brought, but the pickle relish and thick slices of bread were so damn tasty he ate two of them, then a third.

"You're a woman of rare skills," he admitted. Isaac would have liked her, even though he shied away from most women.

"I try my best," she said modestly.

He fed and watered both horses and the mule, which was gazing off at the horizon as if thinking of all the interesting things it could be doing other than hauling luggage. Miss Comet did her personal business out of his sight, which was only proper. While she was gone he dared a nip or two from his flask. For medicinal purposes, nothing else. When Miss Comet came back he saw that she'd loosened her high collar in deference to the heat. He could see a small cut on her neck like the kind he sometimes got when he shaved. He'd seen women before with beards and tiny mustaches, and always felt bad for their misfortune.

"Tell me about this boy you're looking for," he said when they started riding again.

"Kevin is his name. He was one of many young boys orphaned by disease in Massasoit. We took him into our home for children and matched him with a family out here looking for a son. He's twelve years old now, and James and I have received no response to our last two letters."

James. Her husband, he guessed. A rich man who would have been given a commission to serve in the war, not earned it like Landan had. He said, "Just two letters? Hardly seems like a reason to come all this way."

Miss Comet adjusted her hat. "We take our responsibilities very seriously at the Hartvern Home. I have a personal, lifelong interest in each one of our wards. I can't send children west without following up on their safety and happiness."

He resented the implication that the territory was the kind of place where young boys would be neglected or abused. Then again, he'd seen it enough; orphan boys and girls sent from cities to work on ranches and farms, their prospects for education and achievement shunted into years of backbreaking work.

The desert landscape became more rugged and green, the cactuses and shrubs giving way to oaks and acacias, then to junipers and ponderosa pines. From switchback turns on the trail they could see Goldstone in the arid valley below. The heat was still intense, even as the forest grew around them. Miss Comet stripped off her gloves and loosened her jacket. She began singing a tune that he gradually recognized from his days at East Point:

> *Eighty and nine with their captain*
> *Rode on the enemy's track*
> *Rode in the gray of the morning*
> *Nine of the ninety came back*

"You shouldn't be singing about death," he chided.

"And you shouldn't be carrying a liquor flask," she replied.

He wanted to reach for it right then and take a swig, just out of spite. But he didn't. "You don't have the words right."

"There are many variations," she said. "I learned this one in the hospital, after James's injury."

He'd figured her husband as the type to stay behind enemy lines, not brave the front. "What kind of injury?"

"Bullet through the right femur."

One sip of whiskey, that was all he wanted. Landan wiped his forehead. "Did he lose the leg?"

"No. We saved it. I know some medicine on my own, and he had a most excellent surgeon."

Of course a rich man would be able to afford a private physician to coax him through the horrors and hazards of a war hospital. Landan had visited men in wards, smelled the piss and shit and pus, seen the pile of amputated limbs out by the pigpen. At night, on the winds that swept through the desert and up into mountains, he could hear the cries of anguish and anger, of lives slowly being wrung out of suffering bodies. A rich officer in an army hospital would have his own private room, and nurses with clean clothes, and food that wasn't crawling with flies or maggots.

"I think the most fascinating thing—" Miss Comet started to say, but then her pony let out a shriek, reared up on its hind legs, and whipped into a turn. With a yelp she grabbed for the reins. Gravity and force had the best of her, and she was hurled to the ground like a rag doll.

Landan turned his own horse from the ruckus before it too could panic, and pulled his pistol to face whatever threat faced them—rattlesnake, probably, something that slithered off the path into the green forest and was gone before he could get off a shot. Heart hammering wildly, he slid out of his saddle to the ground beside Miss Comet's body. She was loosely curled on her side, her hat skewed and crushed, her dark hair knocked loose. Not dead, but barely breathing.

With a start he realized her hair was a wig—a fine weave, expensive, but now so askew that any passing stranger would see the tight skull cap beneath it. He reached toward it, worried about bumps to her head, but just then she drew in a sharp breath and bolted upright into a sitting position. Her arms flailed in panic.

"You're fine!" he told her, grabbing her hands. "Just fine!"

She gasped for air, her gaze wild. "My horse! A snake—"

"It's gone."

Her hands went to her head, and panic washed through her expression. Landan's gaze shifted downward, as he intended to give her time to fix herself, but then he saw something more surprising then her wig.

Her breasts had shifted. One was riding high, pointed toward the sky. The other had lurched left, toward the trees, in a way unlike any breast he'd ever seen.

"You're…" Landan started to say, but he couldn't finish the thought. He thought of her big hands, the cut on her neck. The fastidious insistence on grooming and apparel. Blood rushed to his face as puzzle pieces came together. He sat back, then climbed to his feet.

"I'll get the horses," he croaked out.

While his back was turned, she hurried off into the trees. He concentrated on collecting and calming the animals, for even the mule needed some settling down.

"Captain Landan!" That was Miss Comet's voice, from behind the solid brown trunk of a pine. Her voice was steadier than he trusted his own to be. "If you could pass me my yellow saddlebag and green suitcase, I would be much obliged."

Her sleeved arm extended expectantly. He got the luggage untied with trembling fingers, then handed both off.

"Are you injured?" he asked.

"Of course not," she replied.

He rubbed his face with his gloved hand, took a nip from his flask. His head hurt just as surely as if he'd hit it on a brick wall. He'd seen boys pretending to be women just for the fun of it. He'd seen girls in boy's clothing sneaking into the camps, sometimes for romantic trysts, sometimes so they could fight in the trenches. But it was safe to say that in all his years he'd never seen a man so determined—or confused—as this one.

It was a good hour before Miss Comet emerged again— impeccably attired, breasts and hair properly restored. Her expression—his? Landan wondered—was resolute.

"It's none of your business," she said, "but as a child, I was seriously disfigured in a tragic accident. It's nothing I like to speak of but it did leave me with certain… irregularities. I would appreciate your discretion and silence on the matter."

He couldn't quite hide his disbelief.

"If it's a problem for you, you're welcome to return to Goldstone. I can continue on my own."

"No," he said. "I said I'd do it. We'd best get going."

She gave him a narrow look, as if judging his worthiness, and then reached for her reins.

The rest of the afternoon passed without conversation. By dusk they were still ten miles out from Kelly's Pass, and the horses needed rest as much as their riders did. On the banks of a slick stream Landan got the animals watered, fed and groomed. With the sun below the trees, the canyons were cool and scenic around them. A man could live out here in peace forever, he thought wistfully. Why couldn't Isaac see that, appreciate it as the truth? He tried hard not to look at Miss Comet, who was cooking up tinned meat over a small campfire. Every brief glance had him studying the curve of her jaw, the thin blade of her nose, the way her wig was set just so.

"Captain Landan, it's rude to stare," she said tersely.

"I'm not—" Landan wrinkled his nose. "I'm just surprised."

"That a woman could be so cruelly disfigured, and struggle all her life to overcome it?"

"Something like that."

"Fate is cruel. Surely you learned that on the battlefield."

When it was dark they bedded down in thin blankets with the stars gloriously spread from one side of the sky to the other. For thousands of years men had been weaving love stories and adventure tales from dots connected into pictures, but all Landan could see were random pinpricks of indifferent light. He wondered, not for the first time since they'd made camp, if he was in danger of any kind. Miss Comet had already proved herself to be deceptive.

For all he knew she'd lured him out here to kill him, and there was no child to be sought after at the Circle W.

"Captain, I can hear your silly thoughts all the way over here," she said from her blankets.

He shifted the saddlebag he was using as a pillow. "You're a mind-reader, too, is that it?"

"You deny it?"

"I can't deny that I'm a little unsettled. Does your husband know? Has he seen you—"

She raised a sharp hand. "Of course he's aware of my tragic history."

He bit back a surge of nastiness. "I've seen tragedies, Miss Comet. Soldiers gone blind, or their eardrums burst, or legs blown off, paralyzed, shell-shocked, maimed, no hands, no arms, boys who'll never grow old, mothers who lost all their children, fathers burying their first-borns and second-borns and last sons, and with all due respect, you don't look like any tragedy at all. Whatever story you want to tell, you tell it. But don't expect my sympathy."

She was silent for a long time. He felt bad about losing his temper, but not so bad that he could form an apology.

"You're right," came her reply, eventually, in the thin voice of someone long exhausted. "My ploy is inappropriate around a man of your history. Around anyone, I suppose. My apologies."

The saddlebag was digging into the back of his skull. He pushed it aside, opted for the hard ground instead. "I suppose it doesn't come up very often."

"Not when I'm careful." She rustled in her blankets. When he glanced over, he saw her watching him by the red light of the campfire coals. Her eyes were wide and solemn.

"I trust you with my secret," she said.

The last time he'd been in this forest, it had been with Isaac. The last time he'd gazed up at the stars, it had been with Isaac's heat and weight against his left side. Then morning had come, with such a terrible argument. Three months it had been, and the wound was still festering.

He rolled away from her. "I give you my word."

When he woke at sun-up she was gone, but he heard the sounds of her morning ablutions just down the dry creek-bed. He fixed breakfast and coffee for the two of them. She returned, looking as pert and well-dressed as any high society lady off to a day of shopping and afternoon tea.

"Good morning," she said.

"Morning," he returned.

Her gaze was speculative. "When we get back to Goldstone, you should invest in a new wardrobe. I think you would clean up just fine if you put your mind to it."

"Putting on airs isn't a priority out here."

"It is if you ever hope to attract a wife."

Landan swallowed the last of his coffee and studied the bottom of the tin cup. He wished he'd put more whiskey in it. Funny, how he'd passed through the worst days of his life stone- cold sober, but now he needed some fortitude to get through even such a beautiful morning.

"Captain Landan," Miss Comet said gently. "You deserve love. Everyone does."

He took the cup to the stream and rinsed it out. "You wanted to go to the Circle W. Let's go."

They made it to the ranch while the sun was still halfway toward noon. The Circle W was a generous spread of land near the Mokumne River, the rounded mountains providing a stunning backdrop. Once upon a time Landan wouldn't have minded a place like it for himself—a place to raise cattle, to have a bed that wasn't a blanket on hard ground, to eat regular hot meals with someone he loved. They passed a corral of men wrangling horses before reaching a log house nestled in a copse of pines. The rancher's wife, Mrs. Bailey, met them at the door wearing a plain blue dress and long apron.

"My stars!" she said, her face full of wonder "It's you, isn't it? Miss Comet! Kevin said that one day you'd come visit. He said you'd show up on the doorstep all fancy, with a very nice hat, and that you'd have your handsome husband with you."

Her gaze shifted to Landan and scrunched up a little in surprise. Clearly he didn't match her expectations.

"Mrs. Bailey," Miss Comet said, offering her hand. "So very nice to meet you in person. This is Captain Landan, who escorted me from Goldstone."

Landan tipped his hat. "I'll let you two fine ladies see to your business," he said, and didn't even trip over the word *ladies*.

"Business!" Mrs. Bailey put her hand over her mouth in distress. "Oh, Kevin. You're here to see Kevin. But he's not here. My husband Hank set off just last week to bring him home."

"Bring him home from where?" Miss Comet asked, her confusion clear.

"From up north, in Flagpole," Mrs. Bailey said. "That's where we think he is. Traveling in the company of Mr. Whitney Waltman, the Amazing Undead Author."

Landan really hadn't planned on sitting down to tea. He'd figured on leaving Miss Comet and Mrs. Bailey to their talk, getting the animals watered, and then heading back to Goldstone for the pleasure of a week-long drunk in the same hotel he'd left behind. But the name Whitney Waltman made his heart pound an extra few beats. The famous poet, balladeer and journalist had been making headlines back east for almost twenty years with verses that shocked, enraged, delighted. As a military cadet, Landan had stashed his contraband copy of Waltman's work in a secret cubbyhole in his desk. Around campfires he'd recited one memorized verse after another to Isaac, who couldn't believe a man could write about illicit love and hedonism in such a way without getting run out of town by church folk.

"Back east, the hedonists outnumber the church folk," Landan had told him.

Waltman wrote not only about pleasure but also of the common lives of carpenters, laundresses, steelworkers, shipbuilders, teachers, and working folk of every ilk; he talked about cities rising out of meadows and forests, of ships that forged rivers bearing passengers, freight, the building blocks of a new nation; he spoke of longing, grief, ambition, tragedy. Landan had felt feverish for days after finishing the book. Other men brought bibles to war; he brought Waltman. But he'd lost his copy, his saddlebag, and nearly his life at the Battle of Ashville. Not until he met Isaac did he think he could share those words. They'd made a special trip to the bookstores of Elizabeth City and found a worn but serviceable copy. Around campfires, with only the trees and owls and stars as witnesses, he'd murmured the words against Isaac's throat and chest, and Isaac repeated them back like prayers.

"—I suppose that it's my fault," Miss Comet was saying, and the admission brought him back from reverie into Mrs. Bailey's sitting room. "I told Kevin he could take any one volume from my husband's library for the train trip out here, and he selected Mr. Waltman."

Mrs. Bailey fiddled with her blue tea cup. "It's not that we don't appreciate literature, ma'am. But perhaps that was too…explicit for a boy his age?"

"Nonsense," Miss Comet said, without rancor. "At Hartvern House, our children start reading classical tragedies before they learn to tie their shoes. We encourage a thorough understanding of the world."

Mrs. Bailey sighed. "Kevin heard that Mr. Waltman was speaking in San Geraldo. It's his final tour, given his recent health calamities. Kevin begged to go. That's almost four hundred miles away! After we refused, he slipped out his window and ran away. Hank brought him back two days later. Then Kevin learned Mr. Waltman would be in Auraria. He jumped on a train like a hobo and got all the way to the theater doors before Hank caught him and marched him home. Three days ago, Kevin found out that Mr. Waltman would be speaking tonight in Flagpole. He was gone before we could talk sense into him. So you see, Miss Comet, I couldn't answer your letters. I didn't want to lie and say everything was fine. The child is a firefly, always flitting off to the horizon. But I never imagined you'd come all this way to check on him!"

"I have a responsibility," Miss Comet replied. "Clearly you are loving parents, even if you underestimate the power of literature on a young man's mind. When I was Kevin's age, I hitchhiked with a gang of camel thieves across an entire desert to hear the poet Gibran speak on the emperor's birthday."

Mrs. Bailey's hand rose to her throat. "A girl so young! You could have been killed! Or molested!"

"To hear Gibran, one should be willing to risk more than life itself." Miss Comet put down her cup. "Now, if you'll allow us some time to freshen up, the Captain and I must be on our way to Flagpole."

"What?" Landan asked, startled.

Miss Comet rose gracefully. "We'll have to leave right now if we're going to see Mr. Waltman's engagement."

"I didn't say I'd take you to Flagpole," he protested.

"Of course you will," she said, with a sweet smile.

Of course he did. Not just for the money, of which she promised more, and not out of fear for her safety. He didn't believe the desert story—camel thieves, indeed—but she was resourceful enough to follow the well-traveled roads to Flagpole with little if any trouble. He went for the same reason a twelve-year-old boy climbed out his window. The famous author, holding court. The Amazing Undead Author, mocking his own mortality while simultaneously lurching toward it. Landan knew a thing or two about Death, and how quickly it could rush over a soul when least expected.

He denied any interest at all in Waltman, of course.

"Read one author, you've read them all," he said to Miss Comet as they rode north. The mule, which seemed to have gotten its hopes up back at the Bailey ranch, trod along on its tether with an occasional bray of discontent.

"You break my heart," Miss Comet replied. "That's like saying every sunrise is identical, every snowflake from the sky. Every drop of precious liquor."

He hid a smirk. "Whiskey's different than gin, and gin's different than bourbon, but they all do the same job."

Miss Comet adjusted her hat. "Make one insensate? Or open a mind to possibilities?"

Now she was quoting Waltman, sonnet twelve. He said, "If you're such a big proponent, you should try a drop or two."

She replied, "I drink plenty. When appropriate, and not while doing my job."

The words made him cross. He hadn't touched his flask today, but another snide remark and he'd reconsider his temperance. Landan wondered if any man could accompany her on an extended journey without the benefit of a nip or two.

"Why didn't your husband make the trip with you?" he asked.

"If you were married, would you insist on accompanying your wife everywhere?"

"I'm not likely to get married, ma'am."

"You could use a partner," she observed.

He was trying hard to keep Isaac out of his thoughts. It was unlikely, but not impossible, that he would have heard of Whitney Waltman's scheduled appearance in Flagpole. That slight flare of possibility made Landan simultaneously hopeful and sick to his stomach. What would he do, if he looked across the room and saw Isaac in the crowd—slim and sinewy, his hands jammed shyly in his pockets, his cornsilk hair slicked back for the occasion?

He realized the horses had stopped at the base of a narrow wooden bridge. The river flowed lazily beneath them. Miss Comet was looking at him in amusement.

"What's that?" he asked.

"You were lost in reverie," Miss Comet asked. "Who's the lucky lady?"

"There's no goddamn lucky lady," Landan snapped, and something flashed across Miss Comet's face.

"I see," she said, with a lift of her eyebrows. Then she nudged her horse onto the bridge and he only had the back of her head to consider.

Hurriedly he urged his gelding to catch up. Hoof beats on the bridge sounded like thunder, and it wasn't until they were across that he got to say, "There's nothing to see about it—"

"Captain Landan," she said, stopping her horse. She raised her hand in a forestalling motion and gave him a look of genuine sympathy. "I am the least likely person on this planet to condemn any kind of love between two consenting adults. You need not worry about me gossiping, spreading rumors, or otherwise sabotaging your reputation. I remain your friend, and would be honored to be your confidant, but simply say the word I shall never mention it again."

He gazed at her hard.

"Never mention it again," he said gruffly.

She turned her pony down the path.

Christ, he needed a drink.

Other men might have been relieved by having their darkest secret pulled into the light and acknowledged by an acquaintance of less than forty-eight hours. Landan felt raw and exposed, as if he'd been stripped and staked out to die a long death in the middle of the desert. The sun was too bright, his saddle suddenly uncomfortable, the gelding just a little too fast despite his attempts to reign him back. He could barely eat his lunch. He drank water from his canteen but it tasted like grit, and he had to spit it out or be sick.

Miss Comet said nothing about his mental state, if she even observed it at all. She was too busy mangling a new set of verses:

> *With bray of the trumpet and roll of the drum*
> *And keen ring of the bugle, the soldiers come*
> *Sharp clank the steel swords, the bridle-chains ring*
> *And foam from red nostrils, the wild chargers sing*

"Cavalry," he finally said. "It's not soldiers, it's cavalry. Scabbards, not swords. And the wild chargers fling. There's not much singing when you're attacking the enemy."

"Are you quite sure?"

He'd heard the song in camps, in public houses, in beer halls after the war. He was quite sure.

"I'm thinking of collecting a series of ballads into a printed volume," she said. "You would be a valuable resource. Have you ever thought of becoming an author?"

"The only good labor is physical labor," he replied.

"I think Mr. Waltman would disagree with that," Miss Comet said.

"Then why did he write so many verses about the common working man?"

"I thought you hadn't read his work."

Damn it. "Just might have heard of him, that's all."

"Captain Landan, I expect a man of your caliber to be honest about literature, even if you can't be honest about anything else."

"I'm goddamned honest!" he protested. "About the things that need honesty. About things that won't get you strung up, or tarred and feathered and run out of town. This isn't Massasoit. It's not a forgiving place."

"They wouldn't forgive you for reading Waltman?"

"Yes!" he snapped. "No. You make a man all confused!"

She gave him a sunny smile. "When I can, yes."

If he liked women in a romantic way, he would have liked her. But then he remembered that she wasn't a woman at all, was something else entirely, and he had to turn his attention to the trail.

"Captain Landan," she said a moment later. "Surely you've heard *The Ballad of William Jane*."

He had to think hard on that one. It was an older song, back from the wars between Cardyr and Kilvemi. A young wife dressed up as a man to join her husband in battle, but was unable to save his life. Unmasked by her fellow soldiers, she was discharged and ostracized. Later she died saving the same regiment of men who'd rejected her.

"It's just a song," he said.

"Songs and poetry tell truths."

"They give you hope that you don't deserve."

She shook her head. "They shed light on the human condition."

"The human condition that made you and me wrong?" he demanded. "That makes us live in shame of being ourselves?"

She stopped dead on the road. Landan noticed, turned. Her face was curiously hard, nearly fierce.

"Whatever I am, I'm not ashamed of it," she said.

He felt his face blush. "That's not what I meant."

"It's exactly what you meant."

Landan nudged his gelding back into motion and didn't answer her.

Soon they reached a junction with a broad road heading north toward Flagpole, and in the next few hours they passed settlers in wagons, men driving stubborn mules, a group of indigenous people carrying buckets on their shoulders, three farm girls with pigtailed hair, six miners with pickaxes, and any number of itinerant cowboys, hoboes, peddlers and madmen. Landan tried not to think about what secrets each might be holding close—who they loved, what they were afraid of, the inconsistencies in their hearts and bodies. In the golden light of late afternoon he and Miss Comet reached the town itself. Flagpole was the largest town for a hundred miles around, an epicenter of trade and logging and industry, with a railroad running along its main street. The best hotel was the Monte Vista and they went there directly.

The hotel was surrounded by a number of restaurants and shops. Directly across the street was a grand theater with an arched marquis and printed playbills: *Mr. Whitney Waltman, the Noted Author, In Performance Tonight Only!* He tried to ignore it while he unloaded Miss Comet's baggage from the long-suffering mule.

Miss Comet asked, "Would you care to be my guest for the show tonight?"

"No, ma'am," he said. Because he'd thought on it, and thought again, and nothing good could come of it. He'd been a fool to think otherwise. "I'm going to find my own room and retire early."

In the diminishing light, with the bustle of folks heading home for the night or heading out for entertainment, she paid him his wages. Then she reached deeply into her carpetbag and withdrew a slim volume. "Here. If you haven't read it, you'll find it quite interesting. If you have, maybe a refresher is in order."

It was Waltman's collection. Landan took it in puzzlement. "You just happen to have a copy?"

"I asked Mrs. Bailey to loan me Kevin's copy," she said. "I thought perhaps I'd have it inscribed. But like a man dying of thirst, you have more need of it."

A bellboy in a smart blue uniform came out to carry Miss Comet's bags. She gave him a brilliant smile, warned him to be extra careful with her belongings, and swept past the doorman into the dim interior of the hotel. Just like that she was gone from Landan's sight, with no final words of advice or goodwill. He wondered if he'd earned her enmity forever by speaking the honest truth. That was his life in a nutshell: missed opportunities, broken relations, regret. Hers would be just one more name added to the list he carried in his heart.

He took the animals to the stable, bought himself the biggest bottle of whiskey he could find, and checked into the Weatherford Hotel. He put the whiskey and the copy of Waltman on the bedside table, and then he considered the best way to start his week-long binge.

Landan dreamed he was back in uniform. Muddy, bloody trenches rose around him, blocking his vision, collapsing in so that he couldn't breathe, couldn't claw his way free. Then he was running in a cold morning fog, isolated, cut off from his men, aware only of his own harsh breathing and the impact of bullets into flesh: the soft, unmistakable horror of it, small thumps as invisible human bodies were pierced and wounded. He couldn't see his men but he could hear them dying. He dreamt of Isaac in uniform, which was untrue to history, and he dreamt of weeping women holding their mortally wounded husbands. You couldn't hold onto a person tight enough to forestall fate.

He dreamed of the morning he'd tossed Waltman's book into the campfire, the capstone of a spectacular argument with Isaac that had nothing to do with poetry and everything to do with Isaac's desire to visit the east. To frequent the beer halls and saloons where a man could hold another man's hand, where he could be affectionate before strangers who shared the same predilections. Frustration swept over Landan like hot oil as he tried to make Isaac understand. That world was elusive, precarious, left a man open to rumors of scandal. It was fine if you were a dandy poet who lived hand to mouth. For a man who had to hold down a good job, it was too dangerous. Did Isaac want to be beaten, killed? It had happened to soldiers. It had nearly happened to Landan himself.

In the dream, Isaac ignored all of Landan's words. Beside them, the fire that consumed Waltman's book rose up, parted the clouds, and scoured the sky. The flames shot back down with heat that boiled away Landan's skin and all the bones in his outstretched arms. The roar of artillery surrounded him like thunder and diminished him to dust. There was nothing, then, no sound or feeling or sense of place in the world; nothing so complete he was surely dead, and it was a surprise when the morning sun woke him.

He lurched upright, heart pounding, sweat pooling out of him. The copy of Waltman's book was on the bedside table where he'd left it.

So was the whiskey, untouched.

He scrubbed his face with dry hands. Picked up the book and read a random line: *Clear and sweet is my soul, and clear and sweet is all that is not my soul.*

Landan kept reading. The clean, clear pages soothed his fingers, made his heart slowly calm. Gradually he reclined back in the bed with the pillow bunched under his head. When his stomach rumbled he got a boy to go down to the restaurant and fetch him some biscuits and ham for breakfast, but other than that and some necessary business with the slop jar, he didn't move off the bed. The good people of Flagpole went about their business without his assistance and very nearly without his notice, aside from the clop of horses in the street, the sidewalk conversations that rose to his open windows, the piano music coming out of the music hall on the corner. Despite it all he remained immersed. Slits of sunlight moved across the small room, warming his legs and then his arms and finally his face, but he rolled onto his side and kept reading.

Gradually he became aware that dusk was coming on, and that he was sore from lying on a lumpy mattress all day, and that the pianist across the street was playing that goddamned *Campside Traces*. On unsteady feet he crossed to the window and sucked in fresh air. Far down the street he could see the arched marquee of the theater where Whitney Waltman had so recently performed.

The pianist finished up his song. In the relative piece and quiet, someone knocked on Landan's door.

Miss Comet was dressed in fine purple dress with a lace throat and lace collars. Her wig was arranged in a spiral of curls, and expertly applied makeup made her eyes look deep and velvety. Standing with her was a neatly groomed boy nervously tugging on his collar, and a tall rancher looking uncomfortable in a suit.

"Captain Landan," Miss Comet said briskly. "May I introduce Mr. Hank Bailey and his son Kevin?"

The men shook hands. Kevin mumbled a hello, and shuffled and scratched like he had ants in his pants.

"Boy, you stay still," Bailey said, sounding both fond and exasperated in equal parts. He made a move to slick down Kevin's unruly hair, and the boy ducked away.

"We're going to be late to the show!" Kevin said.

Landan gazed at the three of them in bewilderment. "What show?"

"Mr. Waltman," Bailey said with a shrug. "Miss Comet here, she convinced me it would be good for the boy's education."

"But that was all last night," Landan said.

"Mr. Waltman was delayed by an inconveniently unreliable locomotive," Miss Comet announced. "The performance was rescheduled for tonight. I have an extra ticket, if you're interested."

Reflexively he said, "I don't have anything to wear."

Bailey said, a little ruefully, "That's what I said."

"The tailor across the street has been told to expect you within the next quarter hour. He'll take care of all your needs." Miss Comet lifted the half-full bottle of whiskey from the bedside table. "I suggest you not indulge in this until afterward."

"I can't," Landan said, and it was unbearable: the thought of putting on fine clothes, sitting in a darkened auditorium, hearing the author himself speak words that had Landan had held so intimately in his hands all day long. The prospect of Isaac being there. "Miss Comet, thank you, but I can't."

"We have to go or we're going to be late!" Kevin complained.

"I'll be departing on the morning train," Miss Comet continued, sounding unconcerned about whatever Landan decided. "I leave in your care the horses, as well as that very unhappy mule. Do with them what you please. I would like to have Kevin's book back, of course. He'll want it autographed."

Landan nodded toward the table, where the book and whiskey sat side-by-side.

Miss Comet looked over, nodded, and then said, "Come, now, gentlemen, off we go." She ushered Kevin out toward the hallway. His father followed, pulling uncomfortably on his collar. Miss Comet made no move to collect Waltman's volume but instead waited until only she and Landan remained.

Somberly she said, "He's down there, Sam."

Goosebumps rose on Landan's arms. "Who?"

"Whoever you're looking for," she said. "Whatever his name proves to be, whatever appearance he might take. If you can imagine it, you can find it. Whatever decisions you've made wrongly in the past, the future is yet unwritten. Do with it what you will. Without shame, without regret."

She closed the door with a gentle snick, and just like that was gone again.

Landan went back to his window. The light of street lamps flickered yellow, and gay music pounded out of the music halls and saloons, and he thought he could hear Waltman's voice beneath it all, murmuring encouragement. When he left the room a few minutes later he took the book with him but left behind the whiskey. Where he was going, he only needed one of them.

Author's notes

1. Surely Mr. Waltman needs no introduction to this audience.
2. Occasionally copies of the manuscript *Diana Comet and the Camel Thieves* appear in auction catalogs or the bright pixels of eBay. These invariably turn out to be fakes.
3. Sam Landan and Isaac Walter first met on a cattle drive near Brokeback Mountain; the Walters, of course, are an important family in Tony Kushner's award-winning play Angels in America.The Weatherford Hotel in Flagstaff, Arizona, has a quite lovely balcony where writers can congregate over beer, popcorn, and a view of downtown.
4. The author is indebted to the book *American War Ballads, 1725-1865*, ed. by George Cary Eggleston, published in 1889.

What You WISH FOR

S ummer comes, bright days filled with the smell of hot dogs and cotton candy. Crowds throng the boulevard day and night. So many people stake claim to the beach with their chairs and blankets that on some days Graybeard can't even see the sand. The beach goers drink Coca- Cola and eat bologna sandwiches and frolic in the waves. Along the boulevard, sailors in white uniforms purchase tickets at Graybeard's kiosk and sneak kisses with their sweethearts in his stairwells and tower. Teenagers lean out of Graybeard's windows, shouting to their friends below. During lulls in the noise Graybeard can hear screams of delight from the roller coaster, and the music of the carousel where wooden horses chase each other day and night.

At midnight the crowds fade and the lights blink out. Graybeard is left alone with the unattainable sea, which taunts him from across the sand, seawall and boulevard.

"When stars sink into the water, do they sizzle and hiss?" he asks the seagull.

An accident has left the seagull with just one leg. Despite the summer crowds she is growing thin, because she can't hunt and peck and hop as fast as the other gulls.

She spends each night now on Graybeard's forearm and leaves feathers behind each morning.

"They hold their fire tight and emerge on the other side of the world, whole and shiny," she says, sounding philosophical.

"Can you catch a star and eat it? Does it taste like candy?"

"They taste like your yellow turban." Wings extend, flap, and then the seagull settles down again. "Like the red jewel on your forehead. Stop worrying about what you don't have."

"I can't," Graybeard whispers.

As the summer burns on, he grows angry at the unruly youngsters who kick his walls and slam his doors. He spies on kissing lovers and is jealous that he can't feel the sweet crush of anyone's lips against his own. He envies the summers in the surf—if they can swim, why can't he? He begins to see greed and longing in everyone. Some want money, some yearn for love, others for alcohol or attention or peace of mind.

"If I could move my arm, I could escape this trap," he thinks. He tries very hard, and hears the faint splinter of wood.

He makes a plan.

Every night, once the boardwalk is closed, he practices movement—the subtle shift of his lips, the flex of his arm, a wriggle of his right ear. Strength builds in him slowly, like a rising tide.

"Silly wood," the gull says. She flaps away, never to be seen again. He misses her.

The children disappear back to their schoolrooms. The bathers stop coming except on weekends. On weekends the roller coaster roars and the carousal spins, but the crowds have diminished. Graybeard misses the company, but now he has more time to twist and shift. One sunset, with the wind blowing hard and the crowds very thin, he moves his arm and hears a sharp, triumphant crack.

"What was that?" asks a woman on the sidewalk below.

"It's the storm, rising fast," someone else answers.

The bald ticket-seller emerges from Graybeard's kiosk. "Just part of the fun, folks. Step on inside."

"It was me!" Graybeard says, though no one can heard him, and his celebration is marred by the oddly charged atmosphere on the boulevard. People seem skittish and uneasy, their gazes pulled toward the horizon. The music from the carousel seems too fast, and off-tune as well. Long before midnight the sidewalks empty. A police car with spinning lights drives by, garbled announcements coming from the rooftop speaker. Come morning, the cigar-chomping man and his workers arrive to board up Graybeard's windows and doors. The tip of the man's stogie glows cherry red.

"Going to be a wild one," he says.

"We've had worse," the bald ticket-seller says, but he doesn't sound confidant.

Pelting rain begins before noon and continues for hours. The sky is a low rumpled roof of gray and blue, undulating like the sea. The howling wind whistles past Graybeard's teeth and pushes against the back of his throat. Just before dark, a white-crested wave spills over the seawall and races across the boulevard.

"Yes!" Graybeard shouts. "Come to me!"

Waves boil up, foamy with sand and fury. The howling wind sends them crashing against the bathhouse and rips away the shingled roof. Great jagged pieces of it bounce and fly toward the roller coaster. The carousel groans and spins as if in its dying throes, and he imagines the wooden horses escaping into the storm. All of the seagulls have long fled from terror but Graybeard feels no fear, only exultation.

"Here! I'm here!"

The entire ocean rises and rushes forward. Graybeard reaches for it with every inch of his desire. Pain rips through his shoulder as nails pop loose and beams splinter. His forearm falls free with a great ripping sound. A moment later his head tumbles forward into the storm surge. Blinded by darkness and water, he finds himself dragged and tossed like driftwood.

The sea tastes like water and brine.

The sea tastes like fury and force.

The sea drags him backward over the seawall and into its turbulent black depths. Only then does he realize his mistake. Only then does he realize what he's lost.

Graybeard longs for the sky.

Half-buried in sand and silt, his gaze fixed eternally upward, he spends every daylight hour staring through several feet of water to the shimmering surface and the tantalizing blue beyond it. Schools of fish and passing freighters sometimes obscure his view, and bits of seaweed sometimes float into his eyes, but even the most obstructed glimpse of sky is better than nothing. At night the blackness is so complete he can't even see the stars.

"I would like to fly," he says. "I would like to soar and dive, and make my home in the clouds."

"You are not a bird," says the lobster who lives in Graybeard's mouth. "Why do you torment yourself with impossibilities? The sea is your home."

Perhaps the sea will one day evaporate, leaving him exposed to the sun. Perhaps a great storm will tear him from the seabed and send him washing ashore. He thinks that a storm is what brought him to the sea in the first place, but all he remembers is darkness and dizziness.

"Are you Cubby?" he asks the lobster.

"No. Who's Cubby?"

Graybeard says, "I don't remember."

The lobster shuffles away.

Daytime fades, blue edging into black. Graybeard longs for the sky.

Author's notes

1. As of this book's printing, the aforementioned Great Hurricane of 1938 remains the deadliest hurricane in New England's history. Because of the speed with which it barreled north from the Bahamas, it was also called the Long Island Express. Approximately seven hundred people died in the storm surge or related calamities.

2. Graybeard really should have known better.

3. The cigar-chomping man's name was Thomas. He originally came from Pouch Cove, Newfoundland, where his forefathers hunted seals. His primary business was building houses for veterans, and Graybeard's Castle was only a side interest. He also liked to build model trains.

The Goddess
AND LIEUTENANT TEAGUE

Stuck on a plane taking her to war, Lieutenant Teague wanted nothing more than for the sergeant across the aisle to shut the hell up.

"Honest truth and nothing less," the sergeant was saying to the two cherries sitting beside her. For hours now she'd been feeding them suspect advice. "You don't want to wear nothing out in the bush. Underwear chafes like a bitch under your cammies. And they get wet, and carry lice. Sooner or late you're scratching at an acre of crotch rot. You know what I mean?"

The sergeant chuckled. She was pretty enough, with honey-colored braids and a thin scar across her chin, but there was something too damn cheerful about her. Beside the sergeant, listening but not commenting, sat a pasty-faced private smoking hand-rolled cigarettes and a corporal scribbling a letter on yellow notebook paper.

Continuing, the sergeant said, "If you are going to wear undies, go for silk. Not cotton. Cotton takes too long to dry out and it's too damned heavy. You can get good silk at Mr. Louvo's, in Little Milia. There's a pleasure bar right next door. The boys there are clean and enthusiastic. The girls, too."

Teague glanced up sharply. The sergeant grinned at her from across the narrow divide.

"Just yanking your chain, lieutenant!" the sergeant said. "Harlotry's strictly against the regs. No girl-on-girl action in this woman's army."

"You just remember that," Teague advised.

She turned back to her magazine, but reading exacerbated her headache. The transport plane was smoky and hot, with soldiers crammed into every available seat. It was a relief, several minutes later, when the wings dipped and the coastline appeared outside the windows.

"Look, ma'am," said the private sitting beside Teague. "Welcome to Ravina, huh?"

Teague tried not to look too interested. The thin white beaches of South Ravina fronted a jungle that hid waterfalls and ancient temples and small tranquil villages. Teague's mother, the highly-respected general, had vacationed there after the war with Cemery. She'd included an account in her memoirs. Somewhere down there might be that same wonderland of colorful marketplaces and bicycles, and little covered boats that navigated the river, and hotels with swimming pools and ceiling fans.

And somewhere down there might be the Goddess of Death and Life, just waiting for Teague. Death by gunfire or explosions or poisoned sticks in pits, death by dysentery or malaria or any other of a dozen diseases. Death at age twenty-two, with only her mother and her fiancé and college friends to mourn her.

Teague touched the ward hanging around her neck and closed her magazine.

The wheels touched down with a thump and rush of rubber. Teague was more than ready to walk on solid ground but it took fifteen minutes of incremental taxiing to reach the terminal, and then another twenty minutes for the ground crew to find a stairwell. The doors finally opened to the humid, steamy air redolent of jungle rot. But then a master sergeant came onboard to have them fill out arrival forms, and it took almost forty minutes to get a hundred soldiers to sign and date the correct boxes.

"That's bureaucracy for you," said the sergeant across the aisle.

Finally they were allowed off the plane. Brutal sunlight poked its way around Teague's sunglasses as she walked on stiff legs across the broad, sweltering tarmac. The heat was no better under the corrugated tin roof of the main terminal. Hundreds of soldiers in sweat-stained uniforms were milling about, some of them shipping home and others waiting for transport to the interior.

"Lookie, lookie," said a corporal from behind Teague. "More lines."

There was no separate queue for officers, which irked Teague. She shuffled along long tables where corporals checked her orders, made sure her immunization records were proper, and exchanged her cash for military scrip. Fans on tall metal stands stirred the air but didn't cool it. Finally Teague reached a master sergeant with dark spiky hair.

"Going on to Firebase Jonathan?" the master sergeant asked.

"As soon as I can," Teague replied.

"Just your bad luck. There was a chopper, but it already left. You can catch the next one in two hours or so."

"There's no faster way?"

The master sergeant grimaced. "You won't be in such a hurry once you get there, ma'am. I've been to Jonathan. It's one of the worst mudholes out there."

"It won't be once I'm through with it," Teague promised.

She sat in one of the sweltering-hot lounges while Armed Forces news played on a black and white television. To kill time she re-read Datch's latest letter. Law school was fine, though his professors were idiots. She imagined him sitting in class and rolling his bright blue eyes at inane comments. He said that he had gone to a fancy dinner supporting the war effort. The protestors outside had been doused with tear gas and carted off to jail.

"They don't understand patriotism," he wrote. "Don't understand sacrifice."

An earnest young soldier came over to Teague and saluted. "Lieutenant Teague? Corporal Narbett, ma'am. I was told to hitch my wagon to yours. Going out to FB Jonathan!"

Teague asked, "First time to the front?"

"Oh, no, ma'am. I've been there before with Colonel Everes. I was her clerk."

"And now you're going to a firebase? You must have really pissed her off."

Narbett's small, round cheeks went pink. "Oh, no, ma'am! I volunteered. Didn't come all this way from the Plains to sit in a nice cold office all day typing up forms."

By the time the chopper came, Teague had heard all about Narbett's parents' farm, their six sheep dogs, the high school Narbett had attended, and Narbett's favorite movie stars. Once aboard the chopper, Narbett shut up and clenched her fists around the safety webbing. Teague peered down at the lush green countryside.

"Better sit back, ma'am," the gunner warned her. "Snipers."

Firebase Jonathan came up quicker than Teague expected. From the air it didn't seem like much at all: trenches, sandbagged tents, a fortified command post. Soldiers in helmets squinted up as the chopper came in to land outside the wires. Teague jumped off, passed her bag to a private, and asked for the platoon lieutenant.

"In the CP, ma'am," the private said.

The command post was a low, camouflaged tent fortified by sandbags and trenches. Second Lieutenant Bawn, a gangly woman with a mole under her right eye, burst into tears when she saw Teague.

"Thank God," Bawn said. "I've been here forever."

Teague kept her gaze elsewhere while Bawn composed herself. Razor wire and mines surrounded the small encampment. A very small tower offered elevated views of the valley below. A dozen or so soldiers were either patrolling, eating dinner, or unpacking the supplies the chopper had brought in.

"Where is everyone?" Teague asked. "On patrol?"

Bawn blew her nose into a handkerchief. "No. This is all we have left after last month's casualties."

The sky grayed into dusk. Hot sticky air made Teague long for a cold shower. She pushed aside memories of Grinnid University's fine swimming pools and athletic facilities. And of the huge dining halls with domed ceilings and long wooden tables. Out here the only food had been cooked and sealed in cans months ago, by strangers in distant factories. She and Bawn both ate from their rations, and Teague's dinner tasted only vaguely like beef.

"Is there a squad going out soon?" Teague pressed.

Bawn blew her nose again. "Not after dark. Never after dark. Come on. Time to hunker down."

And so Teague spent her first night in South Ravina tucked into a trench beside Bawn, both of them smoking cigarettes and keeping their gazes on the black landscape. The crick, croak and click of insects was like a hypnotic song on an endless tape loop. The air grew fractionally cooler but no less humid. Some of Bawn's women came and went out of the trench, circulating between watch posts and the low-slung tents. Teague couldn't see their expressions in the dark. Sometime before dawn she slipped into sleep and woke to gunfire so close it nearly deafened her.

Shouts; more gunfire; the explosion of a grenade. A voice shouted, "Hold your fire!" and two corporals near the tower shouldered their weapons.

"Fucking false alarm," someone muttered nearby.

Bawn whispered, "You scared yet?"

Teague nodded, afraid that her voice would crack if she spoke.

"It's like this every fucking day," Bawn said.

A half-hour after dawn, a helicopter beat its noisy way over the tree line. Bawn disappeared into her tent, then emerged with a half-packed duffel bag. She yelled, "Good luck!" and ran pell-mell for the chopper with no more instructions or advice.

When the bird was gone, Teague turned her gritty eyes to the nearest corporal. "Who's the leading sergeant around here?"

"Sergeant Lyss, ma'am. She just got back."

"Back from where?"

"Three weeks R & R at home."

"Well, find her and tell her I need her in the CP."

Sergeant Modlyn Lyss showed up at the command post a few minutes later. Her honey braids had fallen loose and she no longer looked as cheerful as she had back on the transport plane, but there was no mistaking her cocky smile.

Teague glared at her. "I don't believe much in coincidences."

"Neither do I, Lieutenant. I've got a friend in the Assignments Department, she told me we'd be on the same plane. Thought it might be nice to get to see each other for a spell before working together out here."

"It was lovely," Teague retorted. "How long have you been in Ravina?"

Lyss scratched at a bug bite on her neck. "Finished my second tour last month. This'll be my third. Eleven months and thirty days more to go."

A soldier on her third tour was either crazy or greedy for war pay. Teague gritted her teeth and tapped on the table beside her. "These maps of the Low Valley look like they've been dragged through a rice paddy and chewed on by goats. I need better ones."

"We'll have to put in a requisition," Lyss said.

"Do it. Who are the squad leaders?"

Lyss's gaze was unflinching. "Pederly, she's a short-timer. Wants to go home in one piece and won't do anything to jeopardize that. Amilen's good but too reckless. I've told her twice, keep it up and she'll be in a body bag. Then there's Zooba. Loyal like a dog."

Ten minutes later, the dirty and sweaty squad leaders were standing in the CP. Upon questioning, Pederly said, "Patroling's too dangerous, ma'am," and Amilen said, "Not too dangerous for me," and Zooba, who was short and thin like a man, mumbled something Teague didn't quite catch.

"What's that, Sergeant?" Teague asked.

Zooba fondled the brim of her hat with grimy fingers. "Got to be done, ma'am. Can't let them overrun us."

"You're right. We're going to have three patrols a day. Morning, afternoon and evening. Whenever one squad is out, another is resting and the third is on perimeter guard. We vary the length, the time, the route. I'll be going out with your squad today, Sergeant Zooba."

Alarm tightened Lyss's face. "Lieutenant, that's not such a good idea."

Teague said, "I'll never ask the troops to do something I won't. And I need to get a feel for the countryside."

Of course Teague had gone through field training herself, in muddy fields and swamps back home, overnight and weekend maneuvers rigged to be uncomfortable and arduous. Her teachers had complimented her compass reading and survival skills. She looked forward, in a quietly petrified sort of way, to testing them for real in the field. At noon she joined Zooba's squad out by the latrines. Five soldiers gave Teague squinty-eyed looks and shifted in their scuffed boots.

"Lieutenant, wait up," a voice called, and Lyss came jogging over. She had a rifle slung over her shoulder and a Bowie knife sheathed at her shoulder. "I'm coming with you."

Teague frowned. "One of us should stay here, sergeant."

"We're all disposable," Lyss said. "Pederly and Amilen can manage things."

Zooba said, "This is Sarge's third tour, ma'am. She knows how to stay alive better than any of us."

The other women nodded. Despite herself, Teague acquiesced. They went single-file past the wires and down a narrow trail toward fields of rice. The sun was very bright in Teague's eyes. If she squinted hard she could see the village down the slope. A few dozen thatched huts, some penned animals, smoke rising from open fires. Men and women in traditional Ravinan garb saw to their daily chores while children dashed underfoot. Friendlies, allegedly. Trust no one, her instructors had said.

A half hour later Zooba, who'd taken point, paused with her fist raised in the air. The line stopped and crouched low. Teague felt her thigh muscles strain. The smell of her own sweat filled her nose. Lyss was crouched at her shoulder, solid and unmoving. Up above, a large red parrot flitted from branch to branch. Teague told herself that in a moment or two they might all be injured, maimed, dead. Her hands clutched tighter on her rifle and she stifled the urge to vomit.

A hand signal from Zooba, and they started moving again.

They followed the trail around a thatch of coconut trees and down another small slope to a road rutted by wagon wheels. Zooba started to say, "I think we should—"

A blast concussion knocked Teague back on her ass. She lay stunned for an instant, ears dulled, nose itchy from the acrid smell of blue smoke. She told herself to get up but her legs and right hip started to throb with pain, then burn as if she'd been splashed with acid. She began to shriek. Beside her, a corpse wearing Zooba's uniform smoldered and burned.

Lyss's calm face appeared above her. "Hold on, lieutenant. You've been hit. Going to be fine, though."

Gunfire, a shout, someone cursing. Teague writhed on the ground. Debate raged about whether to carry her back to camp or wait for a chopper evacuation. Consumed by the burning, she lost track of the argument. The next thing she knew, someone was strapping her into a gurney and the world was filled with whirling dust. Lyss's face appeared again, her freckles like golden stars in a pale sky.

"You're going home, lieutenant," Lyss said loudly. "Enjoy the real world."

The chopper rose. Limp bloody bodies pressed in on Teague from all sides. The gunner smoked a thin roll of illegal plant leaves and let off occasional shots into the bush. The engine thudded and thumped as if something wild was trapped under the hull. As Teague's head lolled to the side, fat white clouds coalesced into a woman's face. A great compassionate face with wisdom and peace emanating from every graceful line. The eyes were almond-shaped, like a Ravinan, and her lips were green like moss.

The Goddess stared straight at Teague and smiled.

"My will be done," she commanded, her voice like a river of thunder. "My will, Goewin Teague. Make love not war."

Peace flooded through Teague in velvet waves of blue and gold. The rushing river slowed to a trickle. It became a steady drop, drop, drop, water from a faucet. A heartbeat, muffled. Then a doctor in a grimy evac hospital peeled blood-crusted bandages from Teague's hip and made her arch off the gurney in pain.

"You're lucky the shrapnel didn't take out an artery," the doctor said. "You'll recover fine back home, Lieutenant."

Past clenched teeth Teague insisted, "Not going home." She said the same thing after surgery, and the same thing when the administrative officer came to talk about reassignment stateside, and the same thing when the hospital chaplain said, "My dear, you've done your part."

She groped for the glass of tepid water on her bedside table. "Haven't even started."

The chaplain touched her forehead. "May the Goddess grant you grace, child."

Teague didn't tell the chaplain that the Goddess had come to her in the chopper. Blood loss or shock or the fragrant smoke of the gunner's joint had caused that hallucination. More important was what she was going to tell her mother. It took a special kind of idiot to get wounded on her first patrol. With a flask of whiskey in her hospital robe and a cane for support she hobbled over to the overseas phone booths. Thirty minutes of listening to static and being patched through operators got her to an apologetic secretary in Probyn.

"She definitely said not to be disturbed?" Teague asked.

"She hasn't been feeling well. But I'll wake her if it's important, Miss Goewin."

Teague took the coward's way out and wrote a letter instead. "Minor shrapnel wounds," she reported. "Hardly a scratch. Are you well?"

The hospital was a revolving bay of stench and sour wounds, of harried doctors and bloody soldiers. Teague smoked in her bed and read outdated magazines and flirted with a redhead nurse who looked like Datch. But late at night, as the sick and injured cried around her, she remembered freckles and honey braids and Lyss's voice, Lyss's calm voice. Squeezing her hand and reassuring her as Zooba's blistered corpse was wrapped up in a plastic bag.

The Goddess unfolded in Teague's dreams with arms like vines. "Give peace a chance."

"Go away," Teague mumbled, her tongue thick from morphine.

After two weeks of so-called recuperation she signed out of the hospital and reported to the helicopter pad. The flight back was a blur. Lyss came to meet her when the chopper landed. Her face was scrubbed clean but a smudge of dirt remained on the lower side of her strong chin.

"Heard you were returning," Lyss said.

Now that Teague was back, the ugly mud pit seemed hardly worth the effort. She started limping toward the CP. "Where's the lieutenant who's been filling in?"

"Said she wanted to go on patrol, wouldn't let me go with her. Got killed on ambush."

Teague said nothing.

Lyss added, "Just so you know, you ain't going out anywhere unless I'm on you like glue."

The concern almost made her smile. "You're that interested in my welfare?"

"Hate breaking in new lieutenants all the time," Lyss said. "Oh, and your new maps came in. Of the High Plateau, wouldn't you know."

Teague's tent smelled like someone else's cigarette smoke. Her sheets were wrinkled and dirty. Exhausted, she stretched out anyway and popped an aspirin for the lingering ache in her hip. Through the flap she could see Lyss cheerfully bossing around the troops, getting more trenches dug. North Ravinans would come tonight, or the next night, or some night in the future, trying to shoot and kill, trying to overrun them. She'd known Ravina was full of craziness before she deployed. But knowing in the head and knowing in the gut were two damn different things.

She dreamt of the Goddess that night, wild and crazy nonsensical dreams that she attributed to the stress of returning to the field.

The next afternoon she joined Pederly's recon. Lyss dutifully tagged along. They circled the village, made a circuit past the paddies to the river, and hiked up and down a ridge. Teague's leg ached and her hands were slippery with sweat on her weapon. When they got safely back to camp, Lyss came to Teague's tent flap with a bottle of excellent Scotch.

"You can afford this on an enlisted soldier's salary?" Teague asked.

"And a few favors," Lyss said, cracking that crooked smile of hers.

Teague had no plans to get drunk with her platoon sergeant but she hadn't eaten her wretched canned dinner yet and maybe the pain pills made her soft. Darkness swept in, stealing away the day. From chairs by the open tent flaps they watched for sappers, incoming missiles, hordes of invading troops. Teague confided in Lyss about her mother.

"Big war hero." Teague's head was woozy. She took another drink anyway. "Lots of medals. Killed a thousand Cemerians, or so they say. Then she divorced my father, took over my grandmother's factories and firms, and made her millions."

"That why you're here?" Lyss asked. "Prove something to your mother? You had a gunshot ticket home, ma'am. You were on easy street."

"Says you. Three fucking tours. For what?"

Lyss shrugged. "It's a job. But it's one that ain't ever going to be done."

"You doubt your army, sergeant?"

"Don't doubt the army, no ma'am. Only the folks running it."

Teague rubbed her tired eyes. "I saw the Goddess. Did I tell you that? After I was hit. She's got freckles like you. She said, 'Go back to your women, Lieutenant Teague! Do your job.'"

Lyss scratched her nose and poured herself more Scotch.

Teague burped. "Datch would disapprove. He's not much into theology. Did I tell you about him? We met at Grinnid University. Twelve hours before I shipped off to infantry training we got engaged. He supports the war."

"It's easy to support war from the other side of the world."

"To the other side of the world!" Teague replied, and raised her tin cup in a toast.

In the morning Teague had a hangover of epic proportions. Lyss made herself scarce, maybe a little hungover herself. They didn't drink again until a week later, when third squad got ambushed on morning patrol and Pederly took a bullet to the stomach.

"She kept yelling and hollering," Narbett told Teague later. "Sergeant Lyss kept telling her to be quiet, help was coming, but Pederly kept shouting about how the bureaucrats got her killed. The sergeant should have gagged her, you know? Should have put a stick in her mouth. It took her a while to die."

Teague looked at her closely. "It must have been hard to watch."

"A lot like a war movie." Narbett smiled sunnily. "But no popcorn."

That night, as a warm rain poured down and turned the camp to mud, Teague wrote her first condolence letter. Forty minutes of training in officer school hadn't prepared her in the least. Surely there was a trick to making the sacrifice of Pederly's life sound worthy and sensible to her husband and kids.

Lyss came knocking around midnight. Teague warned, "Don't even show me that bottle you've got clutched behind your back."

"It's only soda." Lyss held out an aluminum can. "Warm as usual."

The soda tasted brown and zingy, with a little caffeine kick. Teague said, "Sit down," and watched Lyss straddle a chair with her long, strong legs. Rain dropped on the tent roof, then stopped. Teague lit a cigarette. She offered Lyss one, was pleased when she refused. One of them ought to refrain from filthy habits.

"Writing Pederly's letter?" Lyss asked.

Teague squinted through the smoke at her own small, slanted handwriting. "One minute she's there, next minute she's gone. All because of a little bullet through the belly."

"Bullet, cancer, car accident, in your sleep." Something flat made itself known in Lyss's voice. "We all go one way or the other."

The braids and freckles made her seem young, but the files said Lyss was thirty-three years old. Teague tried picturing her at Grinnid University, walking the fine stone paths past ivy walls and buildings funded by wealthy alumni.

She asked Lyss, "Who'd you lose, sergeant?"

For a moment the only sound was the insects outside, the constant droning orchestra. Then more rain, a strong smattering of it. Lyss stood up and put her chair back in place.

She said, "Doesn't matter. Enjoy your soda, ma'am."

"Sergeant." The word came out harder than Teague intended. She said, "I'm sorry. Didn't mean to pry."

Lyss gave a sketchy salute and departed.

It was Narbett, in charge of mail call, who revealed that Lyss had no family. She'd come to bring Teague a care package from Datch and a thin letter from the General.

Narbett confided, "Sergeant Lyss's mother took off a long time ago and her father died of cancer. She never gets any mail. But she doesn't want people to know. I think there's other things, too. You know, Lieutenant? That Sarge doesn't want people to know about. Things that are against regulations."

"Carry on with your duties, corporal," Teague said coldly.

"Yes, ma'am," Narbett said cheerfully. "Colonel Everes, she wrote to me. Asked me how life was in the trenches. I've got lots to tell her."

Sergeant Amilen confirmed that Lyss didn't have any family. "But you know, she's got lots of buddies in other places, ma'am. Career army, they want that. They like moving around a lot, free and clear."

If Lyss was lonely, she didn't show it. Teague always felt two arms' length away from the women, but Lyss was constantly clasping their shoulders or helping carry a load. In the camp, everyone followed Teague's orders but always slid a glance to see if Lyss approved. Teague needed to stop that, wanted the troops to respect and follow her without hesitation, but had to admit that Lyss's approval was important to her, too.

And sometimes, if there was some little thing Teague could do to make Lyss smile, if she passed along the chocolate Datch sent her or got her hands on a good bottle of liquor, then it was only because a happy platoon sergeant made for happy troops. Simply an outgrowth of camaraderie, an inevitable side effect of spending so much time sharing the responsibility of command. It would be completely inappropriate to favor Lyss. To have any kind of relationship outside of proscribed regulations, even if Teague found herself attracted. Which she did not. She was no harlot.

If only the damned Goddess would stop bothering her. Several times a week Teague's dreams were overrun by green lips and almond-shaped eyes and jet-black hair filled with writhing vines. A parade of dancing girls gyrated to wild drums. Golden elephants raised their trunks and jewel-eyed snakes flowed between the cracks of ancient temples. Sitar music lifted Teague from her sweaty sheets and twined between her thighs. Like a bird she flew over the Ravinan countryside, swooping over trees and darting through sacred grottos. The Goddess sang and commanded and unfolded the future with prophesies, but Teague couldn't remember a single detail when she woke flustered and spent.

She tried drinking heavily, but that made the dreams even more vivid. She tried prayers, which the Goddess ignored. She contemplated illegal drugs, but not with women to command.

Six weeks after Teague rejoined her troops, the platoon was relieved for a weekend of R & R at the beach. The ocean was too treacherous with riptides to allow swimming, but the landscape was pretty and the bamboo huts screened out the burning sun. The Ravinan men were eager to earn money any way required. Teague hired a masseuse and tried to relax under his small warm hands. Through slatted eyes and beaded curtains she watched Lyss share a beer with a dark-haired local.

"Tight, too tight," the masseuse said, spreading sandalwood oil on her back.

The man with Lyss laughed, his teeth white in the sunlight. Lyss leaned over and cupped his cheek. Then she deliberately turned her head toward the alcove where Teague lay. Across the distance between them, Lyss smiled with confidence and slyness, as if she were privy to all her lieutenant's thoughts and hopes.

The moment held, stretched. Teague's spine tingled under the salty sea breeze and the hands, the stranger's hands, stroking her skin. She imagined the hands were Lyss's, freed from firing guns, hurling grenades or stanching wounds. Lyss bending over her with her hair unbound in long honey waves. Lyss, touching with intent, with longing—

From somewhere nearby came the shriek of a man's laughter. One of Teague's soldiers said, "Here now, sweetie. Keep that coming."

Teague flushed and turned from Lyss's corrupting gaze.

The weekend ended too soon. When they returned to the firebase the platoon that had taken over for them reported two casualties and three enemy kills, though as always the North Ravinans dragged off their corpses and made enemy body counts unreliable. The temporary lieutenant handed over a package of maps that had come in.

"The Western Shore, Lieutenant Teague. Just like you ordered."

Within days most of Teague's women were suffering from crotch rot. The army issued extra vials of antibiotics. But hypodermic needles couldn't save Corporal Swotwill, who died after shrapnel tore through her lungs. Didn't do much for Corporal Anderson, who fell into a pit filled with shit-covered wooden spikes. Teague wept steadily as she wrote Anderson's letter, the screams still echoing in her ears.

The Goddess came to Teague's dreams that night. The goddamned beautiful Goddess with green lips and a tiny darting tongue that delivered nothing but lies. She said, "Draft beer, not girls."

"I don't know what you want from me," Teague said.

The Goddess's tongue unfurled like a snake. "To love others as I love you."

"You don't love anyone," Teague replied. In the dream she was sitting on the steps of a moss-covered temple. Red birds flitted overhead. Sunlight nearly blinded her eyes. "Who made this war, if not you? Who gets soldiers killed?"

"Love," the Goddess repeated, and sent Teague spiraling through the air. She landed inside Lyss, who was asleep in her tent beside three empty beer bottles. Lyss's dreams were gray, muddled, riddled with fear of death. She didn't believe she would survive South Ravina. She feared her death was imminent. A painful death, like Anderson on the spikes. Like Pederly, gut shot and bleeding out. A lonely death, with no one to mourn her.

"I would mourn you," Teague promised. She tried to hold her, to comfort her, but the dream dissolved into blackness.

The morning dawned gray and drizzly, with the smell of cordite on the wind. The nearest firebase, four kilometers south through heavy jungle, reported intermittent mortar fire. Teague saw no reason to cancel Amilen's morning patrol and decided to go with her, but ordered Lyss to stay behind.

"Lieutenant," Lyss said. "You know the rule on that."

The two of them were alone in the command post. Teague lit a cigarette and blew smoke toward the tent roof. "Maybe I want you safe and sound for a change."

"My time comes, it'll come whether I'm on patrol or sitting on the shitter. I'm no more special than anyone else here, Lieutenant. The only thing that matters is what the Goddess wants."

Teague gave her a long steady look. "One last wish, Sergeant. Say you get one. What would you wish for?"

Lyss grinned as she backed out of the tent. Her eyes were rimmed with dark circles, but she otherwise looked fine after her night of bad dreams. "Nothing that's legal in this woman's army, ma'am."

They went out into the morning drizzle, Teague and Lyss and Amilen's squad. Rounded the village, crossed a paddy, followed a narrow trail east. Rain wormed its way down Teague's hood and black flies irritated her face. When they reached a fast-running creek banked by weeds and grass, Amilen called a halt to fill up their canteens.

"Little old temple over there," Lyss observed, scanning the countryside.

Teague could barely make out the stone silhouette beneath layers of overgrowth. A place abandoned, forgotten by time. Or so she believed until a Ravinan woman emerged wearing traditional black robes.

"Down!" Lyss yelled.

Teague hesitated long enough to almost get herself killed. The priestess's first bullet whizzed so close to her head that she felt a streak of hot air. She dropped to the muddy ground, or maybe Lyss knocked her down. Hard to say. Amilen reached for her weapon but was hit by the second bullet. The force of it spun her backward. Narbett turned to watch and got half her head blown off by bullet number three.

"Cover the trail!" Lyss yelled to the two corporals in the rear. "Make sure no one's flanking us!"

Lyss's grenade arced across the creek and landed near the temple but didn't detonate. Teague fired into the trees around the structure and into the tall and camouflaging grass. Accurate fire would have been better than an indiscriminate waste of bullets. But still she pulled the trigger, her hands cold, her tongue dry. She heard a cry of pain behind her.

"Sergeant!" Teague called out.

"Right here!" Lyss said.

Teague fired again. The priestess pitched out of the tree line and splashed into the creek. She was wounded but not dead, and thrashed and screamed in the fast-moving water. Teague rose up on one knee but didn't move to help her. The woman choked, cried out, sank. Surfaced. Her eyes bulged as she flailed in panic. Her hands extended, seeking help.

"Should we save her?" one of the corporals asked.

"Don't be an idiot," the other corporal said.

Teague stayed on the bank. She could have gone into the water, maybe should have, but she didn't. A long moment passed before the priestess was swept around the bend and gone from sight.

Amilen struggled upright, a hand pressed to her bloody shoulder. "Good one, lieutenant."

Narbett was beyond help. Amilen was capable of walking back to the firebase, where they could evac her to a hospital. Lyss had indeed been hit, but suffered only a graze on her arm. She slapped a bandage on it herself. Teague was only half aware of the women doing their jobs and wrapping Narbett in a poncho. Her gaze kept going back to the river, and her knees were trembling so badly she thought they might fold under her.

"Lieutenant?" That was Lyss. "You okay?"

Teague nodded.

On the long, wet trek home, with rain blurring her vision, Teague saw the Goddess everywhere. In the bloodstains on Lyss's arms, in the green plastic containing

Narbett's corpse, in palm fronds and puddles and the gray glowering sky. The vengeful Goddess, furious at the killing of a priestess. The satisfied Goddess, blood spilled for blood. The blond and perfect Goddess of Grinnid University's theology department, her visage captured in marble. The wild Goddess of Teague's dreams, ready to plague her for years more to come.

Back at the firebase, in her tent, she went to her knees and vomited into the dirt.

"Lieutenant?" Lyss was at her tent flap. "Ma'am, you all right?"

Teague sat back against her foot locker. "No."

Lyss entered without permission and stood hunched against the green canvas. "You have to pack your things."

She drew in a shuddering breath. "Every day, someone else. Every day, another bullet."

"Ma'am." Lyss knelt next to her. "Listen to me. Orders came over the radio while we were out. You're going home. Your mom. She's had a stroke. Pretty bad, I guess."

Teague stared at her. "She what?"

Lyss pulled a message from her pocket. "Humanitarian release. You have to go."

Teague read the details twice and then said, dumbly, "But my tour's not over."

"You're going home," Lyss said softly. "Chopper's on the way."

Teague could see herself on a dirty helicopter to the coast and then a crowded smoky plane back to civilization. Could picture a black limousine with leather seats waiting at the airport curb. Important papers to sign wielded by gray-haired lawyers in pearls and tweed blazers. A trip to the hospital, where her mother would be lying in a private suite with only the best doctors to murmur and consult. But every step of the journey had a gaping hole in it, a black spot where honey braids and freckles should be.

She asked, "What am I going to do?"

Rain thrummed on the roof like the Goddess's thousand fingers. Lyss reached a grimy hand to touch Teague's cheek. "You're going home. Which means I can do this," she said, and pressed her mouth forward in a warm, wet kiss.

Teague did nothing, felt nothing.

The rain thrummed louder, turning into the beat of helicopter blades. Lyss pulled back, her expression stricken at Teague's lack of response. Then Teague lunged forward and cupped Lyss's head between her dirty hands and showed her how a General's daughter could kiss. Lyss's lips were chapped and not Goddess green, but they tasted like Scotch and coffee and bliss.

"Lieutenant, they're coming!" yelled a corporal from outside. Lyss jerked back with reddened cheeks but a steady gaze. Dazed, unable to keep her feet from tangling up in one another, Teague shoved clothing and personal effects into her duffel bag. She let Lyss guide her out of the tent and across the muddy firebase. Rain slanted down even harder, camouflaging Teague's tears.

"Lieutenant Teague!" A clean, impossibly young officer shouted over the noise of the chopper. "Sorry to hear about your circumstances. I'll take over from here."

Lyss offered a formal handshake. She looked almost as shell-shocked as Teague felt. "Been a pleasure, lieutenant."

Her tongue failed her. She climbed into the open bay beside Amilen. Firebase Jonathan fell away like a watercolor smear. The twenty-three hour trip home passed in a long ordeal of lobbies and airplanes and bone-weary fatigue that made sleep perversely impossible. The limousine was late to Probyn airport and the chauffeur surly. The hospital was cold and gray, and reeked of disinfectant. A somber-faced doctor with two Goddess wards around her neck told Teague her mother had died an hour earlier.

"She went peacefully," the doctor reported. "With grace."

Datch came. He'd grown a ridiculous little goatee since she'd last seen him and wore a patriotic pin to support the war. Some of Teague's classmates from Grinnid attended the funeral. She remembered their faces but not their names. The paperwork was as tedious as expected, the business concerns as pressing, and if Teague couldn't sleep at night in her penthouse apartment without the benefit of alcohol, if she found herself unable to sit still in board meetings or read the front page of newspapers, she told herself it would all pass in time. She dreamt only of Lyss and Narbett and death, and never of the Goddess. She told Datch she was breaking their engagement.

"Why?" he demanded.

She raised her hands helplessly. "I don't need you."

"You're just like your mother," he said, deliberately cruel.

Two weeks before Winter Solstice she received an old-fashioned postcard of South Ravina. Three relaxed but stylish tourists lounged in a sidewalk cafe in front of a charming old hotel. A woman on a bicycle drove past, her black hair streaming in the wind. "Come Home! Come to Paradise!" the slogan read. On the back were details of an airline flight and the words, "2 weeks leave. Meet me." An order, which Teague found funny.

"Is that from a friend?" asked Teague's secretary.

"War buddy," Teague responded.

The morning of Lyss's flight was bitterly cold. Teague dressed carefully in a blue suit and sensible heels. It wasn't quite a uniform, but it was close. After ten minutes she changed into slacks and a green jersey, but that didn't look right either. Finally she pulled on a blue sweater and suede skirt and expensive boots. She told her limousine driver she'd take her own car.

"Roads are icy, Miss Teague," the driver said. "Best take Riverside Drive."

Riverside wound past high-rises and thin crescents of parks and the half-frozen river. Teague drove carefully. Snow and slush coated the cityscape in white and gray. There would be no snow in South Ravina. No leaden skies or chimneys putting out curling smoke. The army would erect Solstice trees, hang out stockings and play carols, but there would be no peace on earth.

Teague parked in an airport lot near the terminal. She sat with her black gloved hands gripping the steering wheel, the engine still running. Enormous planes descended out of the sky one after the other. She thought, "Make Love Not War" and "Give Peace a Chance." The clock in the dashboard flipped the minutes forward. Lyss's plane would be landing now. Taxiing to the gate. Teague's Grinnid graduation tassel, hanging on the rearview mirror, stirred in the heat from the dashboard vent. She fingered the gold and blue strings. Felt the silkiness through her gloves and down to her bones.

She knew the Goddess had been nothing but a

hallucination brought on by stress. War made women do and say strange things. That part of her life was done and closed, like a book with a moldy green cover.

She wasn't a harlot.

But she was definitely a smoker in need of a nicotine fix. Teague rooted through her purse and came up empty. She'd have to go into one of the terminals to buy some cigarettes. And maybe the newsstand or souvenir shop would just happen to be by Lyss's arrival gate, and Teague would stand there until a familiar face bobbed through the crowds and a crooked smile lifted the world's gloom.

Teague hurried from the car with her head bowed against the strong wind. She didn't see Lyss's postcard flutter from her purse to the dirty gray slush, where it landed face-up in the weak winter sun. The ink detailing Lyss's flight information began to weaken and blur.

Come Home! Come to Paradise!

The words faded away.

Author's notes

1. It is the author's opinion that Teague misses Lyss's arrival entirely, that Lyss considers herself dumped, and that the two women never meet again. Or perhaps they don't meet at the airport, but Lyss calls Teague's office, and they meet later in a restaurant where Teague apologizes for the confusion with an expensive bottle of wine. In some multiverses they live happily ever after, but in most foreseeable timelines Teague breaks Lyss's heart, and Lyss finds happiness with a college professor instead.

2. Narbett was voted "Most Likely to Annoy" in a secret poll among her high school peers. She found out about it, but never told anyone she knew.

3. The author owes a debt to various Vietnam narratives, the television show "Tour of Duty," and to her Uncle Bobby, who served and survived.

The Firemen's
FAIRY

Graduation Day, bright and sunny. The breeze smelled like freshly cut grass. One hundred newly-minted firefighters waited anxiously to receive their diplomas from a magnificent golden phoenix. Steven Goodwin shifted his weight from one foot to the other and tried not to stare at the bird's huge wings. The Supreme Mascot of the Massasoit Fire Department was rarely seen, never photographed, and undeniably amazing. She sat serenely at the edge of the graduation stage with Steven's first station assignment clutched in her claws.

"And so on this fine day…" Assistant Chief Kelly droned on at the podium. Kelly was a short man with steel-gray hair and a paunch that strained his uniform buttons. He'd been speaking for several minutes, but Steven was only half listening. Mostly he was thinking about tough-as-nails Engine 157, with its East Side firehouse and fierce dragon mascot. Nobody messed with 157. Or Ladder 28 on Rymere Island, with a steel-corseted Valkyrie riding beside the driver. Valkyries kicked ass.

Kelly continued, "Their courage and strength will be tested in the field under extraordinary circumstances…"

Beside Steven, Jimmy Linden let out an audible sigh. "We'll be retired before he's finished."

The two of them had grown up together on the same block, had joined the army together, had served in Abbasidia within twenty miles of each other's units. For the last thirteen weeks they'd been practicing ladder ascensions, rescue training, fire suppression and emergency medicine. Steven had aced all the physical requirements. Jimmy received the best scores on the written tests. But none of that meant anything until your first big fire, Steven knew. Until you faced down an inferno and lived to tell about it.

"...and so they'll continue in the tradition of brotherhood..."

Steven shifted his gaze to the audience. His current girlfriend was somewhere in the folding chairs, lost in a sea of blouses and shirts. Steven's father sat right in front, ramrod straight, with the other retired firefighters. Flanking the seats was a line of antique fire engines with gleaming brass and bright red paint. A dozen more modern engines also waited, their crews ready to dash off if needed. Steven could see a three-headed dog wagging its tail eagerly on one truck, and a water nymph filing her fingernails while she leaned against a paramedic unit.

"I present to you the academy's 150th class of brave, skilled, hard-working probationary firefighters!" Chief Kelly finally said.

Steven barely heard the applause and cheers when his turn came to cross the stage. His hand was clammy as he shook hands with his teachers, the school administrators, and Chief Kelly. He knew he was blushing and grinning like a fool. Some days, back in the desert, he'd figured to be dead by dusk. Now he was a fireman like his dad, and both his grandfathers, and all the other Goodwin men whose pictures hung in the fire museum gallery.

At the far end of the stage, the phoenix peered down at him with wide black eyes. He could see himself in those eyes, twin reflections of his black and gold uniform. She lifted her whitish-gray beak and passed a scroll off to Chief Kelly, who pressed it into Steven's hand.

"Good luck, son," Kelly said.

Steven waited until he was off the stage before he unrolled his assignment.

Oh, shit.

Engine Company 13's firehouse was a two-story brick building nestled in a residential neighborhood just a few blocks from the river. The streets were narrow and crowded, lined with wooden triple-decker apartment buildings. The smell of sewage carried on the breeze from a nearby treatment plant The station had its own parking lot surrounded by a chain-link fence. On his first morning of work Steven wedged his battered Honda into an available space, killed the engine, and sat for a long moment with his hands on the steering wheel.

Finally he hauled himself out of the car and walked into the open equipment bay. The fire engine was an old Firestorm II, dazzlingly red and silver. The watch office was empty but sounds of conversation drifted out of the adjacent day room. Captain Ingalls, a large black man with a scarred cheek and short gray hair, was sitting in his office listening to radio traffic and watching a coffee pot percolate.

Steven knocked on the door. "Captain?"

"Probie!" Ingalls boomed. "Come on in."

He went in but didn't sit. The office was only large enough for an old steel desk, two wooden filing cabinets, a leather seat for the captain and some folding chairs for visitors. Official notices and regulations hung on bulletin boards.

"Sir, I wanted to say that I'm glad—"

"Hold on," Ingalls said, raising his hand. Both of them watched the last bits of coffee drop into a glass pot. Ingalls transferred the liquid to a mug ringed with multiple layers of brown grime.

Steven said, "Looks like that cup needs to be washed, Captain."

"Haven't washed it in twelve years," Ingalls said. "I like the grit."

He took a happy sip, fixed his gaze on Steven, and said, "I heard you weren't thrilled with this assignment."

"I'm fine with it, sir," Steven said. "My father was a little concerned."

"Your father called Chief Kelly. They go way back."

"I asked him not to." Which was true. But he hadn't asked very hard.

"The Superintendent told him what I'm going to tell you, probie. You deal with it. Every mascot in the Fire Department is a highly skilled, highly prized supernatural volunteer. The city works long and hard to recruit them, and we're damned lucky to have one. You understand?"

"Sir." Steven squared his shoulders, just like back in the military. "There's no problem."

Ingalls called in Scooter Watkins, the engineer and second-in-command on B-shift. He was a heavy man with a wide mustache and an easy grin.

"Served in Abbasidia, did you?" he asked, after introductions. "People shoot at you a lot over there?"

"Some," Steven allowed.

Ingalls reached for his appalling coffee mug. "Show him around, Scoot. Bob's dying to meet him."

The equipment bay floor was spotlessly clean. The upstairs showers leaked, but the tiles had recently been grouted. The beds in the men's bunkroom were made up with green blankets and tight corners. In the basement were some free weights, a dusty treadmill, and a sofa with tattered cushions. Final stop on the tour was the day room, with its kitchen area and large wooden table. Worn leather sofas lined the walls and two large windows overlooked the river. Pictures of fallen firemen hung on the walls in sturdy wooden frames.

The station's mascot flitted through the air and asked, in a high-pitched voice, "Is this him? Our new probie? I'm delighted to meet you! Ecstatic! We're going to be such good friends. Would you like to stroke my wings? They're finer than silk!"

Tinkerbob.

Official fairy of Company 13.

"Calm down, Bob," Scooter said. "Let the kid sit down for a moment."

Bob danced and twirled and threw little bits of glitter into the air. He was no more than three inches tall and had rainbow-colored wings. His legs were encased in pink tights and glittery ballet slippers. His curly brown hair looked silky soft, and his little cap had bells on it.

"You're very handsome," Bob said as he zipped around Steven's head. "I have a thing for men in uniform. Handsome firefighters all around me. But don't forget ladies, too! Miss Paula is exceptionally beautiful."

"Bob, sit," Paula Little said from her place at the kitchen table. She was the third member of B-shift. Steven knew her only by reputation. A few years earlier, during her first week on the job, she and two other firefighters had been knocking down a fire in a burning brownstone. An air conditioning unit dropped through the roof and smashed the floor out from underneath them. The other two guys died. Paula had spent three months in physical rehab before coming back to the job. Her left cheek and lower jaw were still scarred from burns. Steven pretended not to notice.

"Hope you like our little fellow," Scooter said, with a head jerk toward Bob. "We're mighty fond of him out here."

Bob darted in and kissed Steven's cheek. "We're going to be best friends!"

The kiss felt like the bite of a fly. Steven said, "I'm sure we will."

He hadn't survived the army by being stupid, after all. If the members of B-shift didn't give him positive recommendations at the end of his probation, he'd never make it to full-fledged firefighter. As lowest in the pecking order, he'd have to do most of the grunt work around the station—cooking, cleaning, swabbing down the bathrooms, folding and re-folding hoses, polishing boots. It was going to be hard enough to prove himself without alienating them over a tiny fairy mascot.

"Best friends, best friends, best friends!" Bob sang. He cartwheeled in mid-air and then came to rest on Steven's forearm. "My dearest, will you fix me a bath? Warm water, some honey, and a bit of vanilla oil in a tea cup. Just be sure it's not too hot. I have very delicate skin, you know."

Steven was tempted to pour dishwashing liquid into the mix, but he held back. Give the little guy a chance, he told himself. He was looking for the vanilla oil when the dispatch tones went off and the intercom clicked to life.

"Engine 14, report of smoke, one-two-four Durello Street."

"Report of smoke!" Bob zoomed toward the equipment bay. "Let's go get 'em!"

The shift wasn't even thirty minutes old. Steven had expected just a little more time to get settled. Paula said, "Here, probie," and thrust a heavy turnout coat into his hands. She pulled on her own coat and swung up to the jump seat behind Captain Ingalls. "You sit over there."

He climbed up behind Scooter and tugged his coat on as the engine rolled forward. The wail of the siren caught him off-guard, though he'd never been surprised during academy training. A real call, his first real call. He could sense the curious and envious glares of motorists as Scooter maneuvered the engine through traffic. Men on their way to office buildings, men on their way to crummy jobs. Not him. Never him.

Four minutes after leaving the firehouse, they reached a boarded-up grammar school of crumbling brick and broken windows. It might have been a grand building once, but graffiti marred most of its walls and the playground of rusting equipment was littered with drug debris, excrement, and mounds of trash. A police car was parked on the sidewalk.

"Homeless get in there, try to cook up junk or their dinner," the cop said. "Going to burn the whole place down one day."

Steven couldn't smell smoke. The air was visibly clear, or as clear as city air could be. But he followed Paula dutifully across the playground to a side door that hung loose on its hinges. They inspected inside, finding no people but plenty of evidence of squatters—soiled sheets, candle stubs, a tattered brown teddy bear. The classrooms were ghostly in the boarded-up light. The blackboards had all been shattered or covered with graffiti.

"Nothing here," Paula reported over the radio. She gave Steven a bright-eyed look. "Little disappointing, huh?"

He shrugged.

The rest of the day was no more exciting. In fact, Steven's whole first week unfolded that way. Milk runs and cakewalks. A few car accidents, some building inspections, a diabetic who'd collapsed in a Chinese supermarket. Jimmy, who'd been posted over to Engine 129, at least got some action on a fire in an Italian restaurant.

"Whole kitchen went up," he said over the phone. "All that grease, you know?"

They met to shoot pool at in a private bar called The Hose. The floors were old and scuffed, the booths made of ripped red vinyl, but the pool tables were in good condition and the stools at the bar were sturdy enough to hold the stoutest firefighters. Pictures of equipment and mascots hung on the nicotine-stained walls. The city had recently outlawed smoking in restaurants and bars, but The Hose was owned by a retired battalion chief and Jimmy was puffing on a noxious-smelling cigar.

"Can you believe it," Jimmy said as he lined up the cue ball. "Six medical assists, two car accidents, and a woman too fat to get out her front door. That was the entire shift yesterday. But it's better than getting shot at in Baghdad."

Steven swallowed some beer. "I guess."

Jimmy gave him a mischievous look. "Still. At least we've got a dwarf."

"Shut up."

"Mogol doesn't say much. Good at ripping car doors off with his bare hands. Rest of the time, he sits around cursing and hammering silver."

Bob spent most of his time gossiping, reading celebrity magazines over Paula's shoulder, and playing dress-up with a bunch of other fairies that lived in a nearby oak tree. The fairy men enjoyed draping themselves in colored tin foil, or scraps of pink velvet, or the little tiny firefighter costumes the district chief's wife had made for them. Sometimes they pretended to fight fires in the station locker room. Scooter would issue them mint floss to use as a fire hose. Captain Ingalls would reward them with candy corn for a job well done.

"Thank you, sir!" the fairy men would salute.

The absolutely worst thing about Bob was his whistling. Cheerful little whistles, day and night, in the kitchen and bunkroom and equipment bay, except when Captain Ingalls asked him to pipe down. Station 42 had a goblin infamous for its bawdy ballads, and Ladder 12's minotaur had written a country-music hit, but Bob simply whistled and whistled and whistled.

"Why don't you think up some songs, instead?" Paula asked one night while Steven dried the dinner dishes. "With a melody and lyrics."

Bob draped himself over the back of a sofa. "I'm not good at lyrics. It's my one tragic failing."

Steven said, "I'm sure you have others."

Paula gave him a narrow look.

"My dearest Steven," Bob said, and darted in for a quick kiss on the cheek. "Will you pour me some almond milk? With cinnamon on top?"

A month after Steven joined Engine 13, the shift got their first three-tone. It was two a.m. and he'd been dreaming of being lost in the sand under a hot yellow sky. Over the intercom, the dispatcher said, "Engine 13, Ladder 2, Rescue 8. One-four-five Losco Street." Steven was up out of bed before the announcement finished, and stumbled to the engine with a dry mouth.

"You ready for this?" Paula asked as the engine raced through the dark streets.

"Born ready!" Steven shouted back, and caught the smell of smoke in the air.

Two minutes after leaving the firehouse, they screeched to a halt outside a burning Victorian house. They were the first unit on the scene. Thick gray smoke boiled toward the full moon. Red flames shot out of the blown-out windows of the second floor, melting the aluminum siding. Neighbors in pajamas and bathrobes had come out to watch the spectacle. Some took pictures with their cell phones, while others smoked or chatted. Three kids and a man stood at the curb, in obvious distress.

"My wife!" The man yelled to the firefighters. "I think she's still inside!"

Captain Ingalls turned to Bob. "Go find her."

"Yes, sir!" Bob let out a smart salute and zipped toward the inferno.

Steven supposed the little guy was brave enough, plunging into a burning building like that. His own bravado was turning into wobbly knees. Fire training at the academy had been under intimidating but controlled circumstances. The chances of getting injured or killed had been real, but minimized. Here the hot air was roiling with ash, and the roof might collapse at any moment, and Paula was yelling at him to follow her up onto the porch, hold the line, keep it aimed —

He had his mask on, the heavy rubber and plastic feeding him clean air. But the acrid smells of burning carpet and paint made his nose and throat itch. Heat rolling out of the house baked through his turnout coat and gloves. The most vivid thing about Abbasidia hadn't been the filth, or the desperation, or even the deaths. Instead it was the relentless summer heat baking through his uniform and frying him from the inside out —

Bob darted out of the smoke and passed Steven's helmet. He flew directly to the curb to report back to Captain Ingalls. No signal or order came to rescue the trapped woman. Already dead, then. Paula tugged Steven toward the front door. They crouched low and shot pulses of cold water at the ceiling in the front room. Drenching fires directly was ineffective, old-fashioned. Better that the heat convert the water to cooling mist. It was still hot as hell, but not so bad that Steven couldn't think or act. Soon Ladder 2 and Rescue 8 arrived, and their combined efforts knocked the fire out. Steven felt thrilled and exhilarated at surviving his first fire, then went outside and saw the children weeping for their mother.

"How'd you do, probie?" asked one of the men from Rescue 8 while Steven and Paula folded up their hose.

Bob made a quick dizzying circle around Steven's head. "He did excellent! Very brave. Very manly. But I singed my tights. See? They're all dirty."

Ladder 2's mascot, a Greek sphinx with the head of a woman and wings of an eagle, stretched out her leonine body and eyed Bob as if he'd make a tasty snack.

The man from Rescue 8 said to Bob, "You want a good hosing down? Come on over, we'll get you cleaned up."

"Bob's fine," Paula said firmly. "Go see Scooter, Bob."

That night, while Steven finished the probie job of making sure everything was clean before it was stowed away, he thought more about Paula. Through all his weeks of academy training, he hadn't been sure about women in the department. Sure, they could pass the written tests. They'd done okay in the physical training. But then there was the real world. Plunging into a fire with seventy or eighty pounds of gear on your back, dragging lines filled with hundreds of pounds of water. Paula had done well, but could she carry Steven out if he got injured in a fire? How about carrying Scooter, or even Captain Ingalls? Steven's father, the retired fire lieutenant, didn't think she could do it.

"Upper body strength is the one area where men will always be better than women," Tom Goodwin said as he and Steven watched a pre-season football game. "She lifting weights?"

"Every day, down in the basement," Steven said.

Tom reached for more popcorn. "Never going to be the same."

Steven's newest girlfriend, Katie, was less interested in Paula's physical prowess and more interested in where she slept, where she showered, if she walked around the station in her underwear.

"Yeah," Steven said, pinching her hip. They were lying in bed with the lights of the city reflecting on the ceiling. "We all do. The captain wears a thong, and Scooter has boxers that say 'Firemen do it with a big hose.'"

Katie tweaked his left nipple with her long fingers. "I'm serious."

"She doesn't walk around in her bathrobe." Steven rose up on one elbow. "What do you think, we have orgies while waiting for calls?"

She gave him a pout. "You've got a fairy mascot and a female firefighter. I don't know what goes on down there."

Steven knew some men on the other shifts and other stations gave Paula a hard time. Snide comments here and there. On Valentine's Day she came in and her locker was decorated with red condoms. After she skipped the annual Fireman's Ball, people like Jimmy said it was because she didn't want to bring her lesbian date.

"You don't know she's a lesbian," Steven said, over another game of pool at The Hose. "She takes care of her dad. He was sick. Why are you worried about it?"

"I'm not worried about her. I'm worried about you, with that little pink guy floating around when you're taking a shower. Might rub off."

"How'd you like this pool stick up your ass?" Steven said.

Jimmy said, "See! That's where it starts."

As if there weren't already gay firefighters in the department. Steven knew the rumors. Billy Heller, over at Ladder 12. Living with the same guy for five years, claiming they were cousins. Sam Capodilupo, used to be lead hose for Engine 23 before he got zapped by a fallen electrical wire. His "roommate" hadn't left his hospital room for two days. Things like that attracted attention. Heller's tires had been slashed a couple of times. Capodilupo had come back on the job, but after a couple of accidents—slippery floors, doors that opened unexpectedly and gave him black eyes—he transferred to a desk job in the Safety Division.

Steven thought he was doing a good job of putting up with fairy Bob, even if it wasn't always easy. Before lights out each night Bob asked for a thimbleful of hot cocoa made with real milk and fresh whipped cream. Captain Ingalls had Steven fix it. Bob's breakfast every morning was fresh pineapple cut into splinter-sized portions. Steven was responsible for that as well. Bob slept in a specially crafted, multi-storied oak birdhouse in the watch office. Steven had to keep the windows clean with lemon water, and make sure Bob's handkerchief-sized silk sheets were laundered with the mildest of soaps, and sweep glitter off the birdhouse floors with a fine, narrow paintbrush.

"Don't forget to shake out the rugs!" Bob would cheerfully remind him, and give him another damned kiss like a blood-sucking mosquito.

Worse than the kisses was Bob's whistling, that damn whistling, the day and night whistling. Steven started hearing it when he was at his father's house, arguing over fantasy football rankings with his dad. While he was making love to Lisa, a girl he started seeing after Katie didn't work out. Lisa was dark and curvy, in the habit of leaving bruises on him. The bruises made him feel well-used. He heard whistling on the subway, in the supermarket, when he was standing at the river's edge and gazing at the dark water. Pink tights and butterfly wings and disco music and even the kisses, he could live with. But that ceaseless, high-pitched, off-tune whistling drove him nuts.

Still, he told himself. Better to say nothing. Three months he'd been with Engine 13, no problems. No fires bigger than his first one where the mom was killed. Some gruesome car accidents. Heart attacks and sprained ankles and stranded cats, oh my. Sometimes people came on by the firehouse looking for directions or first aid. All in all far less exciting and dangerous than Abbasidia, and Steven was happy for that.

Then Paula was out sick for a week. She liked the same newspaper comics that he did, and they usually bickered over who got to read them first. It was no fun to have the whole section to himself. Her temporary replacement was a sweaty man from Engine 2 with the unlikely name of Gordon Gordon

"Why do you have two identical names?" Bob asked him at breakfast.

"Why do you have wings?" Gordon's smile didn't show any teeth.

Bob did a somersault in mid air. "To fly like a bird!"

Gordon's fingers tightened around his coffee cup. "Eddie, our satyr, doesn't have wings. Just really sharp horns."

They conducted two fire inspections that day and responded to a heart attack call. Gordon Gordon talked a lot about Eddie the satyr. Steven had seen the half-man, half-goat from afar, but never talked to him. The goat part was weird, Gordon Gordon agreed. But Eddie played a mean hand of poker, could bench-press five hundred pounds, and had personally dragged three firemen out of a notorious blaze down on Pier 52.

"I'm just saying," Gordon Gordon added, watching Bob and his fairy friends play Simon Says in the parking lot. "A mascot like Eddie's a real asset, you know? You can't say that about all of them."

Around four o'clock, just as Steven was thinking about starting dinner, two tones went off. Another car accident, but this one was bad. A flipped SUV had landed on top of a station wagon in the middle of the cross-town expressway. The SUV driver was pinned upside down, his face covered with blood, half his scalp hanging free. He was conscious, somehow, and screaming. No words, just screams. Several inches beneath him, the driver of the station wagon— gender unrecognizable, body in squashed or torn pieces— was beyond anyone's help. But there was a blue plastic infant carrier in the back seat and a tiny kid, maybe only a few weeks old, still alive back there.

"She's crying," Bob reported, as he darted in and out of the wreck.

"Is she hurt?" Scooter asked.

Bob wrung his tiny hands. "Just crying! Can't you help her? She's so unhappy."

"We're trying,"

Two other engines had responded to the call. Police officers directed rubber-necking, frustrated drivers caught in gridlock. A news helicopter buzzed and rattled overhead, the engine noises making Steven's teeth itch. The day was so unseasonably warm that sweat collected under his uniform and pooled at the small of his back. The weight and thickness of his turnout coat didn't help. He could smell burning rubber, scorched metal, blood. Lots of blood. Gunpowder. The stench of rotting bodies, seven of them, lined up neatly beside the road as flies filled their eyes and mouths.

He stood there, the desert glare making his eyes hurt, his breathing tight under his uniform and vest, gun clutched so tightly in hand that his fingers ached.

This was wrong, all wrong, he had left the desert behind him, hadn't he? Had left behind the dead and dying, the bitter and knowing gazes of survivors, the fetid waste and broken cities. Had vowed never again would he be helpless in the grip of politics and war. Not with seven bodies on the road, a family who had offered friendly smiles the last time Steven's squad passed this way. A family. Three adults, three children, a baby with deep brown eyes and beautiful smile—

"Hey, probie," someone said, touching his arm.

He recoiled violently, pulling back with his gun raised. But there was no gun in his hand. Nothing but his bare fingers, pointing at Gordon Gordon. The rumble and stench of traffic made Steven's stomach clench in a spasm. They were standing by the side of the expressway, surrounded by fire engines and police cars, helicopters—goddamned helicopters!—overhead, an upside-down man screaming as blood pulsed out of his skull faster than paramedics could staunch it.

Steven fell to his knees, cement slamming against bone. He retched helplessly, convulsively. He was shivering under his coat, his muscles spasming as if he had his fingers in an electrical socket. When the vomiting stopped he realized a paramedic was taking his pulse, and someone else was pushing a bottle of water into his hands.

"We'd better take him in, just in case," the paramedic was telling someone.

"No." Steven took the water bottle but brushed the paramedic aside. "I'm okay."

Captain Ingalls almost made it an order, but after several minutes of arguing instead told Steven to take the rest of the day off. A police car dropped him off at his apartment. He shed his gear in his living room, crawled into bed with a bottle of Jack Daniel's, and turned on the TV. He didn't eat dinner. He didn't answer his ringing phone. He drank, vomited again sometime around sunset, fell into a restless sleep, and stumbled to the door when some stupid bastard started banging on it.

Jimmy pushed his way in, his expression grim and worried. He was still wearing his uniform.

"You're on shift," Steven said thickly. He could still feel the whiskey burning in his belly and brain. Wanted more, but it was all the way back in his bedroom.

"I'm due back in an hour. Your captain called my captain, said go check on you. You look like hell. And you stink. Go shower off, will you?"

Easier to obey than argue, but the soap and water felt more like chores than any kind of comfort. He pulled on sweatpants but couldn't find a clean T-shirt. Took the whiskey with him to the kitchen, where Jimmy was pulling a hot pizza from the microwave.

"Eat." Jimmy pushed him to a chair.

"Not hungry," Steven replied, which was mostly true.

"Eat. And tell me what the hell happened out there."

Steven lifted a wedge of pizza and watched cheese drip from the crust. "Nothing."

"Nothing, my ass." Jimmy pulled out a chair, turned it backwards, and straddled it. His scrubbed the sides of his head, ruffling his short brown hair. "You froze up? Your captain said you were out of it. Flashback? PTSD?"

The cheese kept dripping. "What are you, a psychiatrist?"

"The department can make you see a real shrink, Stevie boy."

He swigged more whiskey. "Only if I've got a real problem."

Jimmy pinned him with a stare. "You've got something."

Steven shifted his focus to the wall. "You don't think about it? Things that happened back there?"

"Not when I'm awake," Jimmy replied.

Before leaving, Jimmy manhandled Steven to his bed, dumped him on the wrinkled sheets, and confiscated the Jack Daniel's. He searched for the remote to the television, then gave up and turned the volume down by hand. Steven watched from the pillows. He felt sore from the inside out.

"I remember all the dead," Steven murmured. "Their way their mouths hung open and you could see their black tongues."

"You've got to leave it behind," Jimmy said.

Steven closed his eyes. He could feel Jimmy's presence in the room, the solidness of his sturdy body and blue uniform. Brotherhood. Soldiers and firemen, he thought. The room was hot, and he pushed the sheet down to his bare waist.

"Don't shut me out," Jimmy said softly. "I couldn't stand that."

The floor creaked under shifting weight. A long moment expanded, contracted up again. The door creaked. Then, in the soft gray land between waking and sleeping, something gentle brushed against Steven's mouth. Soft lips. Warm breath. A caress—

He jerked awake with a jolt of fear and anger. "Godammmit!" he swore, but he was all alone in the pre-dawn light. But someone had kissed him. He was sure of it. Brief, tiny, forbidden. He wiped his lips and thought he saw the faintest hint of glitter.

"Bob," he snarled, and lurched to the open window and ripped screen.

B-shift was off duty that day. When Captain Ingalls called to see how he was doing, Steven apologized for letting the accident scene get to him. He was sorry he'd become so emotional.

"Can't shut your feelings off," Ingalls said. "Nobody wants you to."

His father called. "Heard you were under the weather," he said, but Steven denied it and that was it, topic closed. His father had never been comfortable with childhood illnesses or frailties. It couldn't have been easy, a widowed firefighter raising a kid alone, but it hadn't been especially sympathetic, either.

"Stop feeling sorry for yourself," Steven told his reflection in the bathroom mirror.

He went to work the next morning with renewed resolve. No more weakness. No more losing control. At roll call, Scooter slapped him on the back and Ingalls gave him a nod. Paula said, "Are you okay?" and he said,

"Sure." Bob spun around him, his butterfly wings quick with concern.

"Dearest, dearest, I was worried for you," Bob said.

Steven dug his fingernails into his palms. "I'm fine."

"I'm so happy to hear it!" Bob swirled and cartwheeled and then he started whistling, that stupid annoying whistling, and Steven's control vanished.

"Stop that!" he snapped. "I swear to God, keep it up, I'll rip your wings off and shove them down your throat!"

Bob froze in mid-air.

"Steven!" Paula said.

"It's all he goddamn does!" Steven said, his vision narrow and blurred on the edges. He felt unexpectedly like weeping, and squashed the impulse with every bit of ruthlessness he owned. "Day and fucking night! It's inhumane. It's cruel and unusual punishment."

Bob sank to the floor, his wings stilled.

Steven stalked off to the kitchen, where he sloshed hot coffee into a cup and over his fingers. Captain Ingalls called him into his office a few minutes later and asked what the problem was.

"Nothing, sir," Steven insisted.

"You bite Bob's head off for no good reason, and that's nothing?"

"The whistling's got to stop," Steven said. "I know you hate it, too. Everyone does."

Ingalls shook his head. "Bob whistles, Paula bites her nails, Scooter stinks up the bathroom and you snore. I myself am exempt from irritating habits, but the rest of you? Not perfect. Never will be. You need to apologize."

Steven stared at a spot beyond Ingalls' shoulder and kept silent.

"Not a choice, probie. Don't get me wrong. You're a good man. Valuable. About a thousand times bigger than Bob, physically speaking. But today? You're the smaller man. Don't make things worse."

"Maybe I should transfer to another station, sir."

Ingalls reached for his coffee cup. "If it comes down to that, maybe so."

The shift passed slowly, with no calls or inspections to break up the long hours. The autumn sun was a stark yellow disk in the cloudy sky. Steven talked to no one unless he absolutely had to. Scooter and Paula spent most of the day trying to persuade Bob to come out of his birdhouse.

"He didn't mean it," Steven heard Paula say.

"He's upset about something else," Scooter added.

Bob didn't respond.

A few hours after a silent, tense lunch, three tones went off. A long, somber list of companies followed. "Engine 8, Engine 25, Engine 5, Ladder 3, Rescue 9, Rescue 156. Four-two-nine Pierre Street."

Not Engine 13, though. Steven felt an irrational anger that they weren't being called out to what sounded like a kick-ass fire, a real scorcher. Twenty minutes later, the tones sounded again.

"Engine 47, Engine 13, Ladder 2, Rescue 10," the dispatcher said. "Support units already on scene, four-two-nine Pierre Street."

Steven jumped up to his seat, saw Paula take her place, felt the movement of the engine as Scooter shifted into gear. They rolled out of the station house twenty seconds after the tone. Bob was with them, perched on Captain Ingalls' helmet. His jaunty cap was askew. He wore bright new purple boots with bells on the tips.

Fairies, Steven thought bitterly, and turned his shoulder.

They raced through the city streets to Pierre Street, where smoke rose from the roof of a five-story brick warehouse. Steven's heart clenched the minute he saw the place. Only a few windows to vent poisonous fumes and broiling heat. Only five exits in and out, including a loading dock by a set of rusty train tracks. Old building, shuttered and abandoned for years. Who knew what kind of toxic or flammable waste might be in there. Drug addicts or homeless schizophrenics might be living inside, might have started the fire. Or a pyromaniac, or arsonists. Collecting insurance on an old warehouse was often a more valuable proposition than trying to clean it up and rent it.

Paula, her face pale, shouted, "This one's going to be bad!"

The district chief was already on the scene, directing crews and equipment. "Reports of people inside," he said, worrying the edges of his mustache with one hand. "Fucker's spread out, hiding. Up on the fifth floor, some on four and three, try to keep it off two."

After a brief conference, Ingalls directed Paula and Steven to take a line up the northwest stairwell to the second floor to support a crew from Engine 4. They lugged their hose over a hundred yards of jagged asphalt and plunged into the gray interior. Smoke rolled thickly through the air, limiting visibility. No sign of flames, but the air was charged with heat. The warehouse was an oven that would grow hotter the longer the flames went unchecked. Three-hundred degree-air at waist level, a thousand or more degrees at the high ceilings. Crematorium heat.

They dragged the hose up to the second floor and into a storeroom with solid brick walls. Tattered sleeping bags and soiled pillows softened Steven's footsteps. From somewhere above, a loud whoosh of inferno. Sweat rolled into eyes, and he couldn't raised a gloved hand under his confining mask to clear his vision.

"Keep going!" Paula ordered, leading him in pursuit of Engine 4's hose.

The radio crackled with reports from other crews. Flames for sure up on the third floor, northeast. Steel fire doors closed off on the fourth floor. The sprinkler system wasn't working. Zero visibility in some areas. Engine 15 was trying to punch holes in the roof for ventilation. A body in the southwest stairwell: after some initial confusion, someone reported that it had probably been there for awhile.

The smoke grew thicker, darker. Fueled by burning kerosene or tar, maybe. Steven caught a glimpse of bright red that was quickly obscured. Ten feet away. Maybe twenty. Hard to tell. Like stumbling around in gray velvet, no stars or streetlights for guidance. They almost collided with two men from Engine 4, one of them Jimmy Linden.

"This one's a bitch!" Jimmy yelled through his mask.

The fire leapt above their heads, a long tongue of bright hot light. Paula trained the hose she and Steven were carrying toward it and opened up the nozzle. The pressurized hose bucked and jerked in Steven's grip. Together with Jimmy and his partner they advanced several feet, but then the rolling flames shifted across the wooden rafters and grew brighter. Oxygen from somewhere above was feeding it, boosting it.

"Back off," Paula ordered. The mask muffled her words, and the roar of fire nearly drowned them out completely. "We're going to need more help."

Jimmy's partner yelled, "We can handle it!"

"Not without more help!" Paula shouted back.

Requests for aid were already filling the radio. Steven could imagine Dispatch sending out more engines, more ladders. Hard-liners lived for these kinds of fires: the terrifying, exhilarating ones, the ones that made legends. At that moment Steven didn't care so much for legends. He wanted out, out as quickly as possible, out to fresh cool air and as much water as he could drink.

Above them, the flames started arcing down like hungry, grasping fingers.

"Let's go!" Jimmy's partner yelled, and the four of them retreated across the storeroom.

One moment Steven's world was dark gray and darker gray. In the next, black smoke swept down like an ocean of ink and cut off all visibility. He couldn't see his own feet, couldn't see the edges of his mask. The light on his helmet illuminated nothing. His only link to Paula was the hose, which jerked out of his grasp and slipped away altogether. He flailed his hands, bent over, but couldn't find it.

"Paula!" he shouted. "Jimmy!"

No answer. None that he could hear, at least. A freight train of noise, the sound of the inferno, rushed down on him. Steven spun in the darkness, tried to remember how many paces they'd come, told himself panic would kill him. He had at least ten minutes of oxygen left. Plenty of time to find a way out. For Jimmy to find him, for Paula to grab his hand. But he was alone, frantically alone, and the heat beating into his brain made it impossible to stay calm.

He keyed the radio, trying not to sound shit-scared. "Command, this is Goodwin. I'm on the second floor. Can't see a thing. Can't see anyone."

No answer. Hadn't they heard him? Steven's chest burned with fear and smoke. "Command, do you hear me? I'm lost."

"Easy, kid," a voice responded. Gruff, an old-timer, maybe the battalion chief himself. "We'll find you. Just stay low and still, got it? Let your alarm lead us to you."

His gear included a motion sensor alarm, geared to go off if he stopped moving for thirty continuous seconds. A minute passed. He couldn't hear the alarm at all, just that dull rushing whoosh of fire eating wood and anything else in its way. His throat closed up, from dryness or danger both. His hands shook uncontrollably. He was on the floor but couldn't remember lying down, was gasping for air but couldn't find enough of it to breathe.

Then a rainbow glow, the flutter of wings. "Dearest!" someone said, high and frantic. Tinkerbob burrowed under the edges of Steven's mask and flitted in front of his eyes.

"Bob," he wheezed.

"You have to crawl," Bob said. "Crawl, crawl! I'll tell you where."

"Can't," he said.

Bob kissed his nose, his cheeks. Little pricks of cool lips. "You have to, dearest. Straight on for fifty feet. I'm right here with you. Fairies always know how to find the sun."

He tried rolling to his knees. Ordered his arms and legs to respond, to obey his will. But his brain and muscles had disconnected. He could do nothing but gasp in hot air and tremble, his whole body shutting down. Above him, the red flames were turning yellow and orange. Like the desert sky, stretching endlessly over a barren landscape He'd delivered death there, or been the cause of it. Seven corpses, black and rotting.

"Oh, dearest," Bob said. "How can I help?"

"Whistle," Steven coughed out. A different alarm was sounding now. His oxygen, running out. If he kept the mask on, he would suffocate on his own carbon dioxide. If he whipped it off, he'd burn his lungs and choke on the toxic smoke. Already he could taste it, the poisonous fumes shutting down his voice and throat. "Whistle so I'm not alone, Bob."

Gloved hands gripped his boots just as the blackness consumed him.

Steven didn't die in the warehouse fire.

But five other firefighters did, as did Bob.

Jimmy and Steven's father broke the news to him while he was in the hospital. His father said, "Two men from Engine 3, three from Rescue 2. Got disoriented, trapped. Ran out of air. Bob was the only mascot we lost. He went looking for you but the fire got to him first."

"He found me," Steven insisted past an aching, seared throat. His whole body hurt from dehydration and heat exhaustion. A headache was squeezing his brain, and the bright fluorescent lights of the hospital room didn't help. "He talked to me."

"He was coming down from the fourth floor," Jimmy said. "Never got out of the stairwell."

"He whistled. Attracted help."

"That was your motion alarm, Steven," Jimmy said.

Three days later, the Massasoit Fire Department gave the fallen firefighters a splendid memorial parade. The ranks were joined by firefighters and supernatural companions from several other cities, and even a unit that drove down from Canada. The mile-long procession made its way down Broad Avenue in long columns of black coats and black boots, with bagpipe music cutting through the autumn chill. Vintage fire wagons carried the coffins. Four white unicorns drew Bob's, which lay atop a bed of roses and daffodils. Thumb-sized fairies sat on the roses and wept behind tiny black veils. Steven wasn't well enough to march but he did so anyway, two hours in the bitter cold, faltering only when they reached the cemetery. Jimmy got him to a low stone wall and sat beside him while a reverend and an elf delivered eulogies.

"You've got to keep going," Jimmy said when the ceremony was over. "You can't quit."

Brittle dead leaves stirred in the breeze, brushing against Steven's shoes. He said, "I was mad at him for coming to my apartment. For kissing me while I was asleep. Bad enough I had to put up with him at work, but in my own place? Never."

Jimmy was rock-still beside him.

"But it wasn't him, was it?" Steven asked. "It was you."

"I don't know what you're talking about," Jimmy snapped. He stood up with his hands jammed into his pockets. "I'm out of here. Shift starts in an hour."

He started to walk away, then turned back with his chin lifted. Twin spots of color stained his otherwise pale cheeks. "I wouldn't," he said. "I'm not some queer. You just dreamt it, whatever it was. Or took too many painkillers."

Steven watched him walk away.

The mourners dispersed slowly, heading off to bars or someone's house for a good old-fashioned wake full of food and booze and reminiscing. Paula was the last left at the graveside. She came to Steven with her long black coat flapping the breeze and tears bright on her face.

"I meant to visit you in the hospital," she said. "To see how you're doing. But then I remembered when I was there, all burned up, and my two friends were dead. Any time anyone asked me how I was doing, I just wanted to scream."

"Are you going to tell me it'll get better someday?"

"Maybe it will, and maybe it won't," she said. "I don't know how it'll be for you. But there is someone who wants to talk to you."

He looked away. "I don't want to."

"Yes, you do. Trust me."

Paula led him past Bob's grave to a copse of fir and pine trees. Steven heard the rustle of branches overhead and glimpsed something gold through the trunks ahead. The magnificent phoenix, the Supreme Fire Chief of Massasoit, was sitting like a statue amid the tombstones and trees. She seemed diminished, shrunken down somehow. Wrapped in feathers of gray grief. Steven flinched under her gaze and took a step backwards, but Paula's hand on his shoulder steadied him.

"It's okay," Paula said. "She just wants to talk."

Later, Jimmy and his father will ask him what the phoenix told him. Steven can't say for sure. He remembers climbing onto the bird's back and holding tight as she lifts into the sky, her wide wings gliding on wind and current, her beak turned toward the sun. He remembers soaring through clouds of twinkling rainbow lights and hearing some whistling, some joyous off-key whistling. Fairies live forever, he thinks she said. They live by their own rules and passions, not yours. Let him go.

He also thinks she told him not to give up on his very important job, but maybe that's something he told himself.

He returned to Engine 13 two weeks later. Some changes had already been made. Paula had asked for and received a transfer over to Engine 25, closer to her home and sick father. Steven had taken her to dinner twice since that day in the cemetery and hoped to take her some more. His therapist was encouraging him. The firehouse had also received a new mascot. Seamus O'Finn O'Flaherty was a three-foot-tall leprechaun who wore a green velvet costume. He lived in a green van in the parking lot, along with Mrs. O'Finn O'Flaherty and their six small children and a tiny dog. Seamus liked to cook and cheerfully took on responsibility for dinner. Unfortunately, Captain Ingalls said, most of his recipes were some variation on corned beef and cabbage.

"I like corned beef, sir," Steven said.

"Not every night, you won't."

Paula's replacement was a firefighter with five years

in the Department who'd been riding a desk over in the Safety Division.

"Sam Capodilupo," he said, offering his hand. Capodilupo was a handsome man, with wide shoulders and a firm handshake. But something in his eyes was wary, cautious. As if Steven might be dangerous.

It took a moment for Steven to remember the rumors about Capodilupo. The insinuations and gossip. He thought of Jimmy, over at Engine 129. Of Bob in his coffin. Of wars fought in deserts, and wars fought in the heart.

"Sorry about your mascot," Capodilupo added.

Steven thought he heard whistling, distant but cheerful.

"Best fairy I ever worked with," Steven said. "Come on. Let's get some coffee. I hear Seamus brews it green."

Author's notes

4. In December of 1999, two squatters in an abandoned warehouse in Worcester, Massachusetts, knocked over a candle and fled the premises. The subsequent Worcester Cold Storage Warehouse fire killed six firefighters who became trapped in the pitch-black inferno. It took eight days to fight down the fire and recover their bodies.

5. The love story between Steven and Paula ends poorly, but Sam Capodilupo proposes to his paramedic boyfriend one Christmas Eve and they marry after Massasoit legalizes gay marriages. They live happily ever after.

6. This version of Massasoit does not exist in our world, but instead in the stories of Nora Neill, the science fiction writer saved by Cubby Salaman when she was a baby in a burning house. Critics of Nora Neill have pointed out that fairy fiction is not science fiction, an argument Ms. Neill refuses to participate in.

7. Fairies do live forever, but not in ways we expect or can understand.

Nets

OF SILVER AND GOLD

As every denizen of the sea knows, lobsters are avid supporters of gossip. It helps pass the dark nights beneath the waves, when the cold briny depths are filled with the mindless chatter of shrimp. Almost every lobster in the seas off Cardyr knew about the talking pirate head embedded in silt with seaweed creeping over its wooden eyes. Grayhead was its name, or maybe Seabeard. It was said to be pleasant but dull, and very melancholy. At some point a lobster mentioned the statue to a dolphin, who happened to pass the information to a killer whale, who in turn commented in an offhand way to the seagull riding on its back. Seagulls are even more avid gossipers than lobsters, so it only took a few years for the information to spread to gargoyles on rooftops, angels in fountains, and war statues in parks.

The boy Cubby, meanwhile, had grown to be a young man with handsome features and a careful, watchful gaze. He became a scholar. Women at the university adored him, but his affinity was for other young men, preferably firefighters, as long as they were both good kissers and excellent conversationalists. After a circuitous route through several fields of study, Cubby found a passion for saving Dynish books from trash heaps and landfills. In the process he read dozens of esoteric myths and forbidden literature: occasionally he even found stories about the founder of Hartvern House, Miss Diana Comet, about whom many interesting and often unbelievable tales were told.

Throughout his life he continued to hear the voices of otherwise inanimate objects. Sometimes, standing by a window at dawn with a sleeping lover behind him, Cubby sensed hundreds of such voices like a distant breeze through trees. In a city the size of Massasoit, such noise was inevitable. After long days in dusty stacks he would often go out and try to ease their suffering. Many times he was successful, and curious notices about stolen masonry, art, or sculpture would subsequently appear in the daily newspaper.

One of his regrets—and he had several, the ardors of his childhood leaving a long impression—was that he could not save his old friend Graybeard. Three summers after arriving at Hartvern House he had jumped a train to visit Cardyr. He was stunned to find Graybeard's Castle gone, replaced by a glitzy ballroom for men in tuxedos and women in gowns.

"What about the pirate's head?" Cubby asked one of the wooden horses on the carousel.

"Washed to sea," the mare said sadly. "Smashed to bits. Can you bring me some of that cotton candy? I bet it tastes like laughter."

When Cubby returned to Hartvern House and told Miss Fay of his sorrow, she replied that every living thing passes on. The spirit of Graybeard, no doubt, was now in a finer and better place.

At age thirty, in casual conversation with a granite lion one winter night, Cubby learned this wasn't so.

Unfortunately none of the stonework that Cubby consulted knew of Graybeard's exact location. Seagulls are infamously bad at directions, whales have short memories, and lobsters have a long-standing animosity toward talking to humans. Cubby learned to sail and scuba dive, bought himself a boat, stocked up on lobster snacks (that is, snacks for the lobsters to enjoy, made of non-lobster ingredients), and set off on a rescue mission. After a month of fruitless searching on the high seas, his spirits began to sink. Then his boat itself began to sink in a terrible summer storm. He hoisted a lace flag that Miss Fay had made him promise to use in emergencies, and was surprised to be rescued by none other by a sailing ship crewed by nuns. They pulled him aboard in a net of silver and gold.

"Thank you," he stammered, after being warmed up from his ordeal with hot drinks and warm blankets. "I'm indebted."

The Captain Nun was a beautiful woman with curly dark hair and regal bearing. "Who gave you that lace flag?"

He explained its origins, and she tapped her chin thoughtfully.

"I'm glad to hear Hartvern House is doing well," she said. "I remember the day it opened, and how many children needed a good home. "

"But you couldn't," Cubby protested. "You're no older than I am!"

The Captain Nun leaned forward. "Every person on this boat has access to the fountain of youth. It's a traveling waterspout as wide as a human hair. Hard to catch, harder to drink from. But once you succeed, you can stay young forever! As long as you never set foot on dry land again. And wear the proper undergarments."

Cubby was sure he did not want to ask about the undergarments of holy women. "Do you mean you're condemned to sail the oceans forever?"

Her eyes sparkled. "Would you like to join us?"

"I'm on a different quest," he said. "Looking for treasure, I guess you'd say."

Never let it be said that nuns could pass up on a treasure hunt or lack the capacity to sweet-talk lobsters. Several days later, Cubby was maneuvering on the ocean floor and scraping sea plants from the face of his old friend. The nuns threw down their nets and hoisted poor Graybeard aboard. Though it was true his paint had peeled away and he was utterly mute, his wood had not softened or disintegrated in any expected ways.

"This proves he's a magical being, deeply asleep," the Captain Nun announced. "If you permit it, we'll fix him up and attach him to the bow. He can sail around the world with us."

Cubby was extremely grateful for the offer. He stayed on until the restoration was complete.

"Every day they're throwing away more books," he told Graybeard. "Throwing them away like dirty rags or scraps of rotten meat, just because no one wants to learn Dynish anymore. Who knows how many stories have already been lost? And if I don't go back to Massasoit, more will be vanish."

Graybeard was silent. Maybe he would speak again, or maybe his story would be quieted forever.

"We'll take good care of him," the nuns promised, and they did.

Author's notes

1. The ocean is loud. You just won't believe how vastly, hugely, mind-boggling loud it is. I mean, you may think your students' ringtones are loud when their cell phones go off during your lecture, but that's just peanuts compared to the ocean.
2. Have you recognized the Captain Nun yet? Cubby hasn't, but he will.
3. Is it dramatic license, or the author's mistake, that the conversation depicted in the ending scene here is not the same as the conversation on page one? Did you really want to read the same conversation again?
4. Yes, that was Douglas Adams in (1).

The Instrument

The corpse calls itself the Instrument of God. It lies flat on a table in a hangar south of Abbasidia's largest airport, its green clothes coated with dust, beard knotted and greasy, tongue thick between stained teeth. The tongue attracts flies in the oven-like heat and disturbs the general of the invading forces so much that he wants to cut it out with his pocketknife. The Instrument's eyes stare at the steel beams high above, and its erect penis juts toward a flickering sodium light. The Instrument speaks, day and night, regardless of whether anyone is nearby to hear:

"God speaks resistance belief defending sons nation rise up planes flew mission ongoing defend duty great country right triumphs despise I am the Instrument…"

Against all principles of science, the Instrument does not rot nor decay nor show any signs of lividity. It is classified above top-secret, its identity never to be reported to the outside world. Only a select few in the chain of command share the secret knowledge. The general, a world-weary man who longs for his wife and children back home, had inspected the corpse the day it was brought in from the ruins of a bombed-out house. "Son of a bitch, that's him," he'd said, and then recoiled at the Instrument's clear, insistent voice. "How can you say he's dead?"

The chief physician replied, "There's no pulse. No respiration or brainwaves, no bowel sounds, no empirical signs of life whatsoever."

"What's it got, a transmitter shoved down its throat?"

Since then, the X-rays have revealed no transmitters, only silver teeth fillings and shrapnel from old wounds and the final, fatal bullet lodged in the Instrument's heart. The shot was self-inflicted, the general knows. The corpse was found with a pistol still gripped in its hand. When the physician and his assistants try to make incisions the Instrument's body deflects their sharpest steel. "Impossible," they declare, but experiment after experiment proves that nothing can pierce its dusky flesh. Skin that feels soft and malleable beneath latex gloves is invincible to metal. Maybe they should try a diamond-tipped drill, someone suggests. Perhaps a laser beam. Meanwhile the Instrument continues to flay the air:

"...regimes arsenals we have seen hatred I am the Lord your God disarm divisive willing and terror cells unyielding patriotism demands people of enemy..."

"Can't you make it shut up?" the general asks. Someone plugs the Instrument's throat with white cotton balls, but the voice rolls out its ears instead, out its pores and orifices, and this is so much more disconcerting that the cotton is quickly removed.

At infrequent times the Instrument does fall silent, and those in attendance hear the desert wind howling down the streets of the fearful city. The privates and corporals who guard the hangar shuffle their feet and double-check their rifles. The high command wants the Instrument flown away for further examination, but each time the general has it loaded onto a plane the tires go flat, or the fuel tanks start leaking, or the cockpit erupts in flames. The general's hand-picked men try driving it out past the schools and factories and overcrowded hospitals, but a series of trucks repeatedly break their axles. "Carry it to the border," the general orders, but the soldiers who shoulder the load collapse from heatstroke.

"Is it the devil?" asks the youngest private, a fair-haired teenager from the heartland, but opinions vary wildly: devil, robot, zombie, vampire, golem, a sign from God, a sign of the impending apocalypse.

In his office across the city the general hears the Instrument's voice beneath the hum of his radio. He imagines the Instrument's tongue enlarging and unfurling, stretching across the distance to envelop him and suffocate him with its heavy, soggy grayness. He slaps away flies that no one else can see.

"...arsenal freedom liberate dissent revenge..."

The cameras set up to monitor the Instrument malfunction constantly, their innards ruined by sand. The microphones propped near its mouth record only static. Among the guards, the initial thrill and mystery wear away to boredom, resentment, bitterness. They play poker and gin, and drink homemade brew, and neglect their duties. On a dare, the youngest private slips beyond a door and approaches the Instrument. He will poke a stick at it or spit in its face. He is full of bravado and has nothing to fear.

But for the first time, the Instrument's head rolls to one side. Its gaze is terrible and bright.

"You," the Instruments says. "Son of so-called liberty. You will take this mantle. You will go into the land and raise up an army unlike any ever seen in any corner of the earth. God in his bountiful beauty will provide. From the first ray of daybreak across the utmost reach of the sky to the eyelids of the disbelievers you will bring faith and strength and order. Your horses will thunder down their doors, your ravens will cry out the new age."

The private tries to flee, but his feet are blocks of stone. Several buildings away the general tosses in his sleep and tries to pillow his ears against the buzzing, the buzzing. Electricity sizzles across overhead wires in abandoned neighborhoods. Across the landscape, dreamers descend marble steps into the gardens and parks of the old city, and glide in boats down a river of sparkling blue, and drift among the flowers of the palace, where exotic birds and fierce creatures delight the crowds. This is what has been lost; this is what must be regained.

"Take it back by blood," the Instrument commands. "Take it by fire and death."

The private walks out of the hangar and into the wasteland. The army lists him as missing in action, though some say he has been taken captive by rebels and others claim he has run off to marry a chieftain's daughter. The burning sun blisters away the general's conviction and resolve. When is a war a war, he wonders, and when is it a trap? Two weeks later the commander in chief arrives under the guise of celebrating a holiday with the troops. He struts into the hanger like a cowboy.

"Ain't so dangerous now, are you?" the commander asks the corpse.

"…terror weapons embrace heart resolve support troops prisoner deaths I am the Lord your God righteous resolve…"

The commander and his entourage strip away the Instrument's clothing and ridicule the scarred, naked body. Its voice does not bother them; they listen to no one but themselves. They pose for pictures with it, cigars in their mouths, thumbs turned up. They cover its penis with a paper bag with a smiley face drawn on it. Afterward the general orders the corpse re-dressed. He is ashamed for it.

The commander returns to his country and announces, "God speaks through me."

The private roams the desert, organizing and stockpiling, the Instrument's dictates burning in his heart.

Night after night the city is bombed by insurgents. The general climbs to the heavily fortified roof of his headquarters to survey the damage and dust and smoke. There are no sirens or gunfire or voices ringing out in fear. There is only the Instrument's litany, rising ever louder, and the incessant nagging flies. The general remembers gardens and parks and the sparkling blue river. What makes a trap inescapable? Who speaks through the dead, or for them? He crosses dark streets full of rubble and grabs the Instrument's gray tongue with his fingers.

"Shut up, shut up, shut up," the general says, just like that, three times.

The Instrument's tongue tears free so quickly and unexpectedly that the general stumbles backward with the prize in hand. Drops of fresh blood fleck the concrete floor. The corpse sighs, closes its eyes and settles onto the table, dust billowing from its ears and clothes. The city is silent, and a hot wind blows over all.

Kingdom
COMING

Jaleesha was eight years old and living with her family in Massasoit public housing the summer the apocalypse started. It was a brutally hot summer, but they could only turn on the air conditioner a few hours a day. "Not enough power," Gramma Nairobi explained. "Them oil sheiks," cursed Roshawn, Jaleesha's seventeen-year-old brother. Without electricity the five ambulatory members of the Holburn family (Uncle Leo, who'd lost both feet to sugar diabetes, was subject to the idiosyncrasies of the building's single elevator) had to either endure the stifling heat of the apartment or go down eight flights of urine-stained stairs to the cement courtyard and the constant risk of stray bullets. "Better the heat," declared Gramma Nairobi, and so they sat with wet towels around their necks and read by flashlight or listened to Sister Ella Cash of the Eternal Church on the battery-operated radio. Heat, sweat, gunfire, the immortal words of Mamie Walker, Caraletta Vaughn leading Sister Cash's choir in rousing renditions of "I Will Be Healed," Gramma Nairobi waving at her own ample breasts with a blue silk fan—these were Jaleesha's memories of the world before everything changed.

"Gramma, listen," Roshawn said one July night. Jaleesha, who'd been sleeping on a mattress beside Gramma in the living room, whimpered and rolled over.

"Go to bed, Ro," Gramma mumbled.

Uncle Leo said, "Can't you hear it?"

Jaleesha blinked open her eyes and saw Roshawn, Uncle Leo and her twin sisters Soozie and TashaLu standing in the kitchen by a battery lantern. The twins were still wearing their polyester uniforms—they worked the closing shift at a neighborhood fast-food joint, and Roshawn walked them home each night—and had brought home French fries and cheeseburgers for Uncle Leo. The smell of grease off their uniforms made Jaleesha's nose itch. The only sounds she heard were the usual nighttime backdrop of helicopters and sirens.

"What's the matter with all of you?" Gramma Nairobi asked crankily. She had sickle cell anemia, which sometimes wracked her with so much pain that they had to take her to the emergency room. Jaleesha's mother had died of sickle cell right after Jaleesha was born. A photograph of her in her coffin was taped to the refrigerator, its edges frayed and worn.

"Can't you hear it?" Soozie asked. "Like thunder."

TashaLu took off her glasses and peered up at the ceiling. "No. Like a flute."

"Like drums." Roshawn's fists were clenched. "A million pounding drums."

Gramma Nairobi rolled off the mattress and lumbered toward the window. Jaleesha stood beside her and rested against her tree-like leg. Gramma Nairobi patted her on the head and looked past the broken mesh of the window to the gray skies over the river.

"Don't you hear anything?" Roshawn asked.

"I hear rain," Jaleesha said. Cool, pitter-pattering rain, refreshing after a long draught. "How about you, Gramma?"

Gramma Nairobi's chin lifted. "I hear the goddess's horn, calling us to Judgment Day."

Jaleesha followed her grandmother's gaze and saw tiny white lights falling from the sky, as if all the stars in the universe had decided to drop in and pay a visit.

They ended up taking refuge in the cramped, windowless bathroom. "It's not a hurricane," TashaLu complained. "Gotta be careful of radiation," Uncle Leo insisted. Through the walls they could hear distant explosions and sirens. The radio played only static. At daybreak Roshawn volunteered to go see if the world had ended. He climbed over Uncle Leo's wheelchair and was gone for several minutes. He came back with a soda in hand.

"The President's on TV," Roshawn said. "Him and some spaceman."

The President and a man-shaped figure in a white spacesuit were posing for pictures in a conference room. "We welcome our new friends," the President said, his face shiny with sweat. The footage was followed by pictures of more aliens shaking hands with governors and actors and the monarchs of far off lands. Soozie tried switching the channels, but all the regular TV shows had disappeared. Despite the reassurances Gramma Nairobi decreed, "No one's going anywhere," and for twenty-four hours none of them did. Surely the world outside was too dangerous, too unstable.

"No, it's fine," said their neighbor Mr. Figueroa, who had ventured out to see if the liquor stores were open. "No more dangerous than it used to be."

Mrs. Morales, who lived in 3F, had also been outside. "Makes you kind of nervous, those aliens everywhere, but they don't seem to be hurting anyone."

"How many are there?" Gramma Nairobi asked.

"Thousands and thousands," Mrs. Morales said. "Maybe millions of thousands."

Uncle Leo trained his binoculars on the street and reported that men in blue shirts were fixing up potholes, painting over graffiti-covered walls and towing off abandoned cars. When Gramma Nairobi relented and let the siblings go outside, Jaleesha saw more workers picking up trash in the park and around the school. Aliens stood at every corner, supervising.

"Good afternoon," one said to Jaleesha.

With a squeak she hid behind Roshawn. The alien's voice was deep and melodic, like men she heard in TV commercials. He had no accent.

"Why'd you come to Earth?" Roshawn asked the alien.

"To make paradise incarnate," it replied. "To restore the Garden."

"Who asked you to?" Tasha muttered, but the alien moved on without answering. That night Jaleesha heard sirens, angry voices in the street, some explosions across the river. It seemed odd to her that people didn't want paradise, but Gramma Nairobi explained it to her.

"Everyone's got a different idea of what paradise should be, little one. Not everyone agrees. Mr. Corporate Executive, he wants one thing. Mr. President, he wants another. People don't want it imposed by outsiders who don't know anything about us at all."

There were riots all over the city, or so people said. Without TV or radio to convey the news, everything was hearsay and rumor. "I heard all the protestors were sucked up into a flying saucer," Mr. Figueroa said, his breath heavy with beer. "The aliens waved their hands and made everyone go to sleep," reported Mrs. Morales, whose brother's girlfriend had supposedly been in the crowd. Meanwhile the electricity came on and stayed on twenty-four hours a day, and the toilet stopped shrieking like a murdered woman every time it got flushed, and all the roaches in the building up and vanished. But Reverend Hatch, during services at the Chicken Coop Church, was not necessarily enthusiastic about the changes.

"We welcome our new neighbors," he said. "We are grateful for their helping hands."

"But what's under their helmets?" Jaleesha asked Gramma Nairobi. The Chicken Coop was an old brick church with black cherubs painted over the altar. They came to service every Sunday, and Jaleesha always had to wear dresses with stiff collars.

Roshawn cracked his knuckles. "Bug eyes and fangs."

Gramma Nairobi slapped Roshawn's knee. "Hush."

The aliens wouldn't say what they called themselves in their own language, nor did they speak that language in front of humans. Some people called them the KC ("They are the Kingdom Come!" Brother Cash declared) but Gramma Nairobi said that was a blasphemous name.

"Fascists is what they are," Uncle Leo said. "Make the trains run on time but ruin everything else."

Jaleesha wasn't sure what trains Uncle Leo meant, but it was nice to walk down the street and not be bothered by crazy people in soiled clothes or crack addicts desperate for money. The prostitutes in their itty-bitty skirts went away, as did the drunks who slept in doorways. In September the twins went back to high school and Jaleesha returned to third grade at McNair Elementary School. The roof had been repaired and the ventilation ducts cleaned of mold. Every student got brand-new textbooks filled with pictures, puzzles and stories about things like molecules.

"They want us all to learn science," TashaLu told Jaleesha. "Makes you smart."

Soozie, who planned to go to hair salon academy, threw her new books in the trash. "Not me," she said, but the next day she brought home two more books, and there was a silver stripe on the palm of her right hand.

Gramma Nairobi examined the mark closely. "What's that?"

Soozie scowled. "Said you get five, you get punished."

Uncle Leo edged his wheelchair closer. "Who said that?"

"The new principal." TashaLu hugged her own books close to her chest, her face unreadable. "He's a Whitesuit."

"Wash it off," Gramma Nairobi ordered, but no matter how hard Soozie scrubbed with soap and steel wool, the stripe refused to fade. Gramma Nairobi asked, "Jaleesha, did your teachers say anything about punishment, about marking your skin?"

"No, Gramma," Jaleesha said, but the very next day her friend Hamdi got in trouble for telling their first-grade teacher that he was going to shove a ruler up her ass. Hamdi was a thin, temperamental boy from Abbasidia with a poor command of English. Almost immediately after the threat a Whitesuit appeared in the doorway. The black visor over his face mirrored back a distorted view of the students.

"You must have respect for your teachers," the Whitesuit said. Like all the others, he had a deep and calm voice. He drew on a stripe on Hamdi's palm with the tip of his gloved finger. "We'll help you, but you must help yourselves first."

Hamdi burst into tears. Jaleesha looked to her teacher, but instead of arguing Miss Rodriguez ushered all the children to the storytelling rug. "Today we're going to talk about the oceans," she said, and pulled out new picture books. "Can anyone tell me how many there are?"

"Seven," Jaleesha said. "Atlantic, Pacific, Lake Manahan—"

Miss Rodriguez smiled the way people do when they're trying not to cry. "Actually, there's just one, with a bunch of different names. One giant ocean around a little bit of land. And the Visitors are going to help us clean up all the pollution we've put into it."

No one on the radio or TV spoke about getting silver stripes on your palm, but a Whitesuit gave Roshawn one for jaywalking and all of the kids in 17C got marks for fighting in the courtyard. Mr. Figueroa racked up five in quick order for offenses that included pissing in the hallway and punching his wife in the eye. One Friday afternoon two Whitesuits came to his apartment, took him outside and lashed him to the basketball post.

"I won't anymore!" Mr. Figueroa said, writhing and crying. "I promise I won't!"

Gramma Nairobi and Jaleesha were just coming back from getting Jaleesha's cavities filled at the dentist. "Let's go around," Gramma Nairobi said as she eyed the crowd, but when they stepped inside the lobby a Whitesuit blocked their way.

"Please report to the courtyard." His voice, like all the others, was deep and smooth and utterly calm.

"This one's too little," Gramma Nairobi argued.

"None are too old or too young to learn," the Whitesuit said.

Gramma Nairobi folded her beefy arms. "This is no place for a child."

Quicker than lightning, the Whitesuit reached out and drew a mark on Gramma Nairobi's hand. She immediately shoved him away. "Don't you touch me!" she snapped, her high voice drawing attention from all over. "You don't get to write on my body!"

Jaleesha threw her arms around Gramma Nairobi's waist. "Gramma, no!"

"No one asked you to come down here and start running things," Gramma Nairobi continued, wagging her finger. "Take off that suit, space boy, and let's see the color of your skin. I want to write on *your* hand."

More Whitesuits surrounded Gramma Nairobi and Jaleesha. The lobby had gone very quiet, with people watching from every corner. One of the aliens—maybe the one Gramma had pushed, but it was hard to tell them apart—reached for her hand and drew another line on her palm. The marks were slim and straight, and almost seemed to glow.

"Please report to the courtyard," the Whitesuit said, no emotion in his voice.

"Gramma, please." Jaleesha tried to leverage her weight against Gramma Nairobi's bulk. She knew that if she didn't get her away, something even worse would happen. But Gramma Nairobi didn't move at all. Her fists were clenched, her chest heaving, and she was glaring at the Whitesuits so fiercely that Jaleesha felt cold and stripped naked under it.

"Gramma, *please*," Jaleesha begged, and finally her grandmother's gaze dropped. Without another word she took Jaleesha to where they could see Mr. Figueroa shivering and pleading. The sun had gone behind a bank of dark clouds.

"I'm sorry," Mr. Figueroa kept saying. "Please, stop. Don't do this."

One of the Whitesuits raised a glowing blue stick as long as a baseball bat. "This is a vhelk," he said, and without further explanation belted it across Mr. Figueroa's back. Mr. Figueroa shrieked and Jaleesha jumped. Several in the crowd made angry noises or jeered. Mrs. Morales from 3F covered her eyes but Uncle Leo, parked in his wheelchair on the far side of the courtyard, didn't turn away.

"Silence," said the Whitesuit holding the vhelk. "Offenses must be punished."

The glowing stick came down again. This time Jaleesha noticed small blue lights flicker at the back of all the Whitesuit helmets at the precise moment of impact. Mr. Figueroa cried, "Stop! Stop, oh God!" Jaleesha buried her face against Gramma Nairobi's belly but there was no blocking out the whistle of the vhelk, the whack against Mr. Figueroa's back, or his agonized screams. After ten strikes the Whitesuit said, "You may return to your homes."

Safe in their apartment, Jaleesha burst into tears. TashaLu said, "Stop making such a fuss. He's not hurt permanently."

"No one has the right to beat us!" Soozie said, her hands on her hips and her expression fierce. "Are we slaves? Our right to self-rule all gone, our Constitutional protections evaporated?"

TashaLu said, "If punishing a man in public keeps him from hitting his wife in private, then I say that's worth the cost."

"I say it's not," Soozie argued. "The Whitesuits have no business being here and lording over us. Things are just going to get worse from here."

"You're wrong, wrong, wrong," TashaLu said. "They're only going to get better."

Gramma Nairobi waved her hand. "Girls! That's enough. Go to your room."

Jaleesha buried her head against Gramma Nairobi's shoulder, trying to muffle the memory of screams.

"What the Lord is telling us is that actions have *consequences*. The Shepherd guides his flock with rod and staff!" said Brother Cash, and Jaleesha took the lesson to heart. She studied hard, always turned in her homework on time and did everything her teachers asked her to. Meanwhile the food at school improved, everyone received a free computer and training on how to access approved web sites, and Gramma Nairobi's doctors gave her new medicine for her sickle cell. They also told the Whitesuits that she was fully employable.

"But these pills might not even work," Gramma Nairobi protested. The Whitesuits assured her their medicines were far better than any she'd had before and told her to report to the custodial department at the new hydroelectric plant being built along the Faarlem River.

"Hydroelectric?" Jaleesha gazed out their living room window toward the river. "The power of water?"

TashaLu, who studied endlessly from new books brought home every day, said, "That's why the Visitors came to earth. To help and teach us to use the ocean effectively, not just fill it up with pollution."

"To steal it, you mean." Roshawn was making himself a sandwich in the kitchen. "The Whitesuits need seawater to fuel their ships. They could have gone to Mars, but all the water there's frozen up."

TashaLu rolled her eyes. "Oh, please. That's just a stupid story people keep passing around. Number one, salt corrodes stuff, right? So you can't use it as fuel. And number two, taking away the ocean would kill everyone and everything on the planet. The Visitors wouldn't go to all the trouble of improving our lives if they meant to kill us in the end."

"It's easier this way." Roshawn popped the lid on a soda can. "Blowing up cities is messy, right? Whitesuits don't like messes. So they pretend to help, and make everything so nice no one notices what's happening with the ocean, and then one day they're going to zoom off and leave us all with nothing but a big desert where the water used to be."

TashaLu scowled. "That's all crazy. They're only going to go away when they know we can take care of ourselves. Parents do the exact same thing with children."

Gramma Nairobi didn't like her job at the hydroelectric plant, but to stay home was to earn punishment stripes. Uncle Leo, however, thoroughly enjoyed manning the reception desk at the Whitesuit police station a few blocks away. The elevator in their building worked flawlessly now, and whenever he wanted to go anywhere he called a telephone number and a van with a wheelchair lift showed up fifteen minutes later. TashaLu and Soozie no longer worked at Burger Queen—all the fast food restaurants had been closed down, their workers and owners reassigned— but TashaLu had a job at a bookstore and Soozie gave manicures for seniors down at the new community center.

"They took Mrs. Kaplan away today," Soozie announced at dinner one night. Her eyes were narrow with anger. "Said she was spreading discontent with that newsletter she's been putting out for years."

"That rag?" Uncle Leo reached for the green beans. "Waste of paper."

Soozie grabbed his wrist. "Used to have freedom of speech, didn't we? You could speak up against the power structure, you could make your opinion known. What did Count Culleny say about dying like hogs and facing the cowardly pack?"

TashaLu was untroubled. "You still have freedom, as long as you accept the consequences."

"Girls, both of you, quiet now." Gramma Nairobi reached for her purse. "TashaLu, take Jaleesha down to the corner for an ice cream cone. Get me one too."

"But Gramma—"

Gramma Nairobi's eyes turned hard. "Are you arguing with me?"

"No, ma'am," TashaLu said sullenly. "Come on, Jaleesha."

TashaLu kept silent all the way down the elevator. The night was warm and clear, and busy with people walking around or dining with friends. Music played in the stores they passed but not too loudly, never too loudly anymore. Jaleesha liked it that way. At every corner a Whitesuit sat in one of their flying aircars, ready to be of help if any emergencies arose.

"Don't you listen to them, Jaleesha," TashaLu said before they reached the ice cream store. She bent down to Jaleesha's height. "People don't like change, even if it's for the better. They don't like to be held accountable. The Whitesuits want to help us because they come from a planet of great power and peace and know how good it all can be. Once their work is done they'll go someplace else and help the people there, too. It's what they do."

Jaleesha squirmed under TashaLu's intense gaze. "But they hurt people, too."

"Only the ones who deserve it." TashaLu kissed her forehead. "We're the opposite of slaves, Jaleesha. We've been freed. We've been *delivered*."

Delivered from illness, Jaleesha heard people say. From poverty and despair. By Thanksgiving Uncle Leo had received two new prosthetic feet. After just one fitting he jogged around the apartment, pumping his arms in victory. True enough the newspapers had stopped printing altogether, and internet access had been curtailed, but

Christmas morning was the most lavish Jaleesha had ever known, what with Gramma Nairobi's new salary and all. On New Year's Eve large crowds took to the streets in Visitor-organized celebration and fireworks exploded over the river. "Happy New Year!" everyone chorused, and Jaleesha thought, yes, it would be. But when school started up again, her teacher Miss Rodriguez was gone without explanation.

"They took her away because she got pregnant and she's not married," Soozie told Jaleesha at the playground. Though it was late January, the temperature was mild enough for them to leave their jackets unbuttoned. There hadn't been any snow at all.

Jaleesha, who'd been propelling herself on a swing, let her feet drag her to a stop. "Mama had all of us and she wasn't married."

"Yeah, well, things keep changing," Soozie said gloomily. She abruptly checked her watch. "Come on. We've got a stop to make."

They went to the Chicken Coop Church. "I left something downstairs," Soozie said. "Stay here and don't cause any trouble." Jaleesha climbed up into the choir loft and pretended she was a famous singer in a music video, but the game grew old quickly and besides, there weren't any music videos anymore. Bored, she crept down the back stairs to the basement. A half-dozen people were crowded in Reverend Hatch's office, arguing.

"They can't ignore the *facts*," said Mrs. Morales, who lived in Jaleesha's building. "The weather changing. The river's dropping day by day."

"Since when have people been able to think for themselves?" Soozie asked.

Reverend Hatch coughed vigorously around the stub of one of his noxious cigars. "You have to talk to the brothers and sisters one-on-one. Spread the word quietly, until we can mount a peaceful protest."

"Peace isn't going to win this," Soozie said. "We have to find a point of vulnerability. Something we can use against them. We've got to grab one, open up his suit, dissect him. Maybe there's a way to make them sick, or poison them—"

"People tried that, down in Old Slit," Mrs. Morales interrupted. "Got killed for trying."

Jaleesha couldn't bear any more. Brother Cash said God himself had sent the Whitesuits. Why would Soozie and Reverend Hatch even think of going against Him? She tiptoed back up the stairs, so upset she wanted to cry. Soozie came looking for her a few minutes later accompanied by a honey-colored girl with straight brown hair.

"This is Daisy," Soozie said.

Daisy smiled warmly and said, "Hey, Jaleesha," but that smile, all gleaming white, wasn't going to save her or any of the others from going to hell.

"I want to go home," Jaleesha said. "My stomach hurts."

Soozie tested her forehead for fever. "All right, let's go." The sun had started to set and the wind had turned bitterly cold. Soozie and Daisy shared a cigarette and school gossip. Jaleesha walked in front of them, unable to look at any of the Whitesuits they passed. At home she ate hardly any of her dinner and Gramma Nairobi tucked her into bed early.

The next day at school, two fourth-grade boys were caught trying to steal a vhelk. "We just wanted to play," they said, but for each it was a fifth stripe and so everyone assembled in the gymnasium. "Actions have consequences," Mrs. Ferguson said, her expression stoic. The boys started to scream when the vhelks hit them, but Jaleesha didn't cringe. She kept her eyes on a large group of Whitesuits standing in the doorway. Each time a vhelk made contact, the blue lights on their helmets flashed and they froze in place like statues. Between strikes they leaned forward, as if in anticipation. Their gloved hands trembled.

"How come they like it so?" Jaleesha asked at dinner.

"Because they're sadists," Soozie muttered.

"They don't like it," TashaLu said fiercely. "It's just as painful for them as it is for us."

Jaleesha doubted that was true.

Spring arrived, with clear blue skies and very little rain. Roshawn began dating a pretty Ravinan girl named Mae-Dee and talked about moving in with her, but the Whitesuits didn't like that unless you were married. Uncle Leo got his own apartment in an old mansion near Gravesner Square and worked at a Visitor office building. Every day he wore a white uniform with gold epaulets and shiny black shoes. "Women love it," he said proudly. Soozie announced that she had changed her mind about hair salon academy and wanted to work at the hydroelectric plant, where her friend Daisy was also going to be working.

"She and Daisy spend a lot of time together," Jaleesha said one night after dinner.

Gramma Nairobi gazed at her steadily. "That bother you?"

Jaleesha shook her head.

But it bothered TashaLu. A few weeks later Soozie brought Daisy by the apartment for Jaleesha's ninth birthday party and everything got ruined by a fight. TashaLu said Soozie was a lesbian and that soon she'd be dragged off "like all the other dykes." Jaleesha knew that Mrs. Chester in 3D, with her short hair and big leather boots, had moved in the middle of the night without taking her things. Soozie said TashaLu was a collaborator, "unable to see what's right in front of you." Which was also true: TashaLu walked right by the dry flowerbeds on the street and said not to worry, that the Visitors would melt some icebergs for the city if the drought persisted.

"Girls, stop!" Gramma Nairobi ordered.

Soozie turned on Gramma. "And you! You always said you wanted us to think for ourselves, be proud of our heritage, and what did you do? Got down to your knees first stripe they gave you!"

Gramma Nairobi slapped Soozie hard across the face. Soozie left in tears. The guests went home early and most of Jaleesha's birthday cake ended up back in the refrigerator in its saggy cardboard box. The next day Soozie moved into an apartment with three other women. Jaleesha dreamed of the Whitesuits dragging Soozie away and woke shrieking in Gramma Nairobi's arms.

"Hush, now." Gramma Nairobi stroked her hair and back. "Your sister's a smart girl. Nothing's going to happen to her."

Jaleesha clutched Gramma even harder. "How come all this happened to us?"

Gramma Nairobi rocked her tightly but didn't answer.

The anniversary of the Visitors' arrival came around, marked with a week of lavish parades and celebrations. As a gesture of beneficence the Whitesuits erased one stripe from the palm of anyone who asked. TashaLu, who was enrolled in summer classes at Columbia and had already moved to the dorms, took Jaleesha to a children's rally at a waterfront park. The day was glorious, the sky and air so clear Jaleesha felt like she could fly away like a balloon. This was the new and glorious city, with musicians playing on every corner, and men and women walking hand in hand in love, and children playing hopscotch while Whitesuits held the rope. Jaleesha and TashaLu boarded a flat-bottomed boat that would take them out to a larger ferry and then to Liberty Island. The receding shoreline had made it impossible for most ships to pull up to the piers anymore.

"Where's the water gone?" Jaleesha said, peering over the side at the gray mud. Seagulls whirled overhead, their cries shrill and loud.

TashaLu adjusted her sunglasses. "It's just a temporary side-effect."

"Cleaning the ocean means taking it away?"

"I said *temporary*. That means it's not permanent."

"You said the Visitors were going to go away when they were done," Jaleesha said. "When's that going to be?"

TashaLu rolled her eyes. "Stop asking questions. You're ruining the whole day."

On Liberty Island they climbed all the way up to the crown of the enormous statue that had stood there for centuries. The wind whipped at their faces, the people below looked tiny and inconsequential, and the blue bay stretched further than Jaleesha could see. If leaned against the safety bars she could see the inscription on the tablet in the statue's left arm: July IVMDCCLXXVI. Independence Day, a holiday her teachers never talked about anymore. She peered down at the statue's feet.

"See the shackle?" she asked TashaLu. It represented tyranny: she'd read that in a book. And it was broken, to symbolize freedom.

"Looking down makes me dizzy," TashaLu said, her gaze on the horizon.

Back on the ground TashaLu went to buy lunch. Jaleesha was supposed to wait for her in the picnic area but wandered instead to a remote section of the embankment, where she could lean against a railing and look down at the piles of exposed rocks. On the grass nearby, a girl her own age was tossing a blue ball to a Yorkie. The girl's parents, the father tall and bald, the mother with a ponytail of red hair, stood further away with their heads bent together. Jaleesha thought they were whispering endearments to one another but then she saw that the father's hand was wrapped tight around the mother's forearm.

"No!" the mother said, quite suddenly. "I'm not your *chattel*, not your slave!"

The girl stopped tossing her ball. A Whitesuit from the ranger station came over to speak to the couple, though Jaleesha couldn't hear what he said. The mother exclaimed, "It's wrong!" and broke away from her husband's grip to beseech the tourists who were beginning to gawk. "Don't any of you see it?"

"Please desist from disturbing the peace," the Whitesuit said.

"Disturbing *what* peace?" the mother demanded.

"Ellen, shut up," the father asked, sounding bored. "You're causing a scene."

The mother kept talking. "This isn't the way things are supposed to be—"

The Whitesuit put a stripe on her palm. It must have been her fifth one, because almost instantly more Whitesuits arrived and dragged her off toward the flagpole.

"Momma!" the little girl cried, but there was nothing to be done. The aliens took off the woman's blouse and bra and slacks. Jaleesha had never seen them do that before. The mother's skin was pale and freckled, her breasts heavy and tipped with dark red nipples. Her panties were a dazzling white. The Whitesuits crossed her hands over her head and bound them to the pole with the same cord that held the flag aloft. One of them slowly ran his vhelk down her spine.

The mother struggled ineffectively. "If you can't stand up for yourself, what about for your children?"

The daughter wept silently. The father still seemed bored. The Yorkie barked once and cocked its head the gathering crowd of seniors and children, and women with tight faces, and men with dark gleams in their eyes. Their expressions made Jaleesha step backward. She felt cold despite the July heat, and nearly yelped when a hand descended on her shoulder.

"All will be well," said the Whitesuit standing behind her. "Actions have consequences."

They were alone, just the two of them, standing by the railing while others drew nearer to the flagpole. Jaleesha swallowed her fear and asked, "Why do you hurt people for having an opinion? Why can't she say what she feels?"

The Whitesuit bent his head toward her. "This is not about feelings or—"

Over at the flagpole, a vhelk whistled through the air and hit the woman's back. The Whitesuit standing with Jaleesha froze mid-sentence, his helmet light aglow. A moment later, as the crowd murmured and shuffled their feet, the Whitesuit resumed speaking. "—beliefs, young one. This is about public behavior."

The vhelk hit the woman again. When the Whitesuit froze, Jaleesha put her hand against his leg and pushed him ever so slightly. He shifted backward. The third time he froze, she pushed with both hands. He teetered and wobbled and then crashed backward, like a statue knocked over by vandals. The helmet cracked open and spilled brackish water on the concrete. A dark and pulsing squid with wavy arms squeezed its way through the cracks, gave out a plaintive cry like a wounded bird, and then dragged itself across the sidewalk and over the railing.

Jaleesha ran. In the public bathroom she locked herself into a stall and squeezed herself into a ball against the cold, clean wall. "I didn't mean it," she whispered, and wrapped her arms across her chest. It took a half hour for TashaLu to find her there.

"What the hell are you doing?" TashaLu demanded. "I've been looking all over for you."

"My stomach hurts." Jaleesha didn't have to fake the tremor in her voice or the tear tracks on her face. "I want Gramma."

They left the island on the next ferry. The woman who'd been punished was still tied to the flagpole as an example for all to see. Jaleesha expected the Whitesuits to question everyone on the pier about the alien she'd broken, but either they hadn't found him yet or were pretending nothing bad had happened. Or maybe they were waiting on land to arrest her. Maybe they'd come to her apartment in the middle of the night and drag her away from Gramma Nairobi. Just the thought made her get sick on the boat. TashaLu rubbed her back and got her a cup of water filled with ice cubes.

"You must have gotten too much sun," TashaLu said.

Back home, Gramma Nairobi tucked Jaleesha into bed and put a wet cloth on her forehead. "You'll feel better in the morning," Gramma promised, and kissed both her cheeks. Out in the kitchen, she and TashaLu debated calling the doctor. Jaleesha wanted to tell them that it didn't matter, but she couldn't make her voice work. All she could do was curl up under the sheets and turn to the window, where the late afternoon sun was streaming like water through the clean glass. She examined her palm, imagining what her future stripes would look like. She tried not to think about how it would feel to have the vhelk strike her. But mostly she remembered the alien slithering across the concrete and making its way back to the sea: making itself at home.

Author's notes

1. Jaleesha's school is named after Ron McNair, one of the seven astronauts who died during the explosion of the space shuttle Challenger in 1986.
2. Although Jaleesha didn't know it, the U.S. government tried to repel the alien invaders by uploading a computer virus to the mainframe on their mothership. The attempt failed miserably and should never be used as a plot device in a science fiction movie.

Diana Comet

AND THE COLLAPSIBLE ORCHESTRA

"Such wonderful music, madam, you have never heard before—songs so beautiful that they engorge the heart, enchant the soul, and all for just ten kinna, such a lovely gift for yourself or a loved one!" says the merchant.

Diana wants to say, I have no loved ones, I have no kinna, but one of those protestations is a lie, and the other only makes her more melancholy. She should have stayed in her rooms today instead of braving the hot and dusty bazaar. The cataloging of her papers is important work. Certain individuals have pointedly stated that it also contributes to her sadness, and the possibility of that is high. The past is a bright landscape of triumphs and joys, sweet on the palate. The present is a sour lump in the mouth of an old woman wearing a blue sari that feels like a funeral wrapping.

"Madam, madam," the merchant says, his eyes imploring, his hands proffering. The toy is nothing but a cube the size of a sugar lump. "Such a fine gift, this tiny collapsible orchestra. For only nine kinna!"

In her younger days she would have haggled but today her ankles ache and her bra chafes, and what are nine kinna? Not enough to feed the dirty children poking each other under the covered table or placate the worried wife clutching a suckling infant. Diana pays the money, collects the brass trinket, and forgets all about it until she is back in her rooms and emptying her drawstring silk purse on a side table. She shakes the cube and hears only a faint rattling.

"What's this, then?" asks her secretary, Hazel, when she brings cool mint tea to the library. "Some strange piece of jewelry?"

Diana kicks off her sandals and leans back on an oversize divan. She has been thinking of getting rid of the divan; it's one of the heavy pieces of furniture she shipped back to New Dalli from Massasoit, and has too many pleasant memories of James attached to it. If she burrows her nose close to the weave she can almost smell his cologne. Five years he's been dead, five years she's been bereft.

"Charity," Diana says, of the cube. "An entertaining story, nothing more."

Hazel examines it and then puts it aside, uninterested. She is a white-haired woman, sixty years old and matronly, often practical but rarely sympathetic. "A letter came today from Lady Moncrief. An invitation to the summer villa for the Festival of Light."

Diana stares up at the painted gold ceiling and fans herself. Elanor Moncrief has always been a delight but her husband is a bore and the children unruly. Their lakeside villa is a stately affair of stone and ancient tapestries, the rooms and gardens much cooler than the oppressive heat of the city, but any visit would require socializing that Diana can not bear these days.

"Send my regrets, Hazel."

"You turn down every invitation these days," Hazel says disapprovingly. "Every would-be suitor, every gentleman caller. It's not good for you."

"Suitors and callers who want my fortune, not my mind and body." Diana wriggles her toes. "You know what would be good for me? That little man who gives foot rubs. Send for him."

The man doesn't come—his hands are swollen today, many apologies. Instead he sends a hijre girl, who Hazel wisely refuses to allow inside. The hijre girls have grown so bold these days, so aggressive—flaunting themselves in the plazas, silk veils fluttering over thick beards. Gone are the days of discretion. The hijre claim allegiance to the gods of both sun and moon, day and night, and they do it so loudly that it's become impossible to ignore them when they demand alms at weddings or funerals. Diana loathes them entirely.

She touches her breasts and wishes, for the thousandth time, that she could cup warm flesh instead of molded cloth.

A shaft of sunlight touches the cube of the Collapsible Orchestra. Diana says, "So what kind of music do you play, hmmm?"

The cube unfolds. All four sides drop down, lengthen. More flaps and folds appear to stretch out and form an elevated stage the length of Diana's arm, fronted by a row of tiny empty seats. A dozen men the size of her thumb rise out of the stage floor with Empire instruments in their hands: trumpets and saxophones and trombones, mostly. One man has a tiny guitar, and another has a set of drums. There's even a piano, and its player wears a jaunty fedora.

The leader of the musicians steps to the front of the stage. His tiny tuxedo is dusty. He bows at the waist and says. "Madam. My men and I are here to play for you."

"Really?" Diana asks, and then remembers her manners. "How very kind."

He gives her a long, unblinking look. "You look less surprised by this than many of our previous audiences."

"To be truthful, I had my doubts about the merchant's claims. But my life has been full of unusual events." She leans forward to study the trombonists, who all smile eagerly; the pianist, who is nipping from a tiny flask; and the lead saxophonist, who is impatiently tapping his leather shoe. "May I ask your names?"

The leader says, "Alton Glenn and His World-Famous Players."

"Forgive me if I'm wrong, but didn't Mr. Alton Glenn and his orchestra disappear eight years ago during the war with the Ivory Alliance?"

"So we've been told, yes," Glenn says, with the air of a man who would rather discuss a more pleasant topic.

"Believed to have died when their transport ship sank in the treacherous straits of Gitras?" Diana presses.

Glenn says, "Would you like to hear 'My Melancholy Lady'?"

For the sake of good manners she should let the subject drop, but Diana thinks it important to clarify the nature of the players before her. "Are you their restless spirits, imprisoned by a curse and waiting for release?"

"We'll play 'In A Mood,'" Glenn announces, rather snippishly. He returns to the orchestra with a click-tap of his tiny shoes and raises his baton. "Gentlemen. One, two, three, four —"

"In A Mood" is one of the Alton Glenn Orchestra's most famous pieces, and Diana has heard it performed on the finest stages of Massasoit. The experience of hearing it now is far different than hearing it performed then, chiefly because these tiny men produce music that is so awful that only decades of decorum keep her from clasping her hands to her ears.

The cacophony of out-of-tune instruments is so loud that Hazel opens the door with a startled, "My goodness! What in the world—?"

"It's this—" Diana starts to say, but the orchestra collapses back onto itself so swiftly that the brass cube rattles for a moment afterward before going flatly still.

"It's this what?" Hazel asks.

"Never mind," is all Diana says.

No matter how hard she tries, she can't make Alton Glenn or his orchestra appear again. No combination of words produces results. Her fingers can find no secret buttons, levers or other physical triggers on the smooth surfaces of the cube. Obviously it was a dream brought on by heat and melancholy. Or maybe she is sliding down an unseen but deadly slope of dementia, and next she'll see former President Eresvoolt smoking a cigar in her bathtub or the famed aeronaut Lamelia Heart floating around the chandelier.

A week later, another fantastical thing happens: the arrival of a note from Elanor Moncrief expressing delight that Diana will be joining her in Dal.

"How very odd," Diana says to Hazel at afternoon tea. "And here I was, certain that we'd declined."

Hazel spoons more sugar into Diana's cup. "I declined to let you sit here all season moping."

Diana grumbles about impertinence but suffers to let her trunks be packed. She complains about the train schedule but lets herself be helped up into a carriage, driven to the rail station, and escorted into a first-class compartment of an iron horse heading north. She chooses to travel in Empire clothes, but the train is so hot and the jostling so wretched that she permits Hazel to unfasten some of her stays and lay a wet cloth on her head.

"I haven't felt so inconvenienced since my passage," Diana sniffs.

Hazel, who knows exactly what lingers under Diana's skirts and who herself has suffered through the changes of age, makes a clucking noise.

"It's true!" Diana insists. "It's true if I'm the person feeling it."

The train passes slums and villages and ancient trade routes, finally overtaking a herd of gray elephants bearing green and blue riders. She feels sympathy for the elephants. Poor beasts should be left in peace to live their long and peaceful lives. James had always been fond of the beasts and once had been arrested for coming to their aid. Diana looks away, unwilling to dwell on the memory. Upon arrival in Dal she and Hazel are met by a carriage from Lady Moncrief and swept from the crowds for another hour of bouncing on dirt roads. The sun is a blood-red jewel at the edge of the enormous lake by the time the villa pulls into sight, which is about the same time Diana vows never to travel again unless she's the passenger of honor in a hearse.

The head servant, Prem, says that Lady Moncrief is busy dressing for dinner. She would understand completely if the travails of the day meant Diana preferred a cold meal and a good night's rest in her rooms. Diana starts to agree, but Hazel rejects the idea.

"Lady Hartvern has been cooped up inside a train car all day," Hazel says. "She would love to dine on good china with pleasant company."

Prem bows. "Of course! I shall have your trunks delivered ever so quickly."

Diana waits until they are behind the closed doors of their apartment before she complains, "You take too many liberties, Hazel."

"You can always terminate my services," is the calm reply. "Now, off with these travel clothes and dress in something comfortable, why don't you? Your green sari would be nice."

Diana sits down in a velvet chair with no intentions of getting up again for hours. "Don't be ridiculous. Elanor would be horrified to see me go native."

"You can't go somewhere you never left," Hazel replies. "This will always be your homeland. You can choose to be unhappy, and you can choose to complain about every single inch of this vacation, but if you choose to be predictable and dowdy as well, you're not the woman I think you are."

Dowdy! As if her skirts and blouses aren't from the finest tailors back in Massasoit, altered over the years to allow for her increasing girth. Certainly silly new fashions in the newspapers had no advantages over her sturdy shoes, woven stockings and practical sleeves. And predictable! Such a dire insult.

"I would wear the green sari but I didn't bring it," Diana sniffs. "You rushed me into packing and made me forget my most essential things."

"I packed it for you," Hazel answers smoothly.

It is heaven to be out of her stiff jacket and long skirt. The sari is loose and flowing, the fabric cool against her skin. Hazel has brought several of her jeweled earrings and necklace sets. Diana drapes purple jewels around her neck, on her fingers, from her earlobes.

"You look beautiful," Hazel says when Diana emerges.

"I look like a beached whale," Diana says.

Hazel steers her out of the apartment and toward the stairs.

Downstairs, in the dining room, Elanor greets Diana cheerfully from the chair where she's been ensconced. Her silver-white Empire dress is impeccable, and her left leg is swaddled in an enormous plaster cast.

"The stairs tripped me," Elanor complains. "How wonderful you look! You remember my eldest, Theodor Albert. And my darling Meridel."

The children are no longer children, Diana notes with dismay. Theodor Albert's handsome face is prematurely lined, and Meridel Moncrief Fitzroy has her hair pulled back so tightly that her eyes look stretched. Meridel's daughters, two fair-haired girls, sit at a side table with somber expressions and impeccable manners. Diana thinks they are like wooden dolls brought to life. Adults and children alike cut their food with silver knives and listen to Elanor and Diana talk with the kind of glazed attention that Diana usually attributes to church parishioners.

Meridel, it turns out, is married to a famous colonel who spends most of his days abroad. Theodor, who spent a good portion of his childhood putting frogs down Meridel's dresses, has little to say and drinks frequently from his wine glass. The only bright news is that Richard, Elanor's insufferable husband, has been delayed by business and will not be joining them anytime soon.

Elanor asks, "And how is your traveling companion, Hazel?"

"She's quite excellent," Diana says. "Always reliable."

"I have such trouble finding good help," Elanor says, and then quiets as the servant girls appear with cold soup.

Diana endures dinner as a lady should, trying to steer clear of mentions of James that would sadden her but increasingly annoyed that neither Meridel nor Theodor Albert put forth the slightest bit of conversational effort. Upon retiring to her rooms she complains to Hazel, "They're ridiculously dull. Like paper cutouts, all flat and gone gray."

"Really?" Hazel folds the book she's been reading by the light of an oil lamp. "I remember Meridel always had a gift for singing. And Theodor Albert, he could dance very well."

"They don't sing and dance now."

"Didn't he fight in the war? On the front, as a commissioned officer? It can change a man."

Diana was away for that most recent and tragic interlude of kingdom versus kingdom. "If he was changed, he should change back."

Alone in the bathroom, she undoes her bindings and removes her wig and looks at her body, all the fat and wrinkles. She pokes at the obscene lumps of flesh hanging between her thighs. If only, in her younger days, she'd had courage to cut them off. Take a sharp knife, make the decisive cuts, burn the flesh to ash. For all their dull exteriors at least Meridel and Theodor Albert and Meridel's children still have youth on their side; anger washes through her that they are wasting the best years of their lives while she is trapped on the declining end, she and the body that has betrayed her.

With her sore head wrapped in thin white silk she retires to her bed and dims all the lamps but one. Hazel must have brought and unpacked the brass cube from the New Dalli marketplace, because it is resting now on the side table and Diana certainly didn't put it there.

"You died young," she tells the invisible Alton Glenn. "A blessing."

In response, the cube unfolds and the orchestra emerges into their places, instruments at hand.

"Our apologies, madam." Alton Glenn bows, stiff and formal. "When we last played, we had let our instruments go badly out of tune. It was a terrible breach of professional musicianship. Hardly befitting of the reputation of the Alton Glenn Orchestra, no matter how unfitting our demise. We've now remedied the situation."

Head nestled on her pillow, one hand curled beneath her sagging chin, Diana says, "At least you don't have to suffer the indignities of waning strength and lost beauty."

The pianist says, "Ma'am, you try living in a metal cube and tell us how lucky we are."

"Shut up, Henry," says one of the trombonists. "Nobody cares about your sour grapes anymore!"

"You shut up, Charlie," someone else chimes in.

A tiny voice pipes up. "Hey, lady? Got a cigarette?"

Alton Glenn whacks his baton against his bandstand. "That's enough! Are you musicians or children?"

This sets off a new round of squabbling. Diana interrupts long enough to ask how it is they came to be imprisoned, and a saxophonist named Arty Haws tells the tale.

"See, we came to New Dalli to play for the troops," Arty says. "And in the audience, but we didn't know it, was this magician who liked us so much that he made his own tiny version of the band out of sacred metal from blessed mines. But we didn't know it. Until later, when our boat sank in the Gitras Straights, and we all drowned, and we woke up inside here. The magician, he was a little surprised. Not what he intended. And he thought we were bad luck, being dead and all, and so he sold us off, and then someone else sold us off, and then you bought us."

Diana is not sure she wants to bear the karmic responsibility of owning a dozen dead musicians. Still, it's not a problem she can solve tonight. She rolls onto her back and places a scented pillow over her tired eyes.

"You say you've fixed your instruments," she says. "Won't you play something soft and soothing?"

The men start a song so immediately awful Diana almost bites her tongue off.

"Really now!" she snaps.

Abashed, they lower their instruments.

"We've been in here so long we've gone tone deaf," Alton Glenn says miserably. "We're just wasting everyone's time."

"All we've got is time!" says Henry the pianist, pounding his off-tune keys. "All the dead have is eternity!"

"Shut up, Henry," says the drummer, and Diana pulls her blanket over her head until the band collapses again.

Diana tries to sleep but is annoyed that Hazel hasn't come to investigate the cacophony. How irresponsible. Diana could be in mortal distress, dying alone and unloved. But what if Hazel is the one who's ill, lying stricken on the floor? A knock on their adjoining door produces no reply. Diana lets herself in and sees an empty bed. A faint noise in the outside hall has her opening the outside door but to her surprise she sees only Theodor Albert, sneaking across the stone floors like a thief.

"Lady Hartvern! I didn't expect to see you."

Well aware that she is not dressed at her best, Diana closes the door to a mere wedge. "I didn't expect to see you either, Teddy."

He flushes at the long-ago nickname. "I forgot to—I was meaning to—er, I got turned around. Wrong wing. Good night!"

In the morning, Hazel has the distant smile of a woman well-loved.

"Who is it?" Diana asks tartly. "The stable boy? A footman?"

Hazel's smile disappears. "Never you mind."

"I would tell you."

"You most certainly would not."

That Hazel has a secret lover makes the day more depressing. Diana finds herself scrutinizing every member of the staff, looking for tell-tale love marks or satisfied expressions. Elanor has organized a boat ride on the lake for the morning's diversion, Hazel included, and Diana watches to see if her gaze lingers on the carriage driver or the boatman or, heaven forbid, Theodor Albert, who is at least twenty years her junior.

If Theodor has any interest in Hazel, he doesn't show it. His attention is almost unwaveringly devoted to a small notebook in which he scribbles, pauses, scribbles again. He wholeheartedly ignores Meridel, who flushes easily in the heat and whose two daughters resist their grandmother's exhortations to look at the water, look at that silver fish, imagine being a mermaid.

"Are you writing epic poetry?" Diana asks Theodor Albert as the boatman glides their shikara over the placid waters.

He blinks in surprise. "No. I don't read poetry."

"Are you making observations of the sun and moon?"

Theodor Albert frowns at the crescent moon, barely visible in the bright sky. "These are calculations. For my investments."

Hazel says, "I've never had a good head for math, myself."

"It's all I do," he replies.

"Not true," Meridel protests. "You also make watches."

He pats the thin gold chain leading into his side pocket. "I tinker. But you paint! Very nice landscapes."

"Good enough for my own amusement," Meridel says dismissively. "You do scrimshaw. Very fine engravings on whale's teeth."

Diana fans herself impatiently. "I once saw a man get swallowed by a whale."

One of Meridel's daughters darts Diana a skeptical look. "You did not!"

"I did," Diana insists, and launches into an epic tale about crossing the Great Ocean on a luxury liner with a passenger list that included royalty, scoundrels, adventurers and poor but ambitious immigrants along with a virtuous young maiden and her two rival suitors. The first suitor was the spoiled son of an investment tycoon. The other was a man of common Corish stock commissioned as a third officer on the ship. The spoiled son wooed the maiden over fine china and scrumptious food, and sent roses to her cabin; the third officer brought her to the bridge one night and let her steer the great ship under a sky full of diamond stars. Six days into the voyage, discovering the rivalry, the spoiled son challenged the third officer to a pistol duel for the maiden's affection. The third officer declined to trade lead and instead dared the spoiled son to a swimming race around the ship. The third officer had been a very fast swimmer at home, but he didn't know the spoiled son had been captain of the swim team at Coxford University. The captain stopped the ship so the competition could take place.

"I don't believe you," says Meridel's older daughter. Her name is Eloise and she has the look of a girl sucking a lemon. "The captain wouldn't stop the ship for a swimming race."

Diana fans herself. "This captain did. He had painful memories of his own bachelorhood, when he was a horse jockey, and how he lost a lover to a rich breeder."

Theodor Albert quirks an eyebrow. "He was a jockey who became a captain?"

"He had many talents. Do you want me to keep telling the story or not?"

The younger girl, Adalyn, nods energetically. "Yes, please!"

"It was a hot day, the sea flat like a big blue tablecloth. The passengers and crew all watched from the railings while the two men dove off the poop deck in their white swimming suits. Into the water they plopped! The maiden's young brother blew a whistle. The men started swimming very quickly in opposite directions around the ship. Great cheers and shouts filled the air to encourage them."

"Who won?" Meridel asks, her hand near her throat.

Diana fans herself some more. "The third officer started strong, his pale arms flashing in the water. But then he foundered and fell behind. The spoiled son pulled ahead—"

"You said they were swimming in opposite directions," Eloise accuses.

"When I was a child," Diana says, "I never interrupted my elders."

Adalyn tugs on Diana's arm. "Please, please, continue. Who won?"

With a dramatic flair, Diana says, "Neither! Before the race could conclude, a great gray whale rose up out of the deep. The captain called for harpoonists, but the beast was too quick. It swallowed the spoiled son whole and then dove down with such force that the subsequent wave nearly capsized the ship."

The girls stare at her, entranced, and then Eloise says, "It seems too much of a parable that the whale swallowed the spoiled son and not the third officer."

"Fortune had nothing to do with it," Diana says. "The spoiled son was winning the competition because he had poisoned the third officer. Spider venom in his morning coffee, delivered by an unscrupulous steward. The third officer never had a chance. The spoiled son, knowing that victory was his, started throwing insults over his wet shoulder. Which drew the attention of the whale, because leviathans of the deep can't abide anyone with egos larger than their own."

Adalyn asks, "Did the third officer marry the maiden and they lived happily ever after?"

"No," she tells them. "He drowned."

After a moment of startled silence, Adalyn bursts into tears.

Hazel discreetly kicks Diana's ankle. "He did not!"

"He did!" Diana insists.

That's Diana's version of the story, anyway: the glow of infatuation, the thrill of romance, followed by the invariable disappointment of drowning or being eaten by sea beasts. But everyone is frowning at her as if she's spoiled a sweet cake by spitting on it. As if she's ruined a precious secret that the children mustn't learn until they experience the heartbreak themselves.

"You're cruel." Eloise turns away from Diana with her arms folded.

The shikara has made a wide circle and is heading back to shore now, passing old Empire houseboats and lovely gardens planted in the honor of the goddesses. The daughters are quiet, as is their mother. Hazel still looks annoyed. The heat is unbearable. Once they are safely back in their apartment, Diana takes to her bed with a wet cloth over her face.

"It's your own fault for telling such a terrible story," Hazel says.

"It's the world's fault for being full of them," Diana sniffs.

Meridel and the children do not come to dinner that night. Elanor says nothing about poisons, drownings, or whales, and instead makes small talk about the beautiful temples at Calir. Theodor Albert shows no interest in the temples. He pushes chickpeas around his dinner plate as if studying their mathematical trajectories. Diana hates her own food but forces it down, piece by piece.

Hazel sneaks out again that night to her secret lover, and Diana despises her.

The night seems insufferably hot, even within the villa's stone walls. Diana stares at her ceiling and listens to faint music over the lake. Her legs hurt. Her stomach is upset. Conversation would be a welcome distraction but Alton Glenn and his orchestra refuse to come out no matter how much she cajoles. She threatens to drop the cube into the villa's blue wading pool, or toss it into the swill piles that get collected by the pig farmers.

"I will," she tells the cube. "I'm very vindictive."

The musicians stay silent. Diana hears footsteps in the hallway and opens the door in time to see Theodor Albert skulking about in his soft-slippered shoes, a wine bottle in hand.

"Lady Hartvern!" he says.

"Teddy. You're lost again."

His hands flutter. "You've caught me. I couldn't sleep."

Diana would invite him in, cajole him into sharing the wine, but he's a man still in his prime and she's an old woman whose breasts and wig are hanging in the bathroom.

"Good night, Teddy," she says, and crawls into her own lonely bed.

The next morning Elanor begs off the trip to Calir, citing the pain in her broken ankle. Hazel also stays behind, because a woman of good Corish stock has no interest in heathen temples, thank you very much. That leaves Diana to travel with Theodor Albert, Meridel and the girls to the marble temples, which are located in the forested hills on the far end of the lake. The roads through the eucalyptus and bamboo groves are lined with travelers, tourists and merchants. The grounds of the temples themselves—sprawling and grand, crowded and loud—remind her of the bazaar back in New Dalli, a conglomeration of food grills and relic stalls, with flea-ridden dogs and children underfoot, sitar music and drums filling her ears, the air thick with curry and roasting meat. Brilliant flags flutter from every tree branch within reach, and even from branches higher up: purples and reds, and yellows so dazzling Diana can't gaze too long before her eyes start to water. She wishes James could see them.

The only refuge from the noise and gaiety are the temples themselves, with their domed roofs and enormous arches and thousands of reliefs depicting the pantheon of a million passionate gods. White light fills the spaces and muffles every sound. The temples could swallow up entire regiments of soldiers. Diana sits near a row of white candles and watches the tiny flames flicker. She thinks about dead James and the dead spoiled son and the dead third officer, and all the other people who have died and left her alone in her old age.

She has brought Alton Glenn and his orchestra with her. Diana has half a mind to donate the cube to the temple priestesses, who may know how to break the sorcerer's supernatural magic. But perhaps breaking the spell would lead to an even worse fate.

"What's that?" a querulous voice asks from behind her. Eloise stands there, looking uncomfortable in the white dress her mother has made her wear.

"None of your business,"

"Is it a toy? I want it."

"The world is not responsible for meeting your wants," Diana says. "Nor am I."

Eloise's eyes turn into a narrow squint. "I know what you are. You can't hide it."

Diana's heart begins to quicken. "And I know what you are. A vile little girl with nothing better to do than cause trouble."

"I'm going to tell everyone you're a nasty old man!"

Diana slaps her. Not very hard, but enough to leave a pink mark. Some nearby tourists gape at them, perhaps marveling at the gall of a woman in a sari touching a girl of Empire descent. The Collapsible Orchestra's cube tumbles from Diana's lap and clatters to the floor, unbearably loud.

Eloise scoops up the cube with her nimble little fingers.

"I hate you!" she says, and runs off with slapping footsteps that bring even more attention their way.

Diana can't bear the accusing eyes of strangers. She hurries from the main gallery into a side chambers, her fingers stinging and her eyes wet. She will not stand for such impudence from a child. When they get back to the villa she and Hazel will depart immediately for the train, and Elanor can send her things after her. No, better yet, she will hire a coach to carry her directly to the nearest depot, and she will ban the Moncrief family from her memory forever.

Her legs threaten to buckle under her. Diana stops at a low bench in an alcove, far from other tourists. Surely she is dying, but the relief she expects to feel is sour with fear. She wants a quick sudden end, like the drop of a guillotine. Not pain that twists inward and inward like a knife. A horrifying prospect looms: stricken ill, confined to bed, months of slow decline while Hazel sneaks off to her secret lover and leaves her to the ministrations of hijre nurses, their painted eyelids fluttering over their mustaches.

In a gallery across from her, a man and woman stand in shadow; embracing, passionate, her arm curled up on his shoulder, his head tipped down to meet hers. It's incredibly rude for anyone to be enjoying such passion while Diana's own life slowly leaks out of her. Nevertheless the tableau fascinates her. It's almost as if she knows them, these strangers, the woman with the auburn hair, the man's strong chin—

Abruptly she recognizes them both, and is glad she is sitting on a bench.

Such a strange thing, knowledge, that it can make the goosebumps on her neck more vivid than the tightness in her chest. For so long she has thought herself beyond surprise in the realm of forbidden love. She lets out a surprised cough. The two lovers break apart and turn her way.

Diana isn't sure who is the most mortified.

"Lady Hartvern," Theodor Albert says, his voice strangled.

Meridel's mouth moves, but no words actually emerge.

"Good day," Diana says, and flees as if her skirts are on fire.

She comes to rest outside in the heat and sun, sitting by a crowded water fountain. She feels curiously free of a long-carried weight: for once, hers is not the most crushing secret in her social circle. When Theodor Albert and Meridel emerge from the temple it is separately, as if they are utter strangers, and the carriage ride home is full of excruciatingly polite silence except for Adalyn, who jabbers on about Calir with all the enthusiasm of her age. Eloise glares dourly at Diana, but Diana stares stonily back until the girl looks away and starts pulling threads out of the window curtain.

"Eloise, stop that," her mother finally says.

"I won't," Eloise replies. "You can't make me."

"Don't be unpleasant," Theodor Albert tells her.

"I can be anything I want to be."

"And you can have a bowl of fish oil for supper," Meridel says sharply.

Back at the villa, Diana tells Hazel that they will be leaving the next day.

"We can't!" Hazel blurts out.

"Honestly now! It's not as if your affair with the footman or the stable boy is bound to end happily, unless you plan to leave my employment for drudgery among the servant class."

Hazel lifts her chin. "Lady Elanor would hire me if I asked."

"She wouldn't dare steal you out from underneath me."

"She would, and she will!"

Diana harrumphs. "We're leaving tomorrow to return to New Dalli. I expect you to have all our things packed by breakfast."

Hazel takes the tea tray and leaves, her shoulders and jaw rigid.

Diana resists the urge to throw a pillow after the closed door, but she will not resort to childish tantrums no matter how much Hazel deserves one. When a soft knock sounds on the door Diana is vindicated that the silly woman has come to her senses and says, "Come in."

Instead of Hazel, Meridel appears. Her face is as white as bleached linen.

"Lady Hartvern," she says, her voice sounding strangled. "I must know your intentions."

With a desultory hand Diana says, "Your secret is safe with me."

Meridel bursts into tears.

Diana had hoped to avoid this part—the tearful confession, replete with mortification, protestation, a shamed acknowledgement of how her love for Theodor Albert violates deeply held and perfectly valid taboos. Diana pats her knee and offers a laced handkerchief and tries to be patient. The young can be so very silly in their self-centeredness, their narrow-minded insistence that theirs are the most important secrets in the world, that they are the first to sin or stray.

Finally Diana says, "My dear child, I believe you that you never meant for this to happen, that you understand how forbidden your love is. Certainly the only recourse is to end it quickly and precisely, like the clean cut of a surgeon's knife."

More tears. "Lady Hartvern, don't you have an alternative? Surely with your wisdom and worldly experience…"

"There is no cure for a problem like this," Diana says. "What will you do? Leave your husband and fine home? Lose your status in society, lose your children when a judge sides with your husband? Will Teddy leave his occupation, abandon his home and any semblance of good status? You will both be ruined."

Meridel dabs her eyes. "However wrong our love is, it still feels true and strong."

Diana shakes her head. "You cannot survive it. You will kill yourselves in the attempt. For the sake of your daughters, you must return to good behavior and proper morals."

Meridel departs with a resigned air that Diana knows all too well.

Fifteen minutes later, another knock sounds on her door: Theodor Albert, fiddling anxiously with his pocket watch.

"I know our behavior has been reprehensible," he says. "I hope you will not let it color your stay."

Diana says, "Reprehensible behavior is nothing new to me, Teddy. I've given my option to your sister and that opinion stands, as old-fashioned and puritanical as it may be. As for myself, I'd already decided to return to New Dalli before I witnessed your rendezvous. I'll feel more at home there, with my old familiar things."

He tilts his head. "You can't leave. The festival won't be nearly the same."

"My will is resolved."

He sighs. "My mother doesn't want you to know, but she has arranged for an elephant tribute for your late husband. It's been paid for and planned for weeks. Would you refute her generosity so?"

"I didn't ask for anything," Diana says, a little sourly.

Theodor Albert considers her for a long moment. She has the sudden irrational fear that he's looking past her skin into her soul and finding it wanting.

Sternly she says, "If that's all, I'm very tired."

He makes a thoughtful sound and then pulls the brass cube of Alton Glenn's orchestra from his pocket. "As it so happens, I also came to return this to you. Eloise was showing it to her sister. After some interrogation, she told me it fell from your pocket at Calir."

The prospect of accepting its return makes her chest feel unbearably tight. Diana says, "You keep it. It's broken. Broken like a human heart, never to be repaired."

He ponders the cube, pockets it, heads for the door.

"Teddy," she calls after him. "I'll stay for the festival. But then I must return to my ordinary life, and you must as well."

He dips his head in acquiescence.

Hazel doesn't return that night; Diana feels infinitely resentful. Breakfast is as gloomy an affair as a funeral, even though the servants have decorated the main hall with garlands and scattered red petals on the marble title.

Meridel and Theodor Albert don't look at each other. Adalyn, when she appears, is giddy about the prospects of snake charmers and caged tigers, but Eloise is cold.

"Don't you have something to say to Lady Hartvern?" Theodor Albert prompts her.

Eloise arches her eyebrows. "I'm sorry you dropped your toy at Calir."

"How sincere of you," Diana says.

Theodor Albert says, "A toy it most certainly isn't," in a way that makes Diana think he has discovered the cube's secrets, but nothing in his face gives him away.

Lady Elanor's foot is still aching and Hazel again refuses to respect heathen rites. A colorfully festooned shikara bears Diana and the unhappy Moncriefs across the lake. As they draw nearer to the north end of the valley, music from horns, lutes and drums clashes in the air, delightful when the notes complement one another, annoying when disharmonious. The festival is all about clash and surrender: icons of the sun and moon twisted together, life and death symbols in sinuous embrace, food both sweet and sour, incense that stimulates and sedates. The riverbank is full of families, old couples, widows like Diana; hijre girls with mock wedding veils over their faces, priestesses anointing the sick. The elephant parade forms a long line, each beast bedecked with wreaths and flowers, each mammoth leg painted brightly with the shapes of snakes, vines and blossoms.

The tribute elephant for James Hartvern is a magnificent old animal with eyes that regard Diana serenely. The ladder up its mammoth flank looks ridiculously flimsy.

"I'm afraid of heights," Diana says, not quite a lie.

Theodor Albert says, "The children can do it, and so can you."

"I would never do such an unladylike thing," Eloise sniffs.

Adalyn grabs hold of the ladder and swings up, her shoes and stockings flashing in the sun. "I would!" she says boldly, and within moments she is seated on the leather saddle strapped to the elephant's middle.

"Well, then," Diana says, determined not to be outdone by a ten-year-old. Her grip has not lessened after all these years and soon she is seated behind the girl, both of them gazing down at the plaza and the revelry, and the enormous beast patient beneath them. Something shifts in Diana, something she didn't actually realize was unaligned; her vision clears a tiny bit and her hearing sharpens.

"You can come down now, Adalyn," Meridel says, shading her eyes against the sun.

Diana encircles the girl's waist with her arm. "I think she's good for me. Can't I keep her?"

Adalyn giggles and leans back against Diana's ample chest. The child's amusement turns into a squeak of fear when the sitar music begins and the long line of elephants ambles forward.

"Now, now," Diana says. "It's just forward motion. Nothing to worry about. Most elephants are very gentle, because they remember their former lives as caterpillars and how easy it is to get trampled."

"Caterpillars don't turn into elephants," Adalyn protests. "They turn into butterflies."

"They turn into many things," Diana says, eyeing the gilded temples and dervish dancers and the deep blue reflecting pools filled with white lotus petals. "It's people who get stuck in one shape or other."

"I won't get stuck," Adalyn said.

"An admirable goal," Diana says.

She feels James like an old elephant in her heart, heavy and lumbering, and in the blinding sun she frees him from a cage of blood and flesh, sends him off to whatever pasture or prairie awaits him. It doesn't make her feel better. It doesn't give her peace or clarity, because an elephant-sized hole is still a hole, and under the broiling sun with dust clogging the air she realizes just how many weights and holes await her in the years to come. Beauty, strength, vitality. All will continue to flee no matter how hard she holds tight to the elephant's reins. Hazel will leave for the arms of a lover. Memories will drift away like clouds. There is nothing to look forward to at the end of this ride but there is still the ride itself, with a painted elephant carrying Diana forward, with crowds waving flags and palm leaves, and incenses sweetening the thick air so that her head swims and she has to hold on harder.

She glances backward to see Meridel and Theodor Albert standing apart, faces pinched in misery, while Eloise throws pennies at beggar children and smiles in her cruel little way.

When they get back to the villa Diana soaks her legs in a tub of salted water, and when she stands up dripping she hears the sounds of Alton Glenn's orchestra rising from a balcony far below. She peeks over the stone railing to where Theodor Albert is watching the musicians with apt fascination, tiny tools in hand. He has tuned their instruments into perfect harmony. A door clicks open and he looks up. Diana doesn't have to see Meridel to recognize the tender longing on his face. When they begin to dance together, legs and arms pressed close to the sounds of an old waltz, Diana tells herself to withdraw and give them privacy. But she cannot; she watches raptly, and wishes the world could accommodate their love.

Movement at her side brings her attention to Hazel, whose mouth is set in a prim line.

"I was never that close to my brothers," Hazel murmurs. "Sheep farmers, all of them. Couldn't dance to save their lives."

Diana says, "Come to deliver your notice, have you?"

"Don't be silly," Hazel replies, gaze fixed firmly below.

Diana waits a moment before asking, "Did he break your heart?"

"We break our own hearts with unreasonable expectations," Hazel says, briskly, and Diana knows there won't be any further conversation on the topic. Which is fine. Diana think it is possible that she has talked too much in her life, and curiously too little as well; she thinks the hole in her heart is beginning to fill with something strange and liquid yet still indefinable, a magnetic wellspring that is going to draw her and Hazel into new adventures beyond the horizon until she is a frail husk drawing her last rattling breath.

"We should get you ready for dinner," Hazel finally says.

"Dinner can wait," Diana says. She folds her arms on the railing and rests her head dreamily. The waltz is a song to stir the heart. "Listen to the lovely music."

Author's Notes

1. Alton Glenn Miller, the famed big band leader, was on his way to Paris to entertain the troops when his plane vanished over the English Channel. Many wild and fantastical stories have been told about his disappearance, but the truth remains unknown. He was forty-three years old at the time he went missing.
2. Did you guess who Hazel's secret lover was?
3. The story of the swimming competition is entirely false, except to those who participated in it.

Women

OF THE LACE

Before you ask why I'm robbing this civil war museum, let me tell you how my grandmother and I spent several years stranded on a tropical island, and how she taught me to make lace using coconut shell needles and pig-hair thread.

As we worked she would say, "Kings and queens, and brides all a-flutter, and starry-eyed housewives, and gentlemen dandies, and even lowly milkmaids, all dreaming of knots and patterns, and willing to poke each other's eyes out for the finest they could get. Those were the golden years, child, before machines started crapping out lace by the mile. Ladies of the castle started it, something to do while their men were out hunting boars and infidels. The merchants' wives followed, and then the farmers' wives, and then the peasant girls, who had to pluck the hairs from their own heads because they couldn't afford anything else. Lace was a precious commodity, a fine art, and a secret source of women's power. But then Mattie Bellingham went and ruined it all. Yes, Mattie Bellingham and the great lace factories of Mount Hernon.

"Now, Sue Lu, I can see from your face that you're thinking me a liar. Your own grandmother, weaving stories to pass away the hours until some cargo ship rescues us from the middle of the ocean. I have the sinking feeling our ordeal will last many weeks, and I intend to keep your spirits buoyed as we search for edible breadfruit and fight off the amorous intentions of the grunt-pigs, who even now are peering at us from the bushes with unnatural lust in their eyes. But everything I tell you is true, and can be used as a warning about our family's history and power. There's a saying, 'Give a woman some lace and she'll dress fancy for dinner; teach her how to make it, and she'll have needle pricks in her fingers for the rest of her life.' You, my darling girl, are going to have the pricks.

"So. Mattie Bellingham. Her story really starts long ago with a little girl named Caterina. Caterina was an orphan, you see, never knew the kiss of her mother's lips, never bounced on the knee of her father, but she came from a well-established hoity-toity lineage, and her fate was always controlled by the knobby hands of men. Her uncle, the Pope, made sure she was raised properly, at the knees of nuns. The murate, they called them. A secluded order living at the top of a treacherous mountain. Little did the Pope know that they were pagan sorceresses who had long hidden their magic, lest they be burned alive. They taught little Caterina how to knot the powers of the earth so that she could protect herself wherever the winds of politics blew her. They also taught her the most sacred rule of their order: magic lacemaking must never, ever, be taught to boys or men.

"'No problemo,' little Caterina said. 'I understand completely.'"

Grandma continued, "When she turned fourteen, the Pope took Caterina from the convent and married her off to the future king of another land. Unfortunately, the future king was already in love with someone else—a very powerful witch, a wicked and terrible woman. You must believe in witches, Sue Lu. They roam the earth even in these modern days, and you can see their power in the winds that dashed our ship on the rocks and stranded us here. Anyway, all Caterina could do was squeeze out royal babies, endure the humiliation of her husband's whore living in the suite of rooms directly above hers, and continue her needlework. She didn't dare weave any magic against the mistress-witch, for everyone knows that evil sent forth returns twofold, but for her ladies-in-waiting she made lace that could cure a woman's monthly ills, or bring on a child when one was dearly wanted, or eradicate the venereal diseases so common to the royal court. Many tried to learn her secrets, but Caterina trusted them only to a little girl named Marie, a child-queen who was also the pawn of powerful men.

"Caterina and Marie—oh, the lace they made! Their silver needles flashed like lightning long after the rest of the court had gone to sleep. Their designs were so beautiful even the most cynical hearts in the palace wept with awe. The mistress-witch grew mottled with envy and tried to drive a wedge between them. She spilled turkey gravy on Caterina's finest threads and made sure Marie was blamed. She swallowed Marie's bobbins and had the servants tell her Caterina had stolen them. But none of the mistress-witch's plans bore fruit, and eventually she was sent into exile. Marie married Caterina's son, sealing the women by law as well as magic. Then the son died, and heartbroken Marie returned to her homeland to do battle with her fierce, duplicitous cousin, a slutty queen who called herself a virgin."

Dear Reader, I can see you making connections in your mind. Dimmed memories of history lessons are starting to surface. But at the time I heard these tales, I was just a small girl with no access to encyclopedias or textbooks. Sometimes Grandma changed the story. In one version, the mistress-witch succeeded in poisoning Caterina's heart, turning it black with loneliness and pain. In another variation, the mistress-witch filled Marie with vile ambition and deception. The only constant is that Marie did go back across the sea, to the land where she was called Mary, and was immediately arrested.

"The so-called Virgin, who was anything but, feared Mary so much that she kept her locked up for twenty years, in castles and manors and fine country estates. There wasn't any television in those days, and hardly any books at all, so Mary got herself some bobbins and thread and began to stitch away the hours of her life. Pinto in aria, gros point de Venise, bobbin lace, needle lace—there was no technique she couldn't master, no pattern too difficult. She was a master of guipure roses so pure, so delicate, that the lacemakers of the Low Countries went crazy trying to imitate them and were carted off to insane asylums to build windmill blades instead. Great oceans of lace spilled from Mary's hands and into the hands of authorized smugglers, who sold it for money to support her cause against Liz the Slut. But even Lizzie adored her cousin's lace, seized from the holds of rebel ships. She wrapped herself in it, she wallowed in it, she hung it from her ceiling and pretended it was the sails of a magic ship carrying her to the Great

Lost North, to men with fur hats and strong hands and borscht breath, and to canopy beds built from ice and whale ribs.

"Eventually Lizzie got so jealous of Mary's lace that she ordered her put to death. The Secret Society of Lady Lacemakers, an organization headquartered in the Low Countries, immediately dispatched secret agents to Fotherington Castle, where the dreaded sentence was to take place. Those petite but brave ladies used ancient knowledge to fashion a golem—that's sort of like a robot, you see, but without all the wires and light bulbs—to take Mary's place, but the golem was having none of that. She escaped out the castle door to wander in woods and marshes, where she lives to this day, protected by the Heritage Foundation. Mary, meanwhile, was taken to have her head chopped off. They stripped her of all but her simple dress and petticoats, made her kneel down, scooted her little dog out of the way and thwack! The executioner swung his axe."

"They cut off her head?" I cried.

"Who's telling this story, you or me?" Grandma said, with a gimlet eye toward the sea. Yapper, her Yorkshire terrier, raced back and forth in the surf, barking at crabs and dolphins and sea-monsters that only he could see. "Back in London, Liz the Unloved passed all sorts of laws saying who could wear lace, where you could buy it from, who was authorized to make it. There's nothing like outlawing a thing to make it more alluring. After the Slut Queen went to sleep in her cold stone grave, thousands of little shops sprung up like wild mushrooms. Lacemakers sailed to the New World and started the first shops in Massasoit. They went with the outlaw outcasts to the lands Down

Under, because even the cruelest criminal's heart softens when he's wearing something frilly under his trousers. Lace missionaries sailed all the way to the Eastern Empire and sat outside the walls of the Forbidden City until the Dowager Empress herself took up needlecraft. Is that a rescue boat I see?"

No, not a boat, just a strange shape of clouds on the horizon. By then we had made several inches of lace, using the patterns grandmother had drawn on palm fronds with turtle blood ink. Bit by bit she was teaching me the secrets of the murate, as passed from Caterina to Marie to one of her most trusted ladies-in-waiting, who in turn passed it to her daughters, and their daughters, and eventually to a young woman of Cardyr named Martha Custis.

"Mattie, as she was known, was a sheltered little thing, gentle and refined, quite unaccustomed to hardship. Then her husband went and died on her, leaving her two small children and a fortune to manage. Those were unsettled times—revolution was in the air, and sickness in every household—but soon she met an army colonel named George Bellingham. He loved Mattie more than any man had ever loved a woman, though sometimes his wooden teeth cut her lips while they were kissing. She, in turn, loved him so much that she laced murate spells to protect him from bullets and fire and drowning in rivers. In every portrait you ever see, any painting or print in museums or books, you can be sure George is wearing Mattie's lace under his clothing. Close to his root of power, if you know what I mean.

"Now, George was no fool. He asked Mattie to make lace for all of his soldiers, so they too would be protected in battle. 'But George,' she said, 'magic on such a large scale may not be a wise course of action.' In turn he said, 'Mattie, my dear, the fate of a nation rests entirely on your milk-white shoulders.' Reluctantly but patriotically, Mattie agreed. A thousand orphan girls were brought to Mount Hernon for training. Eighteen hours a day, seven days of the week, while the drums of war beat outside, those brave girls stitched lace squares that soldiers could tuck under their trousers.

"'It's not enough,' George said. He told her they needed more, more, ever more. The enemy soldiers had their own magical powers, you see. Their leather belts had been crafted back home by the vengeful mistress-witch, who had used bloodshed and violence to unnaturally prolong her wicked life.

"Mattie and the poor girls of Mount Hernon couldn't keep up with the demand. Every evening they slumped over in exhaustion, their vision gone dark, their dreams tormented by needles. George brought in a thousand boys too small to carry guns and said, 'Teach them your magic, my dear.'

"'George,' she beseeched him, 'is this war so necessary? Is there no chance of peace?'

"'Mattie,' he said, his gaze stern, 'if you love me, you will do this thing.'

"Poor Mattie was so in love, so desperate to save her country, that she broke the number one rule of the murate and did as he asked. The boys bent to their task with sharp eyes and nimble fingers. But no matter how hard they tried, the lace the boys made was defective. On the battlefield it attracted bad luck, ill fate, the ricochet of bullets, the scourge of infection. Thousands of soldiers died."

Sometimes, at this point in the story, Grandma would excuse herself to go walk in the jungle. I would sit by our signal fire with Yapper in my lap, thinking of dead soldiers in bloody meadows, until she returned.

"What happened, finally?" I would ask. "Didn't we win?"

Grandma rubbed her hands by the flames. "It took several years and a costly infusion of foreign magic, but George's army eventually triumphed. That, of course, is a different story."

Eight years after we first washed ashore, Grandma and I finished making an enormous lace banner and affixed it to the highest tree on our island. A year after that, a wooden ship came sailing into the bay. Affixed to its bow was the figurehead of a pirate with a yellow turban. The ship's crew of hearty nuns hoisted us over the side, and the Captain Nun, resplendent in black lace and white boots, said, "That's enough of a vacation for you, Martha!"

"'Martha?'" I asked Grandma. "Are you—"

The Captain Nun pointed a finger toward the blue horizon. She was a beautiful woman, though with a chin shaped somewhat like a man's. "While you've been lollygagging, the world has gone to ruin! Invaders from outer space have descended to impose galactic tyranny! The seas themselves diminish! I have been thrust into the role of superhero, and you must join my legion of sidekicks. Meet Mr. Cubby there, at the helm."

A stooped old man waved to us.

"And my cabin girl Jaleesha," the Captain Nun said.

A dark-skinned girl with long braids gave me a grave nod.

Grandma said, "Now, Diana, surely you exaggerate—"

But the Captain Nun was already stalking to the bow with her spyglass in hand. "Set sail for South Ravina, Graybeard! We have a world to save."

I couldn't be sure, but I thought I heard a rumbling voice from the pirate figurehead.

Below decks, over the first tea and biscuits we'd enjoyed in a long, long time, I asked my Grandma why the Captain Nun had called her Martha. Surely Grandma was not Mattie Bellingham herself?

"How could I be?" Grandma replied, brushing sand from her feet onto our cabin's floor. "To believe that, you'd have to believe that two hundred years ago, riddled by guilt and compelled to make amends, George's widow faked her own death, fashioned her own life-extending potion from the fertile fields of Virginia, and began traveling this wide, crazy world as a vagabond, a gypsy, a crazy old woman who tells tall tales to children. You'd have to believe she planned to recover every piece of lace made by the boys at Mount Hernon and return them to the headquarters of the murate. Much was destroyed or buried, but the rest resides in far-flung attics and museums and antique shops, or in the grimy hands of the mistress-witch herself. Mattie's goal was simply to return the lace to its rightful place, but now it seems likely to be the only thing that can save the planet."

"You believe that story about alien invaders?" I asked.

"Captain Diana certainly stretches the truth now and then, but she would never lie about global destruction."

Grandma finished off the last biscuit. "I will keep on my quest, and you must retreat to the nearest safe haven."

"No," I said. "I want to go with you."

I thought I had convinced her, but when we put into port she ditched me on the docks by jumping onto the back of a speeding lettuce truck. She cried out, "Farewell, Sue Lu! Remember the pricks!" and I haven't seen that beloved woman since.

"She has her own destiny to follow," the Captain Nun told me. "As do we all."

So now you know why I'm cracking open a glass cabinet in the middle of the night and stealing away a square of lace that bears the telltale knots of the murate. You know why I'm shimmying up a lace rope to the museum skylight, and why after that I'll weave my way through cities crawling with Whitesuits until I rejoin the Captain Nun and her crew. There are thousands of us secreting through the night even now—rebels and adventurers, storytellers and cowboys, sailors and soldiers and magicians. I believe we will triumph against the terrible odds and emerge victorious, no matter how many long years of danger stretch ahead of us.

Meanwhile, if you happen to see a woman who looks like Martha Bellingham, tell her I love her and miss her. Women of the lace have to stick together, after all.

The End

Afterword

This collection represents some of my published short fiction, but not all of it. The themes, games, and (what I hope are) sly references represent some of my interests and social concerns, but not all of them. The following thanks go out to people who most deserve them, but surely not to all: the human memory fails. Thank you to my family, to Stephanie and Terry, to my comrades at Blue Heaven and the Online Writer's Workshop, to the members of the Jacksonville Science Fiction and Fantasy writers' group, to the magazine *Strange Horizons*, to Alex Jeffers and Niki Smith, and to Steve Berman and Lethe Press.

LaVergne, TN USA
28 September 2010
198785LV00001B/11/P